Don't Call Me Katie Rose

Don't Call Me
KATIE ROSE ❀

by Lenora Mattingly Weber

THOMAS Y. CROWELL COMPANY

New York

jW 383 do

Don't Call Me Katie Rose

One

❀

HONESTLY! You'd think a girl was guilty of high treason just because she wanted to stay home instead of going with her family to Bannon.

Every Labor Day as long as Katie Rose Belford could remember, her family had driven the fifty-seven miles from Denver to Bannon to visit her mother's folks. When her father was alive they had always gone. Last Labor Day—the first one after his death—when Mother said she couldn't bear to go without him, Grandda O'Byrne had driven in from Bannon, loaded Mother and all six of the children into his car, and taken them out. Going to Bannon for Labor Day was like going to church on Sunday.

Bannon was a little farming town, and they always came home with tomatoes, thick cream, maybe bacon or sausage, and *always* eggs, so that all the way home Mother kept warning, "Careful of the eggs now." Katie Rose could never remember ever getting home without many of them cracked or broken—not with all the scuffling about in the back seat by the three youngest of the family.

For convenience' sake these three were always lumped together as "the littles."

This morning Katie Rose dawdled in the kitchen waiting until the hubbub of getting ready had started. Her mother glanced at her daughter's black hair wrapped up on roller curls and the checked shirt hanging outside blue shorts.

"Hurry, lovey, and do your hair and put on a pretty dress."

Katie Rose's eyes under their dark fringe of lashes were a deep blue that was almost purple. Now they flickered uneasily. "I'm not going to Bannon with you. I've decided to stay home today," she said.

And that was when Mother, her older brother Ben, her younger sister Stacy, and the three littles stopped in their tracks and stared at her as though she had suddenly turned into Benedict Arnold.

What would Mother say to that? She was not the gentle-voiced, unruffled, cookie-jar type of mother, but a redheaded Irish, impulsive, loving—but tempery—

· 2 ·

one. She had married at nineteen, so folks were always saying to Katie Rose, "She looks so young and pretty to have children in high school."

She never read books on child psychology, or worried like some mothers about giving her children "psychic scars." Once she had clouted Stacy with a stock of celery, and she found the pancake turner just as handy to whack with as to turn pancakes.

But now she only gasped out in unbelief, "Not going to Bannon with us! Mother in heaven, why?" and turned helpless eyes on Ben who was the oldest and the one she leaned on.

Ben gave the offender a scorching look from his blue, blue eyes. He was seventeen, and redheaded like Mother, but already a head taller. He had a maddening way of not speaking *to* Katie Rose but to an invisible someone behind her. He did now in a la-de-da voice, "The Duchess of Belford is of finer clay, don'tcha know, from the rest of the peasants."

The so-called Duchess ignored him. "You see, Mom, tomorrow is the first day of school, and I've got a lot to do."

Stacy was putting a rubber band around her auburn blond pony tail. "Silly!" she laughed. "What's to the first day of school?"

Nothing for you, Katie Rose thought ruefully. You're fourteen and you haven't an inhibition in the world. You sing and prance when you're happy; you shed bucketfuls of tears when you're sad, and erupt like a volcano when you're mad. You're more like Mom and all the O'Byrnes than I am.

Stacy added, "The first day you just register and say hello to everybody and then come home."

She would be saying hello to everybody because she was going back to St. Jude's. Katie Rose wasn't. She and Ben were beginning in a brand new high school, and just the thought of it started a flutter of wings under her ribs.

It was hope. Emily Dickinson had written, "Hope is the thing with feathers that perches in the soul." And that scrabbling about inside Katie Rose was her hope that at the new John Quincy Adams High, she would be as popular and sought after as her beautiful Aunt Eustace had been when she was young.

Aunt Eustace was the real reason for Katie Rose's staying home today.

The littles chanted out, "Katie Rose, go blow your nose."

Mother hushed them and sent the three scampering through the side gate and to the car parked at the side. Katie Rose carried out a carton of yarn for one of the relatives.

Ben got in behind the wheel of the old Chevy and yelled out, "All aboard!" Stacy went dancing through the gate and climbed into the front seat with him and Mother. Their dog, Cully, was whimpering to go, and the littles argued that there was room for him, but Mother said, "Good heavens, no," and called to Katie Rose to hold him so he wouldn't race after the car and develop athlete's heart.

Even as Ben started the motor, part of her wanted to call out, "Wait! Wait, and I'll go."

Instead, she watched the car turn onto Hubbell Street and head north for Bannon. She knew so well how Gran and Grandda O'Byrne would welcome them, and the platters of fried chicken they would all sit down to. And how all the other O'Byrnes and Callanans and Tracys —the shirttail relatives, Mother called them—would be bobbing in and saying, "Sure now, you must stop for a cup of tea before you leave." And sometime during the day, Grandda would say, "Rose, play us an Irish jig." Mother would sit down at the piano, and Ben and Stacy —and in other years—Katie Rose would dance for them. Uncle Brian, Mother's youngest brother, would join in.

And because Katie Rose danced with more dignity than Stacy, one of the relatives would be sure to nudge another and say, "Look at *her* there. Belford through and through.

They meant that she took after her father's side of the family, which was English. "The booky Belfords," the Bannon folks called them.

Well, she was different. She didn't like being *poor*. Stacy didn't mind wearing clothes Mother bought at rummage sales, but she did. "You, and your airs and graces," Mother would say. "God help us, I'd think I got the wrong baby at the hospital if you didn't look so much like your Aunt Eustace."

That reminded her. Aunt Eustace, Father's only sister, would probably call today. She usually dropped in a day or two before school started to bring the children something special. Sometimes when the family returned from Bannon in the evening, a package would be left at the front door, and Mother would say with relief, "Ah, so she came while we were gone."

Funny about Mom, Katie Rose mused, standing on in the September sun. She was so gay and easy with everyone except Aunt Eustace. But Katie Rose alway felt ill at ease when her aunt dropped in, either alone or with frail old Grandfather Belford, to their noisy, untidy house. Aunt Eustace and Grandfather lived in a big stone one people called the Belford mansion. It was a landmark near the university.

Aunt Eustace's life had a fairy-tale fascination. As a little girl, Katie Rose had been far more enraptured by her scrapbooks, full of her pictures, her trips, her parties, than by Snow White or the Sleeping Princess. The nicest thing anyone could say was, "Katie Rose, you certainly favor your Aunt Eustace." For didn't all those newspaper write-ups constantly mention, "Her brunette beauty was enhanced by a white ermine wrap," or, "The Homecoming Queen, Miss Eustace Belford, graced the float with regal beauty"?

And Katie Rose's visits in that serene, well-ordered gray stone house were paradise. A room and bath all her own. No slaphappy Stacy helping herself to her blouses and bath powder, or leaving chocolate smudges on her books.

Katie Rose let go of Cully and looked back at their red brick house. It sat on the corner and even though it was a two-story with four rooms upstairs and four down (if you counted the reception hall) it always looked as though it were bursting out the seams into the yard. Clothes on the line. A ladder under the apple tree. Bicycles and roller skates on the walk. Even the lawn mower was sitting where the littles had left it after cutting half the lawn.

Two of the littles were twins and they had been duly christened Matthew and Angela, but were called Matt and Jill. They were eleven and Brian was ten, but the three were all of a size with slate-blue eyes and hair the color of cornflakes. Ben bought the same Levis and T-shirts for all three. When he took them to the barbershop, they all came out with the same haircut. Mother laughed and said they deserved more paddlings than they got, but it would mean paddling three because they were always in everything together.

They shared a paper route, getting up at five every

morning. They fought among themselves, but if a neighborhood youngster picked on one he had three wildcats to fight. Ben said that Jill didn't know yet that she wasn't a boy.

The littles were one of Katie Rose's crosses.

She hurried into the kitchen to make cookies to serve Aunt Eustace with her tea. If only she had ready-to-bake ones instead of mixing them from scratch! She had voiced that thought aloud once, only to have Ben, the grim watchdog of finances, say, "Nothing doing. You pay too much for what you get. Besides we already have butter and eggs."

But the butter came from Bannon relatives, and was in bowls instead of cubes; the eggs were often cracked and leaky. She had exploded once to Stacy, "Other people buy breakfast food in boxes. I just hate all those sacks of corn meal and cracked wheat from Bannon. I wish we got bacon in flat little packages, instead of chunky old slabs they send in. You know what they all say, don't you? 'Poor Rose, with all those mouths to feed.' "

"Oh pish and tush! Don't be such a sensitive soul. You notice they all stay at 'poor Rose's' when they come in to the dentist or for buying new clothes—or whatever."

Yes, and Katie Rose didn't like that either. That doubling up to make room for Bannonites.

This morning she had to juggle a recipe for drop

cookies in order to use up the thick sour cream. Last school term when she walked home from St. Jude's with her best friend, Marge, Marge had only to take a roll of ready-to-bake cookies from the refrigerator, slice them, and slide a panful in the oven. The cookies would be ready by the time they made chocolate.

But Marge and her family had moved away from Denver at school's closing in June. That was one of the reasons Katie Rose had decided to switch from St. Jude's to John Quincy Adams High with Ben, who wanted to work in its up-to-the-minute chem labs. Stacy was quite content at St. Jude's. Besides she, a freshman, couldn't go to Adams because, like other public highs, it took only tenth, eleventh, and twelfth grade pupils.

Again the wings fluttered under Katie Rose's ribs. She hoped she would find friends at Adams High.

She put her first panful of cookies (spice, but without nuts) into the oven, and went out to clean the front porch.

The littles had hunched the chairs together to make a fort. She was bent over pulling them apart when someone yelled out, "Hey, I came to borrow the purple ballpoint you said I could."

She straightened up and stared at a gangling, sunburned boy grinning at her. His snub nose was scarlet and peeling. His straw-colored hair was so long it curled at the neck. He had a cut on his chin, and his shirt looked as though someone had grabbed it at the shoulder and all but ripped out the sleeve. One of his huaraches was held together with twine.

He stared back at her in just as much surprise. "Gee, I thought you were—Do you have a redheaded sister?"

"Yes. Stacy."

"She's the one. She's a doll. I saw her yesterday at that little store where the bell rings when you open the door, and it smells like cheese and garlic—"

"Wetzel's," she supplied.

His grin came back. "That's right. And Mamma Wetzel didn't have a purple ball-point—only blue and green and black. But it has to be purple for what I've got to do, and Stacy said she had one I could borrow."

Leave it to Stacy to meet weird characters and invite them to the house. Katie Rose said, "You never know where to find anything of Stacy's, and I don't have time to hunt and hunt. I have to clean up this whole place for some very important company I'm expecting. Besides I'm baking cookies."

"I can smell 'em." He moved closer to the screen door with a rapt expression on his face. "Look," he appealed, "I'll clean up this whole mess out here and finish cutting the grass, and you hand out a broom and I'll sweep the porch and walks—if you'll just give me something to eat."

He did look hungry. He did have a melting grin. "Okay." She gave him the broom, and raced back to the kitchen.

This having to use unorthodox ingredients in recipes! The first panful of cookies were so rich they had spread all over the pan. She added more flour, more liquid to her dough. She worked, hearing the whirr of the lawn mower and thump of bicycles being leaned against the back porch. He finally came back with the broom, puffing for breath.

It was noon now, and she poured milk and fixed sandwiches for two. Her caller went through his before she had even cut around the runny cookies and put them on a plate.

"You know what I had to eat yesterday?" he asked, and then answered himself. "Quince preserves and mustard pickles. Know what I had for breakfast today? The rest of the mustard pickles."

She stared past the red, peeling nose into his deepset gray eyes. "Why? Don't you have a mother?"

"She died ten years ago."

She made him more sandwiches, and found potato salad in the refrigerator. "Don't you have any other folks?"

"Yeah, but kind of few and far between and far away. Pop and I were living in Mexico, but I left him five days ago to drive up here."

"You left him in Mexico? Why? Why didn't he come with you?"

He hesitated. "He travels a lot—first in this country and that. He's an itinerant worker."

"You mean he goes around picking fruit?"

He studied that a moment. "Yeah, he goes to a country and lives there a year or two—maybe longer—and picks the plums out of the country."

"I shouldn't think it'd take a year or two, or longer, to pick plums."

"You'd be surprised. You have to pick them and sort them, and maybe throw out the ones you thought you could use but on closer inspection—"

"You're zany as a zombie. You could tell by one look whether a plum was good or not. Why did you drive all the way from Mexico to Denver?"

"It's like this. Mother came from Denver, and Grandma and Gramps were always writing and wanting me to come and stay with them. So when Pop finished his—his picking plums in Mexico, suddenly everything cleared for him to go to Alaska. Besides, he thought it was time I was getting back to home territory."

"I didn't know they had plums in Alaska."

"Oh yes, very *unpicked* ones there. So Pop and I wrote the grandparents I'd be coming, and it took me five days to drive up in my ratty little convertible—"

So that explained the sun-bleached hair and peeling nose!

"—and guess what? When I pulled in day before yesterday they were gone. Our letter from Mexico was still in the mailbox. A neighbor across the alley, who's tak-

ing care of their cat and their lawn, said they took off
to visit a nephew in California and stay a month or two.
The house was locked tighter'n a drum except for a
basement window open enough to let the cat in and
out.''

''What'd you do?''

''This fellow across the alley helped me open the cat
window wider, and I crawled in. So I have a cat named
Oscar, laundry facilities, recreation room with a fireplace, half a bath—but no light in it—and access to
Grandma's fruit closet. Mostly pickles and preserves.''

''Don't you have any money to buy food at Wetzel's?''

''I was robbed,'' he said on a heavy sigh. He told her
how a friend had ridden with him from Mexico City as
far as Santa Fe in New Mexico. After dropping off the
friend, he had driven on alone. That night he had pulled
off the road to sleep in the front seat—

''I woke up, and here were three hoodlums making off
with my suitcase and guitar, and the woven bag I was
bringing Grandma with a bottle of tequila tucked in it
for Gramps. I gave battle, but three were too much for
me. One of them whammed me across the chin with the
guitar.'' He fingered his cut chin. ''Seems kind of trea-
sonous for my own guitar to injure me.''

''Did they steal your money too?''

''Yes, and that's one of life's ironies. If I'd had it on
me, I'd still have it. But Pop and I decided it'd be safer

pinned in a pocket in the suitcase. Good thing I only had one day's driving ahead of me or I wouldn't have had enough for gas.''

She thought of his landing at his grandparents, broke, hungry, and bunged up (from his own guitar) only to find them gone. She slid more cookies onto the plate. ''What's your name?''

''Michael in England, Micky in Ireland, Michel in France. I've been called Miguel for the last two years in Mexico. What's yours?''

''Kathleen Rose Belford. The family calls me Katie Rose, but beginning tomorrow when I start to school I'm to be Kathleen. In the morning I'm telling them I will *not* be Katie Rose. Aunt Eustace always calls me Kathleen.''

She glanced at the clock. Almost two. She got up. ''I still have to clean the house for the company I'm expecting.''

''How about my giving you a hand as long as I ate you out of house and home? I'm a good cleaner-upper.''

He was. He ran the vacuum while Katie Rose picked up and put away. He stopped and pointed to the bookshelves that covered a whole side of the living room. ''Who's the bibliophile?''

Maybe he thought she didn't know what the big word meant. ''My father. But I've read almost all of them,'' she bragged. ''Summer before last after he died—I missed him so that I read, read, read from morning till night.''

He flashed her his nice grin.

He mopped the big front hall. He leaned on the mop to ask, "How early can you remember something clearly?"

What a surprising fellow he was! "Why?"

"You and your *whys*. Why because Pop and I were arguing about it. I read his— Well, just before I left, a man told him about something that happened when he was three, and Pop wondered if you could trust your memory that far back. He wants me to think about it and then write him. How far back can you remember?"

As she thought back, vague, jumbled pictures came to her mind. Of her father's reading or quoting from a book while Mother fed or maybe bandaged one of the littles. "I remember when I was three or four, Father read something to Mother about filling a cup. And she said, 'Do I fill your cup?' and he said, 'Yes, my sweet, full and running over.' So whenever she'd pour him coffee or tea, I'd watch to see if she filled the cup running over."

"That's a swell something to remember."

Katie Rose polished their dented silver sugar bowl for Aunt Eustace's visit. "But there's one time that's indelibly engraved on my mind," she said. "It was when Uncle Brian went in the Army, and came in from Bannon to tell us good-by. He brought the girl he was engaged to—Colleen—and they were so in love."

"How old were you then?"

"That was ten years ago when Uncle Brian wasn't

nineteen yet. I was five and a half. But I can still see him in his uniform plain as day—he's tall and red-headed. And he had Mom move the buttons over so his jacket would fit tighter. She cried, and Uncle Brian hugged her and said, 'Rosie, you goose, there isn't even a war on. I'll be home in two years.' I remember Colleen saying she'd have her hope chest full by then. She was so pretty. She was in a flowered dress with a real, real full skirt, and her waist was so small she looked like an upside-down hollyhock. Mom sat down and played an old Irish song, and they danced to it right there in our living room, and Uncle Brian sang the words to Colleen — 'You hold my heart in your two little hands.' And then he tipped her face up and kissed her.''

''And I suppose he came back in two years and married her?''

''No, he didn't come back in two years. He went to Korea, and I don't understand about it all, but he was wounded and captured by the Communists. It was five years before his folks finally got word he was alive and coming home. And somehow gossip in Bannon had it that he was disfigured and lamed for life. But he wasn't —just nervous and weak and rundown. Anyway, the night before he came home, Colleen eloped with a fellow named Fred Kleim. He has a garage here in Denver some place.''

''The snide little wench! How'd your Uncle Brian take it?''

"It was Mom who had to break it to him. She said he laughed as though it were a big joke, and said, 'Then, Rose, I guess you're going to have to use this set of silver I bought in San Francisco.' It's still there in the cupboard in the box it came in. Mom's saving it for when he straightens up and finds another girl. If he ever does! He drinks too much."

"No wonder. Pop says grief turns a person to hard work, prayer, or drink. Ten years ago," he mused. "That was about the time Mother died. Only I can't remember it clearly at all. We all got sick from food poisoning in a little town in Greece, so it's just like a blurry nightmare. Only when I woke up, I couldn't say, 'I had a terrible dream that Mother died' because it was true."

Katie Rose filled the sugar bowl. "I know. Dad's death still seems like a nightmare too—even though it's going on two years. He and his partner in the book store started out for a little town to buy some old books, and the car skidded off the icy road and turned over. Dad was killed, and the driver was paralyzed for months. The phone call came late at night. Mother called to Ben and me—and I remember coming down the stairs and seeing her still holding on to the phone so dazed, and saying over and over, 'It's a mistake—it can't be true—Ben, Katie Rose, it can't be—' " Her voice lumped as she told it.

They worked on in silence until he asked, "Who is

this important personage we're scrubbing and polishing for?"

"My Aunt Eustace. I'm the one who should have been named after her instead of Stacy. That's Stacy's real name, Eustace, but she doesn't like it."

The house was shiny clean now, and her helper said, "You'd better go on and dress up for your company. And don't forget Stacy's purple pen."

Two

KATIE ROSE found Stacy's purple pen on the floor of their upstairs room where she had used it for initialing her gym shoes. Nor was she long in climbing in and out of the bathtub, yanking out curlers, reaching for lipstick, and putting on her prettiest dress. No rummage-sale bargain, this coral-colored cotton, cut on princess lines with tiny ruffles outlining each gore. Aunt Eustace had bought it for her at "Madeline's."

She took a Band-Aid out of the bathroom cabinet, and her two pictures of Aunt Eustace off her dressing table to show Miguel from Mexico. She saw the admiring look in his eyes as she descended the stairs and while she covered the cut on his chin with the Band-Aid.

She held up the pictures. "This is my aunt we cleaned up for. Everyone says I look just like her."

"You look like a ruffly petunia."

"This one is a copy of the huge painting over the fireplace in the Belford house that an artist painted of her in England when she was presented at court. She was twenty. And this is a copy of another picture painted just recently, and there're twenty years between, but see!—she's still just as beautiful."

He gave the picture only a cursory glance. "Don't look like she'd be very handy in a kitchen," he commented.

The nerve of him! "She has more important things to do with her time. She devotes it—as the papers say—to the cultural arts, and—and—"

"And she entertains celebrities, I bet."

Suddenly Katie Rose wanted to impress this raggle-taggle boy with his impudent grin. "Do you know who gave the land for our university? The Belfords. Do you know that my grandfather Belford was chancellor there till he retired? And do you know that the society editor calls Aunt Eustace all the time to ask if she's entertaining"

"Did you get the purple ball-point?" he interrupted.

She thrust it at him. "There!"

He sat down at the dining table, and pulled an envelope out of the back pocket of his grimy khaki pants. "Now you go on and do something. I don't want you watching me. Why don't you go get some flowers for the table?"

"Don't worry, I don't want to watch you," she flung back, and went out to pick some of the hardy asters at the side of the house.

He called to her as she came in, "Petunia, come here. Tell me the question that grown-ups are always asking you that throws you the most."

She didn't know what to answer. His mind moved too fast for her.

"Then I'll tell *you*." And in an adult, patronizing voice, he said, " 'What are you going to be when you finish school, young man? Are you going to follow in your father's footsteps?' "

She laughed, and they were back again on the old confidential footing. "Yes, they do. Especially at St. Jude's where Mom plays for all the school performances. The nuns just adore her, and they're always asking me, 'Are you musically inclined like your mother?' "

Slowly she picked withered leaves off the asters. And then, because he was so easy to tell things to, she blurted out the *one* thing she hoped no one would find out at John Quincy Adams High where she was starting tomorrow, "Mom plays the piano and sings at Guido's Gay Nineties. From seven-thirty to midnight. Giddy's, everyone calls it."

"She does? One of these places with checked tablecloths and candles, and the waiters with handlebar mustaches? And she wears leg-of-mutton sleeves and her hair in a pompadour. She sounds swell."

"But I—I wish she had another job. Because—well, Aunt Eustace doesn't know, and I'm so afraid she'll find out. She'd be horrified. I mean—well, she goes in for symphonies and operas and—"

"So what? After all, your dad is dead—and a buck's a buck. So why doesn't she tell Aunt Eustace and let her flip?"

Before Katie Rose could get in a huff again over her aunt, he handed her back the pen. "There now. I've done what I lay awake for a whole night and planned on doing."

She looked down at the card on the table in front of him. "Is that your school transcript?"

"So it is. For Miguel Barnett. See?"

"St. Jude's wouldn't give me my transcript. They said the school always *sent* them to whatever school the student was going to."

"They're not so orthodox in Mexico. I asked them for it and—bless their loving, trusting hearts!—they handed it over to me."

His transcript was made out in purple ink. And he had made such a point of finding a purple pen. "Did you change something on it?"

"Just two little pen strokes—neither one any bigger than an eyelash," he admitted.

"That's forgery," she said, aghast. "You'll be found

out because you know how teachers and schools always check everything. You'll have a day of reckoning."

"A dread day of reckoning," he sighed. "I suppose I will."

"Are you going to school here?"

"Sure. Grandma was always writing and telling about this wonderful John Quincy Adams that's just finished and in walking distance of them."

Her heart skipped a beat. "You're going to Adams?" Somehow, all the time they had worked and talked together, she had thought of him as a chance acquaintance she would never see again. And here she had spilled out the whole story of her life, complete with family skeletons. "What year are you?" she asked faintly.

"Soph, I guess. I'm almost a year older'n you, but I've changed schools so much. I can talk in just about any language, but I'm poor in grammar and syntax. I know all about Marie Antoinette being done in, but I'm not even quite sure who John Quincy Adams is."

"His father was our second President, and then he came along and was our sixth. It's a new school for me too. I'm a soph too." She looked at him and couldn't help feeling—well, *maternal* toward him. "First impressions are very important, Miguel. Were all your clothes stolen except what you've got on?"

He nodded, and looked down at his streaked and grimy khaki pants. "How long would it take these to dry if I put them through Grandma's washer?"

"They'd be dry by morning. You can't wear those flappy huaraches. You ought to get a haircut too."

He riffled his fingers through his long, straw-colored hair, and grinned ruefully. "More of fate's ironies. Pop and I decided to hold off on shoes and a haircut so I could get good old American ones."

She offered impulsively, "I've got some baby-sitting money I could lend you for a haircut—"

A knock at the back door interrupted.

The Japanese workman who always put on the storm windows next door had come to borrow back the ladder which the Belford littles had left under the apple tree.

Miguel said something that was evidently Japanese to the man, for his face lighted. He answered back in what was to Katie Rose unintelligible jargon.

Miguel shoved his transcript into his hip pocket. "I asked him if he could use any help and he said yes. Says he needs someone to lift and hand him the heavy windows and doors. Says his arthritis is bothering him. I might make enough for a haircut."

"You might make enough so you won't have to eat marmalade and pickles for supper."

Before he hurried off, he bowed and kissed her hand. "I was hungry and you gave me food," he said soberly. "I was wounded and you gave me a Band-Aid. I needed shearing and you offered me your baby-sitting money. *Adios,* and *vaya con Dios,* Senorita Petunia."

Zany as a zombie!

And he was going to John Quincy Adams. She was suddenly paralyzed with a fearful thought: of his flap-flapping down a hall in his huaraches, torn-shirted and unkempt, and yelling out, "Hey, Petunia."

As Gran O'Byrne always said, "The saints have mercy!"

The kitchen clock said four now. She strained the lukewarm tea into a pitcher. Iced tea for Aunt Eustace on a warm September day. Katie Rose's family drank strong *hot* tea out of a big earthenware teapot summer and winter. She hunted through the cupboard for two glasses that almost matched. Silver, china, glassware, linens always matched at the Belford mansion, but at the Belfords' on Hubbell Street one was hard put to find two of anything that did.

The scene was all set for callers. Four-thirty. She hesitated about phoning Aunt Eustace. What could she say that wouldn't sound like, "I'm waiting for you to come with my starting-to-school present"?

But at five she dialed the Belford number. She could mention casually that the rest of the family had gone to Bannon without her. The housekeeper answered and said Miss Eustace was unable to come to the phone. "Who's calling, please?"

"It's Kathleen, Mrs. Van." (Her name was Vanderburg but her aunt and grandfather had shortened it to Van.) "I—well I—"

"I'll tell her you called."

Aunt Eustace must either be resting or having company herself. Then all Katie Rose's staying home from Bannon and baking cookies and shining up the house (with the zombie's help) had gone for naught. Not to mention her looking like a flower—petunia, he'd said—in the coral-colored dress with its ruffly skirt which her aunt had selected for her.

A half hour, an hour dragged by. She dawdled about the house, let-down and lonely, and feeling that life had somehow done her wrong.

Then Cully's bark announced that someone was coming up the front steps. She opened the door and stood transfixed. The setting sun was bathing the whole world in a rosy glow. And there, coming to the door was the kind of boy every girl dreams of. His eyes were dark. So was his hair that was a thick, curly mat on his head. He was built like a football player, but he was wearing a blue sport shirt and navy tailored shorts—and a heavenly smile. Why, it was like a roll of drums sounding in a technicolor movie for the Enter-the-Hero scene.

He was carrying a suit box, and he said, "I guess you're Kathleen. I'm Bruce Seerie. I'm the messenger boy from your aunt Eustace."

"Oh, you are! Oh, come in—come on in," she fluttered.

He stepped into the hall and handed her the box. There *was* such a thing as love at first sight. She couldn't bear to have him turn and walk out the door and out of her life. "I was just going to have some iced tea. Would you—do you like iced tea?—I mean, it's all ready." She couldn't keep her eagerness from showing.

He answered nicely, "Thanks. Sounds good."

She scuttled about in the kitchen fixing a tray with glasses of tea and cookies. Thank heavens for the polished dining table and the flowers. Thank heavens he hadn't caught her with her hair in curlers. And a special thank heavens that the noisy family was gone. The littles would have chanted out, "Katie Rose has got a beau! Whatta you know—whatta you know!"

Where was her poise? For once she envied the O'Byrne trait of being easy and friendly without being gushy. Mother had it. Stacy had been born with a gift of blarney that made everyone warm to her.

"I made these cookies. They're better with nuts. Is the tea too strong? You were certainly swell to bring this box over from Aunt Eustace."

He had poise and lots of it. He liked spice cookies without nuts. The tea was just right. He was glad to drop off the box from her aunt. "My dad is the Belford lawyer and handles her rentals and finances, plus little odds and ends she wants done."

That prompted her to run on about wonderful Aunt Eustace. He didn't say a word about whether she was handy in a kitchen or not. His old man and his mother gave her a high rating, he said.

An uneasy lull, which Katie Rose filled, "I'm starting to John Quincy Adams tomorrow." There went the scrabble of that thing with feathers under her ribs.

"Good enough. I'm switching over to Johnny Q too."

Johnny Q! She hadn't heard it called that before. "Oh—you are? Are you a soph?"

"Junior this year."

She couldn't help gushing on, "If I'd been born a *month* sooner, I'd be a year ahead, but at St. Jude's they had this gruesome rule that you had to be six before Christmas or you couldn't start in the first grade. My brother Ben is only a year and a half older, but he's *two* years ahead of me. And Stacy's a year and a half younger, and she's only *one* grade behind me. All because they were born in the fall and I was born in January."

His beautiful smile. "The moral of that is: "Don't get born in January. I was sixteen just in time to get my mitts on a wheel in time for school. I still haven't got a car of my own. Just promises. I share this one with Mom. She says her half has the gas tank and mine the wheel."

Katie Rose shoved the plate of cookies at him. "Won't you take another one?" But inside she was saying, "Won't you please like me?"

He talked football. Johnny Q had a coach that was hard as nails—a regular slave-driver—but that's what it took to win games. Bruce was an app gym man too. At her blank look, he explained, "Apparatus gym. You know, horizontals, parallels, and rings."

Magnificent Bruce Seerie. And so exactly the opposite of her earlier caller. His tan was smooth as bronze. His hair didn't need cutting. He didn't surprise her by asking, "What's the earliest you can remember?" He wouldn't tamper with a transcript. No, and neither would she dream of saying to this terribly clean, healthy, polished—even blasé—boy, "Uncle Brian drinks too much," or "Mom plays the piano at Giddy's."

Instead of chomping down cookies, he ate only one. Half his iced tea was left in his glass when he stood up and said he guessed he'd have to be pushing on. He was going to a cook-out, swim party.

She felt suddenly Cinderella-ish. "I hope your bringing Aunt Eustace's box hasn't made you late for your date," and ached to hear him say, "I haven't got a date. How about your coming with me?"

But he said easily, "Oh, Jeanie's no clock-watcher."

Jeanie. She had never known what jealousy was before. It was an ugly green monster that turned the tea in her throat bitter. He tossed off a crumb of comfort as he went out the door, "Be seeing you at Johnny Q."

She watched from behind the screen door as he climbed into a cream-colored convertible. She envied, even hated the Jeanie who would soon be sitting beside him.

In the box from Aunt Eustace was a kelly-green cardigan for Stacy, who wore a uniform at St. Jude's, and a plaid skirt and turquoise blue slipover for Katie Rose.

Even though Cully was nudging at her to feed him, she had to try on her new clothes. She had to walk through the house and dream of walking through unknown corridors at school with Bruce Seerie's hand on the soft cashmere sleeve of the sweater.

The family returned at dusk. They weren't as noisy and high-spirited as usual. Katie Rose helped them carry in cantaloupe and canned peaches and a loaf of Irish bread which had come, as she knew, from one of their relatives named Liz. Liz seemed to think the young Belfords would drop dead of hunger without her round, lumpy loaves made of whole wheat meal.

Mother deposited her load in the kitchen, and glanced at the clock. "Heaven help us, it's time to dress for Giddy's."

"Swish a lot of cold water on your eyes, sweetie," Ben said. He was both protective and tender with his mother.

Katie Rose saw that her mother's eyes were red from crying, and she followed him into the hall. "Is Uncle Brian drinking again?"

"Not again—*yet*. He got fired from another job. I guess drink is the only way he knows to escape what's eating him. He's such a lovable guy."

Pictures of a young, high-headed Uncle Brian passed swiftly through Katie Rose's mind. His stirring tenor voice when he taught them to sing "Cockles and mussels, alive alive-o." So had he taught the three older ones to dance and to skate. She thought of his taking her and Stacy Christmas shopping or to a circus when they were little. When they were tired, he would carry the two of them on his shoulders.

"He's had almost five years to escape it," she said, nagged as always by what Aunt Eustace would think. "I can't see why—"

Ben stopped her with his dark look. "There's a lot you can't see. You can't see that he was starved and brain-washed and tortured by the Communists for years, and that he only held out by thinking of the girl waiting for him at home. So he comes home sick and beat and—well, you know what he found. Did you iron my white jacket?"

Ben worked from eight to eleven as sandwich man at the Ragged Robin drive-in down on the Boulevard. In all her furor of getting ready for Aunt Eustace, she had never thought of his jacket.

While Stacy sorted over the Bannon eggs in the kitchen, Katie Rose ironed the jacket. "Your battered zombie that you told to come for your purple ball-point came," she said.

"He did! I fell madly in love with him. His name's Mugell."

Stacy and her manhandling of words. She pronounced misled, *mizzled* as though it rhymed with *drizzled*; and ecstasy as though someone put an ec in front of her name, *ec-stacy*.

"Not Mugell," Katie Rose corrected. "Meeg-u-ale, or Meegwale if you say it fast."

" 'Meeg' or 'Mug,' 'gell' or 'gwale,' he's still a ginger-peachy."

Oh no, Bruce Seerie was the ginger-peachy. What was Jeanie like? And how far gone was he on her?

Ben was waiting in the hall for his white coat. He called up the stairs, "Hurry up, gorgeous, or we'll both be late."

It never ceased to be a thrill for the young Belfords to hear the rustle of those long and full silken skirts at the head of the stairs. All day Mother would be working about the house, making apple tarts or maybe putting up shelves in the basement. She would be in whacked-off Levis, and wondering where she left her shoes; she was a great one for stepping out of them.

Then the breathless and dramatic moment of her coming down the stairs transformed into a glamorous entertainer. Tonight she was wearing the emerald-green taffeta with its black lace yoke and the long, gored skirt heavy with bands of black velvet. Her red hair was combed into a pompadour. One of the littles muttered, "Aw gee, I like the red dress better."

She said as she pulled on black lace mitts, "Were many of the eggs broken on the way in? Now what is the line that comes after 'Oh, how we danced the night we were wed'? There's a wedding anniversary party out there tonight, and they'll be asking for it."

They all briefed her on the lines. It was a nightly ritual for Katie Rose to put on her lipstick; Mother's slapdash job of it never got in the corners. Stacy hurried to get her black velvet wrap with its gold satin lining. It was too warm to wear it, and she threw it over her arm.

It was an event for the neighbors to watch her set out for Guido's. The middle-aged couple next door (the ones whose storm windows were now on) stood in their yard to beam at her and say, "We said we bet you'd be wearing the green tonight."

The family across the street, where Stacy often baby-sat, was watching too. The man went through his usual routine of singing out, "Oh, you beautiful doll!" and starting to run toward her, with his wife hanging on to him and pulling him back, while their children jumped up and down in high glee.

Ben drove off with her. After taking her to Giddy's out on the Henderson Road, he'd swing back to his job at the Ragged Robin. Mother got a ride home with the cashier and her husband. She was supposed to be off at midnight but it was usually one or two in the morning. She worked every night except Friday and Sunday.

Stacy said happily as she and Katie Rose watched the Chevy out of sight, "Aren't we the luckiest? All the kids at St. Jude's wish they had a mom like ours."

Mother liked her job at Giddy's. "Just think of getting paid for doing what I'd rather do than anything else.'' And Uncle Brian always said that playing and singing came as natural to an O'Byrne as yowling to a cat. Katie Rose would think they were lucky too if it weren't for Aunt Eustace who would be *scandalized* if she knew about the job at Giddy's.

Three

✿

IT WAS ALWAYS scrambled eggs the morning after a
trip to Bannon.

Katie Rose, an apron over the new Aunt Eustace
sweater and skirt, stirred the cracked and broken ones
in the skillet, and salted them with a fluttery hand. She
was shivery and shaky. Not only was she registering
today at a new school, but she had that Don't-call-me-
Katie-Rose bit to get across to her family.

Breakfast was the usual bedlam. Stacy was ironing
the white blouse she would wear with the plaid jumper
and green tie to St. Jude's. She had forgotten and left
it on the line, and a rain in the night had soaked it.

Jill, with her short hair and tanned, chapped face,

looked like a sulky boy in her uniform. Ben pulled her to him to retie her tie. He gave her a fatherly swat on her behind. "Someday you'll be pretty and all the boys will whistle at you," he said.

"That'll be the day!" Stacy laughed.

Mother stood, waiting for the percolator to give its final burble before she poured herself coffee. Her eyes were heavy, and her lipstick was still a faint smudge. Ben scolded as he always did, "You ought to stay in bed, woman, and get your sleep out." And she said on a yawn as she always did, "I can catch a nap later on." But she seldom did.

They ate breakfast in what they called Mom's dinette. Her father, Grandda O'Byrne, was a builder, and she always said some of it had rubbed off on her. One morning when he had driven in from Bannon and was having coffee in the kitchen, she asked him if it would be much of a job to take out the wall between the kitchen and back porch in order to make the porch into a dinning nook.

"Heck, Rose, I could rip it out in a couple of hours."

She had leaped to her feet and said. "Then what's stopping us?"

Her enthusiasm carried them all through the great mess of plaster dust, trips to a salvage yard for lumber and glass, and stepping over paint buckets. She scarcely stopped pounding and painting for ten days and nights —except for playing at Giddy's—until she was hanging the curtains she had found at a Goodwill store.

The family now had another project: Putting half a bath in the closet under the stairs. The tips Mother got at Giddy's for playing and singing requests went into a sugar bowl with a broken handle. For two years they had been trying to get enough for the plumber's estimate. The up-and-down fund. The dipped-into fund. Always a present to take to a birthday party, maybe a rabies shot for Cully—"Well, take it out of the half-a-bath," Mother would say.

It was a morning ritual to count the bill or two and the silver she took out of the pocket of whichever swishy skirt she had worn the night before. One dollar and seventy-five cents this morning, which brought the total to fifty-three dollars and forty cents. The littles kept counting and recounting it until Ben admonished, "Stop fiddle-faddling with the money and eat your breakfast."

Mother said, "Yes, always eat a good breakfast. Breakfast is the most important meal of the day. It's like putting gas in a motor, or stoking a furnace."

Ben caught Katie Rose's eye, and his wink at Mother said, "Listen to her! And her with her black coffee and cigarette."

Those rare moments when Ben made her one with him always warmed and lifted her heart. She hated to break the spell—but now was the time. She cleared her throat. "I have something to tell you all. It's very important. Now that I'm starting in a new school, I want to be called Kathleen, *not* Katie Rose."

The spell was broken with a vengeance. Again that Benedict Arnold stare from all of them. Ben's eyes flashed, and he addressed the invisible someone behind her, "So Katie Rose isn't high-toned enough for the Duchess. Oh deary me, it has a low Irish sound."

One of the twins mumbled, "But Katie Rose is your name."

"I *loathe* Katie Rose," she said.

Her mother repeated in amazement, "You—loathe —Katie Rose—"

Stacy giggled. "Want to trade with me? I wouldn't mind Katie Rose, and then we could call you Eustace."

"Stacy!" Mother scolded. She looked around the table out of troubled eyes. "Listen to me, my dear owns. There's so much sorrow and heartache in the world—" (She must be thinking of Uncle Brian) "—so if we can do anything to make someone we love happier, then let's do it." She smiled shakily at her one dark-haired child. "Uncle Brian always calls you Kathleen Mavourneen, so we'll all remember and call you Kathleen." She handed her her cup and said very formally, "Please, Kathleen, I'd like a little more coffee."

Katie Rose wished right then she was more like Stacy. She would have thrown her arms around her and said, "Mommie, you're swell." All she could do was fill the coffee cup and set it before her mother. She had won her point, but somehow she wanted to cry.

So Katie Rose, five-foot three and weighing a hundred and six, was ready for her new life in a new school as *Kathleen*.

Ben took them all in the Chevy. He dropped off Stacy and the littles at shabby old St. Jude's, and then headed east.

The Belfords lived west and south of the university. Just since Kathleen could remember, the part of town east of the campus had built up into block after block of pretty new ranch houses. This exclusive residential district was called Harmony Heights, and the older section, of which Hubbell Street was part, had been dubbed Hodgepodge Hollow.

The Hollow was not at all exclusive. Old brick houses like the Belfords' rubbed shoulders with low frame shacks. Some homes had fenced yards, some had none. One house across the street from the Belfords' had even started as a hot-dog stand at the park. It had been moved onto ground under a big cottonwood, and was still having wings added to it.

Wetzels' neighborhood grocery, where Ben stopped this morning for a notebook, occupied the front of a house with the owners living in back. Next to it was an untidy shop with a sign, AL FLOOD, BODY AND FENDER WORK. The Flood family lived behind the shop on the back of the lot, which was cluttered with bent and rusty car parts. The parents yelled and fought with each other, and so did the children. The Belfords' mother often said, "Those fightin' Floods—common as pig tracks." And though she had no trace of snobbery in her, she warned, "We'll give poor Al Flood any business we can, but let's not mix with any of the family."

And Matthew had chimed in with, "Not us. They're tough, those Flood boys, and once one of them took Jill's bicycle and wrecked it. But he can't now because he's up at the Reform School for breaking in Downey's Drug."

Rita Flood had been in Kathleen's class at St. Jude's, but had not been one of her friends. She was sly and pushy—yes, and cheap.

They were nearing the school. Looking toward the east, Kathleen could see the blurred outline of the old stone Belford mansion sitting on high ground. Ben swung into the parking lot at John Quincy Adams. He studied it with interest—the split-level architecture, and the amazing glass and wood panels. "You can hardly tell where the door is," he mused. "They've got three stereomicroscopes in their lab."

"Ben, are you scared about starting to a big, new school?"

"What's there to be scared of? This isn't a big school as schools go. It was just put up between two other highs to catch the overflow from them. Someone was telling me the principal wants to make quite a thing about its being a friendly, everybody-know-everybody-else one."

"Do you suppose any others will be coming here from St. Jude's?"

"I doubt it. They're out of this district. We were over the edge ourselves, remember? Grandfather Belford had to see the school authorities and get a permit."

At that moment a cream-colored convertible swung into a corner of the parking lot and Bruce Seerie leaped out and joined a knot of other boys. The thing with feathers fairly flapped its wings under Kathleen's ribs.

"That's the boy that brought the box from Aunt Eustace. His father is her lawyer, and they all know each other real well." She added painfully, "Ben, I don't want anyone at school to know that Mother works at Giddy's because—"

"Because why?" That cold flash of his eye again.

"Because—well, she says herself she doesn't want Aunt Eustace and Grandfather to know."

"Get this through your stuck-up noggin, if you can. It isn't because she's ashamed of it—though I suppose Aunt Eustace would feel it was sullying the name of Belford. It's because Mom doesn't want Grandfather to know that Dad cashed in his insurance and put it in the book store. She wants the old fellow to think Dad left us enough to get by on. He'd only worry and feel he should help. And he doesn't have it. Sure, he owns the Belford mansion and has his retirement pay, but it's Aunt Eustace that has the dough—she inherited it from one of her mother's relatives."

"But, Ben, this is a new school, and if I make new friends—"

"Friends, she says." Again he appealed to his invisible ally behind her. "As though a friend worth having would drop her like a hot potato because her mother plays the piano to make house payments and buy groceries and pay on our bills so's to keep one jump ahead of the sheriff." He lowered his eyes to her. "I'm darn proud of the woman myself. Giddy's is no honky-tonk. They serve the best lasagne in these parts, and they're not even licensed to sell hard liquor. Nobody gets drunk on beer or wine. Guido and all of them out there treat Mom like one of the family."

"But I still think—as long as we're just starting here—"

"All right, all right. I won't shout it out to the multitude that Mom's the leading attraction at a Gay Nineties club. Come on now. Who'd ever have thought that was a door where all of them are pouring in!"

They went through it and into the smell of new plaster and varnish, and a noisy maelstrom. They were routed through corridors and down steps into the gym, where tables were set up for registering. Ben said, "We belong here at the A to M one."

They gave their names to a teacher behind the table, who then told them to wait until she could assign them counselors. As they turned away someone said, "Hi, Ben. Hi, Katie Rose. Fancy meeting you here!"

Kathleen looked at the sharp-faced girl in her too short, too skintight red dress with big polka dots, and at her ratty hairdo. She couldn't believe that fate could be so cruel. Fancy meeting Rita Flood of the fightin' Floods here at Johnny Q! She had supposed that of course Rita would be safe at St. Jude's.

She was too jolted to answer, but Ben said, "Hello, Rita. I'll let you in on a secret. It's Katie Rose no longer. It's Kathleen from this day forward."

"I get you. And I'll buy it," she said with a conspiratorial wink. As though, Kathleen thought, they were all buddy-buddies!

The extra thump of her heart told her that Bruce Seerie was at the side of the gym looking over the apparatus that had been pushed out of the way. She didn't want him to think she was *with* Rita Flood. She turned away and pretended to read a notice on the wall.

A teacher at the A to M table called out, "Benjamin Belford. Kathleen Belford."

With that, a ruddy, tweedy man came hurrying up to shake hands with Ben. He was their principal, Mr. Knight. He was proud, he announced, to welcome a boy named Benjamin Belford to his school. "I went to the university under your grandfather, *Chancellor* Benjamin Belford. I knew your father. And this is your sister, Kathleen." The school was honored to have her too, he said in a hearty voice.

Ben looked embarrassed, but she was hoping all the enrollees would hear, and say afterwards, "There goes Kathleen Belford," so that she wouldn't feel so lost in this new school. Mr. Knight boomed on to the teachers at their table and other tables that no name was so revered in educational circles as that of Belford—

Why were some of the students looking behind him, and having all they could do to keep from snickering? Kathleen followed their eyes. There was her zombie. He had his thumbs in his ears and, without making a sound, was going through the *hee-haw, hee-haw* motions of a donkey. Ben had to cover his twisting lips with his hand.

Mr. Knight went his busy way, and Miguel pushed up to Kathleen and said, "Hi there, Petunia. Thought maybe you wouldn't recognize me with my hair cut."

As though she wouldn't recognize that peeling nose, wide grin, and Band-Aid on his chin. "You shouldn't make fun of Mr. Knight. He's the principal."

"I know. Swell guy too. He okayed my transcript."

"But he did get a little thick," Ben admitted.

Rita Flood's name was called. Kathleen watched with relief as Rita left the gym with her white slip.

"How do I look?" Miguel asked Kathleen and Ben with childish pride.

He looked terrible. The short haircut showed up a lump on his head. And where in heaven's name had he found such an *old-man* shirt with pin stripes in it, and two sizes too large for him?

He enlightened them happily, "I looked through an old trunk of Gramp's in the basement and found this shirt and look!" He lifted a foot in black *laced shoes.*

She said faintly, "Your grandfather must be a big man."

"Portly is the word. And I washed my pants like you said with a lot of soap and bleach, and hung them on the line and they'd have been perfect if it hadn't rained in the night. I ironed them dry."

But they were still damp at the seams and pockets, and smelled of chlorine. She felt a sudden lump in her throat. But why should she feel responsible for him and his makeshift attire?

A girl turned away from the A to M table and came toward the three of them with a beaming, crinkly smile. "I know who you are," she told Kathleen. "I knew when Mr. Knight said Belford. You're Kathleen that Bruce took the package to last evening. I thought for a while I'd been stood up."

So this was Bruce Seerie's date whom Kathleen was sure she would envy and hate. She could envy her for being so petite and winning. Her hairdo was just right with her pixie face, and her white-trimmed jacket dress was the same golden brown as her eyes. But you couldn't hate her. She included Ben and Miguel in her "I'm Jeanie Kincaid."

Even while Kathleen made introductions, Miguel from Mexico said brashly, "You know what you look like? Like a cookie all sprinkled with sugar and cinnamon. Umm-mm-m."

Her smile exploded into a laugh. "Well now. I've

been told I'm nutty as a fruit cake, but nobody ever called me a cinnamon cookie.''

Ben looked at her with appreciative eyes but said nothing.

An announcement came over a speaker: ''Will the pupils who have received slips please go to the room designated on them?''

Jeanie looked at hers. ''Do you go to one thirty-one, Kathleen?''

She nodded and they started out together. Ben called after them, ''You'll have to get home on your own, Sis. I want to look over the chem lab.''

She and Jeanie found Room 131 just as Rita Flood was coming out the door. Rita stopped her. ''Golly, Kathleen, we've got to get all sorts of things, like a gym suit—they're in one piece and you get them at Penney's. What I mean is, we could go shopping in the morning because there's no school on account of teachers' meetings.''

''I'm busy tomorrow,'' she said shortly. What right did Rita have to act as though they were bosom pals?

Kathleen's and Jeanie's class schedules were made out after much consulting with a young and helpful counselor. They were walking down the hall toward the front door when Kathleen caught a glimpse of red dress and white polka dots. She drew back and clutched Jeanie's arm. ''Is there any way to get out besides the front door?''

Jeanie peered ahead and then back at her. This was Kathleen's first experience with the way Jeanie Kincaid could size up a situation without having it put into words. "There must be. Let's sneak down to the gym. Bruce ought to know."

Again Kathleen's heart gave its Bruce Seerie thumpety-thump. Here was her chance to tell whether or not it was love everlasting between Jeanie and Bruce.

The registering was so nearly over in the gym that the boys were moving the equipment back on the floor. Bruce came over to them, a hard-breathing gladiator in gym shoes, black T-shirt, and white pants. He asked if they needed a lift home.

How could Jeanie refuse so lightly? "No, thanks. We just want you to help us get out without going through the front door."

Was it because Kathleen was along that he looked relieved? He escorted them to a side door, opened it, and called after them, "Be seeing you tomorrow."

Outside, the sun was glaring. Jeanie pointed in the direction of Harmony Heights where she lived. Kathleen said she lived on Hubbell.

"It'll be the long way round for you, but let's go to our house," Jeanie said, "and have a Coke with lots of ice. Maybe Mom will be home, maybe not. This is her morning at Mount Carmel nursery."

Kathleen walked beside her, puzzled, and again Jeanie surprised her by reading her thoughts. "If you're thinking that Bruce would have been panting to drive me home if you weren't along, you're crazy. He wanted to stay and try out the horizontals. And he doesn't like a sticky girl.'' They paused on a corner while a truck lumbered by. ''And that's all right with me. Because, to tell the truth, Kathleen, I'm not passionately wild about Bruce.''

''You're not! I think he's—'' She almost said ''magnificent,'' but tempered it to ''nice.''

''Yes, but have you ever dated a fellow who was always so nice, who—well, never got worked up about anything?''

''No, none of the boys at St. Jude's were like that.'' Jeanie's very candor prompted her to admit, ''I guess I haven't dated as much as you. I was always asked to our school parties and dances, but none of the boys was the kind to take your breath away. Stacy—she's my younger sister—thinks I'm too choosy.''

''I'm not,'' Jeanie said, ''but my dad is. He embarrasses me the way he third-degrees boys that drop in. He can put down a firm foot too. But back to Bruce—he's so well brought-up it gets monotonous. I'd like to trade him for someone hot-blooded who has tantrums, or walks a picket line in the rain, or hates his mother— or something.''

Kathleen couldn't believe such heresy. ''He has a beautiful smile,'' she said.

''Yeah. He wore braces on his teeth till he was fourteen. How did that Miguel get the goose egg on his head and bash on his chin?"

She laughed when Kathleen told her about his trip up from Mexico, and his losing battle with the three hoodlums who were making off with his belongings.

"He's a goof-ball," Jeanie laughed again. "But such an appealing one."

They walked past blocks of new, low houses with velvety green lawns and clipped hedges, while the noon sun beat down. Kathleen's new slipover felt hot and scratchy.

She couldn't help worrying about Miguel and his showing up at Johnny Q looking like a comic valentine. And she couldn't help wondering how long Rita Flood had waited at the front door for her.

"Jeanie, does it make you feel kind of scroungy to have to dodge someone you don't like?"

"You mean the girl in the polka dots? I'd feel scroungy if I dodged someone just because she dressed like a slob."

"No, it isn't the way she dresses." Kathleen told her about Rita's rowdy older brothers who were constantly in trouble with the law, her screeching mother, her grumpy father who looked as though he'd been sautéed, clothes and all, in rusty oil.

"Don't worry about it," Jeanie said. "She looks a little on the vixenish side to me."

Kathleen couldn't tell Jeanie her biggest worry. Rita

Flood, like many of the St. Jude pupils, knew that the Belford mother supported the family by playing at Giddy's Gay Nineties. If Rita knew Kathleen didn't want it broadcast, she'd take delight in doing it. Why couldn't Rita Flood have stayed on at St. Jude's instead of coming to Adams to be a thorn in her side?

Four

JEANIE LIVED in a low, rambling white house with a rosy tile roof and shutters. It was laid out like many of the new ranch-style houses where Kathleen baby-sat; the kitchen faced the street, the living room was behind it with French doors opening onto a patio.

Mrs. Kincaid was there, relaxed in a deck chair. She said she was limp from her morning at a day nursery down under the viaduct. She was as friendly and warm as Jeanie but, unlike her, was tall and blond. When Kathleen helped Jeanie gather up potato chips and odds and ends in the kitchen, she said, "You must look like your father, Jeanie."

"I don't look like either of them. I'm adopted," she

admitted freely. "They took me when I was about seven weeks old."

They sat on the shaded patio with Cokes and food. Jeanie's mother said, "And you're Kathleen Belford. I was in your father's class at the U—so now you know how old I am. He'd be forty-two?"

Kathleen nodded. "Mother is younger."

"Six years. I know that too because their romance was the big thing on the campus. Your father was working on his Master's thesis, and was in the library a lot—that's where I worked. Your mother, a freshman, came up from a little town—"

"Bannon," she put in.

"Yes, to major in music."

Kathleen squirmed a little, thinking of someone who wanted to be an opera singer ending up at Giddy's. She said, "She and Dad used to kid about it. Sometimes when our three littles would be howling together, he'd say, 'Would you call that an orchestral ensemble?' "

Mrs. Kincaid went on, "Your father had never given a second glance to any girl until your mother came in the library. But when he saw her—why, it was like that song about taking one look at you and then my heart stood still." Her eyes lighted. "Yes, all the campus basked in that romance. Your mother was so beautiful. Even her name, Rose O'Byrne, had the lilting sound of an old ballad. And she hasn't changed much. I saw her in Wetzel's store last spring when I stopped to get some cheese." Mrs. Kincaid said then what Kathleen was used to hearing, "She looks so young and pretty to have six children."

"Tell her about the library," Jeanie prompted.

"When your grandfather Belford retired as chancellor, they named the library after *him*. But I always like to think it was called Belford Library because your father and mother met and did most of their courting there."

"Mom's the romantic type," Jeanie said. "She's told me about it, and that's why I wanted to know you."

Kathleen said, "I suppose you know Aunt Eustace too. She must have been terribly popular. She's got scrapbooks—one for each year—and they're just crammed full of pictures and write-ups."

Jeanie's mother said, "She was the daughter of the most-loved chancellor the university ever had. She was sought after, made over, and looked up to. She was Homecoming Queen, Maypole Queen, and I don't know how often she was Prom Queen. She was Junior League, and presented at court in England. So, as I tell the doctor—" She didn't finish the sentence, but ended with, "I mean Jeanie's father, Dr. Kincaid."

And Jeanie said with her ready laugh, "As long as our parents knew each other way back when, that should make us related or something, shouldn't it?"

"Kissin' kin, at least," her mother said.

Jeanie walked two long winding blocks with Kathleen when she left. "Someday I'll walk all the way home with you, and go in for a Coke."

"It's a long trek. But maybe Ben could drive you home."

Jeanie's cinnamon brown eyes danced. "That's what I had in mind."

The sidewalks were cottony clouds as Kathleen walked on alone. She had made a friend at Johnny Q. And she had found out it wasn't undying love between Bruce Seerie and his last night's date.

Stacy was waiting for her on the corner outside their house. Perhaps because Kathleen was so happy, she looked at her sister objectively for the first time. And she saw her not as pure nuisance value in her life, but a pretty, vital girl with shiny, auburn-blond hair, transparent skin, and eyes almost as green as the tie she wore.

Kathleen then noticed Uncle Brian's red car with its nicked fenders and Bannon license sitting at the curb. Its doors gaped open, and the littles were struggling through the side gate with sacks and packages. Their redheaded uncle waved to them both in high spirits and yelled, "We finally made it."

"What's going on?" she asked Stacy.

"Uncle Brian brought Liz in from Bannon to stay with us."

Liz was the relative who always sent in her Irish bread. She had come over from Ireland about five years ago. "Good old Liz," everyone spoke of her. Over in Cork County she had raised a nephew after his parents died. When he was grown, he emigrated to Bannon and was nicely settled when he came down with polio. When Liz got word of it, she had closed up her cottage on the river Lee, and caught the first plane over to care for him.

"How long's she going to stay with us?" Kathleen asked.

"I dunno. Her blood pressure is either too high or too low and she's going to a clinic."

"Where's she going to sleep?"

"Oh, Mom and Ben have been juggling beds around, and she'll sleep in the alcove off Mom's room. Ben's down at the dime store to get castors for the bed. The reason I waylaid you is because Liz didn't want to come for fear she'd be crowding us. Mom told her no, we wanted her and needed her. And then Liz perked up and wanted to know did we take our lunch to school because—"

"Don't tell me. I know. She'll bake her lumpy old bread. I'd be caught dead before I'd take it in a lunch."

Stacy's eyes flashed fearsomely. "Kathleen Rose Belford, if you go in there with your nose up in the air, and don't act pleased as punch because she's come—" a moment of wracking her brain, "I'll kick you out of bed every night. I'll burn holes in that new sweater you've got on. Yessir, and I'll paint mustaches on your two precious pictures of Aunt Eustace."

And Kathleen knew she would.

Because the Belford house sat on the corner, the garage opened not on Hubbell but on the side street. Most of their coming and going was not through the front door, but through the side gate and the door which opened into the dining room was just a step or two from the kitchen. (Kathleen thought it crude of the family to call it the back side door; she called it the side back.)

Uncle Brian was still unloading the car. "What in the world is that?" Kathleen asked, pointing to a frame almost as long as a bread board but narrower, with wool yarn stretched across it like strings on a harp.

Uncle Brian answered with his roguish grin, "That, my beauties, is a loom, and if you're good girls maybe Liz will weave you a scarf on it."

Stacy nudged Kathleen as they walked up the back steps, "He's in high spirits—and I do mean *spirits*."

They went through the screen door and into more clutter and commotion. Liz was bending over a full and bulging woven bag. She straightened up with a jar of jam in one hand and in the other a huge dressed chicken, its legs and neck protruding from the waxed-paper wrapping.

She was a sturdy woman with a moist, rosy face, and always a little out of breath. "Our black-haired, gray-eyed Mavourneen," she greeted Kathleen. "And lovelier each time I lay eyes on you."

The O'Byrne side of Kathleen answered to Liz's warmth with, "I'm so glad you came, Liz," and meant it. But the Belford side thought: Wouldn't it have been awful if Jeanie *had* come home with me into this hulla-baloo—and the smell of whisky on Uncle Brian?

Mother came in from the kitchen with the teapot and said, "Sit down now, Liz, and we'll have tea before we carry your things upstairs."

Liz put the chicken on the table, and pressed the jar of jam on Kathleen. "Open it, do, for the little ones. I promised them blackberry jam on their bread."

She was opening it in the kitchen when she heard Liz say to Mother, "Ah, Rose, I did all I could to keep the lad from stopping at the bars as we came."

"I know, I know." Mother raised her voice to call out, "Lovey, put on some coffee—and make it strong." The three littles at the table in the dinette were now drinking their Cambric tea—tea made pale beige with milk and sugar. All the while Kathleen put on the coffee, they were clamoring for the blackberry jam.

Stacy came into the kitchen and snatched up a piece of Liz's oatmeal-colored bread and spread it thickly with butter and jam. She was taking a bite that left a big half-moon in the slice when the door knocker sounded.

So few people used the front door. Family, or friends they knew well, drove up to the side and came through the picket gate and to the *side back* door. But Aunt Eustace and Grandfather Belford *always* stopped on Hubbell and came to the front door.

"I'll catch it," Stacy said blithely, and streaked into the hall, still carrying her sticky piece of bread. Kathleen's heart turned leaden as she heard her bright, "Why hello, Aunt Eustace. Hello there, Grandfather. Come right on in. You're just in time for tea."

Just in time for a horrible mess! Kathleen thought.

She turned to the three at the table, who by now were well smeared with jam, and shook a threatening finger at them. "You stay out here, do you hear?"

She wished she could say the same to Uncle Brian!

Aunt Eustace laughed happily at sight of Kathleen in the pullover and skirt she had sent by a very special messenger the day before. "I wanted you to have something new for the first day of school. I knew that shade of turquoise would be perfect with your coloring."

She had come laden with gifts as usual. Leather-bound looseleafs for Kathleen, Ben, and Stacy, and real pens—not ball-points. For the smaller three, she brought notebooks and pencil boxes full of colored pencils.

As usual, Aunt Eustace was all fragile, feminine loveliness in a pink linen dress with matching sweater over her shoulders. Such slender pink pumps! Such soft leather in the white pouch bag. So like a rose, Aunt Eustace.

The minute she came into the room and sat down on the couch, Kathleen saw the room and everyone in it through her eyes. It was always like that. Even while she was thanking her aunt for her gifts, and feeling Grandfather's feathery kiss on her cheek, she was wishing her mother didn't look so—well, tacky.

Because of her pompadour hairdo at Giddy's, she had let her hair grow long. Around the house, she combed it back into a ponytail that looked pretty much like Stacy's except for its being longer and redder.

Mother and her clothes! Mother and her pawing over bargain tables in basements and saying, "Look, girls! Imagine only seventy-nine cents for blouses—and these shorts." And what a wonderful time she had at St. Jude's annual rummage sale. Then, once having bought a peculiar assortment of clothes, she felt she had to wear them.

This afternoon she was in faded pants with a screw driver sticking out of the pocket. Her blouse was one the twins had given her; the print in it was of clowns and performing dogs. She also, in her sentimental fashion, thought she had to wear anything anyone gave her.

As usual in Aunt Eustace's presence, she looked flustered and ill at ease. She was glancing about for the shoes that she had probably discarded when she and Ben were juggling beds.

Kathleen glanced sideways at Liz. Dear knows, she had enough bulk of her own without wearing such a baggy skirt, and bulgy sweater she had knit herself. On a day as hot as July, why did she have to look so bundled up? Mother said once that it was always misty and chill in Ireland, and people got the habit of wearing heavy woolens.

But Liz was quite unflustered. She was saying to Grandfather, "Sit down, sir." He was the kind everyone called *sir*. "Wait, let me clear that chair for you. Brian came for me before I was ready and, bless us and save us, I just had to snatch up all my bits and pieces. Have a cup of tea now."

Grandfather Belford was tall and thin, with a skin like tissue paper that has been wadded up and then smoothed out. He was the only man the young Belfords knew who wore vests with his suits.

He turned his kindly, scholarly smile on Mother and Liz. "This is one place you can be sure of a real cup of tea. Yes, milk and sugar, please."

Aunt Eustace preferred lemon with hers, and Stacy went to the kitchen for it. All the while, Kathleen was conscious of that plump, picked hen on the table with its insufficient wrapping. Cully kept sniffing at it, and she hurried to put him out before carrying the chicken to the kitchen.

Stacy had cut the lemon into chunks instead of slices. Oh, why couldn't Aunt Eustace have come yesterday when the house was clean, uncluttered, and quiet?

Then Uncle Brian came bursting in the door. A book was tucked under one arm, and he was carrying Liz's loom as though it were a harp. He strummed on the strings of yarn stretched taut on it, and sang out in his strong, melodious tenor about the harp that once through Tara's halls the soul of music shed—

Stacy giggled. Aunt Eustace's smile was perfunctory. But Grandfather chuckled and said, "Sing the rest of it, Brian."

He finished about the harp hanging mute on Tara's walls, and Kathleen could only wish he had been the same. Could Aunt Eustace tell he had made many stops on his way in from Bannon?

With a flourish he gave Liz her loom. He took the book from under his arm and waved it dramatically, "This is Liz's very precious book that goes every place she goes. Her *Ireland, Yesterday and Today.*"

"By Michael Parnell," Grandfather said. "A fine writer."

Aunt Eustace smiled gaily. "I know Michael Parnell very well. When his *France, Yesterday and Today* came out several years ago, I arranged for him to speak at our Alliance Française. I gave a buffet supper in his honor afterwards. He autographed one of his books for me."

"Autographed, is it?" Uncle Brian said, and his Irish brogue was thicker than usual. "He did more than autograph Liz's. He paid her a loving tribute. Just listen to this!" And he read: " 'For Liz, our ministering angel, who sheltered and mothered the boyeen and me when we were sore in need of it. God willing, we'll meet again.' Signed, 'Mike Parnell.' ''

"How nice," Grandfather said to Liz. "You must have known him well."

"I boarded him and looked after the boy when he was traveling up and down Ireland," she said simply.

"He put Liz in the book too," Uncle Brian went on with a look of triumph at Aunt Eustace. "What page is it that he tells all about you, Liz?"

"Never mind, never mind now." And Liz took the book out of his hand. "It's just a bit where he tells of tramping down the boreen through the rain, and being warmed by my tea and a surf fire. Here, Brian, have your cup of tea."

Aunt Eustace stood up and said they must be going. Grandfather dropped his thin, veined hand on Uncle Brian's shoulder. "So you're fond of Thomas Moore's songs?"

"Sir Tom's? Ah yes."

"I have some of them on records. Come out and listen to them with me sometime. Maybe you'd sing some of the old favorites yourself. Yes, I wish you would, Brian. After an old fellow like me retires, he misses having people about."

Kathleen didn't hear what Uncle Brian answered, for she was walking to the door with Aunt Eustace. She didn't drive; neither did Grandfather since his heart attack a year ago. Their housekeeper's nephew acted as chauffeur for them. The Graven Image, Stacy called him, and Kathleen had to admit that he sat behind the wheel of their shiny blue car with no more expression than one.

Emil came to help Grandfather down the steps. Aunt Eustace lingered to ask Kathleen if she had signed up for French with Madame Miller. Kathleen had.

"I'm so glad. She's a French war bride, and you'll learn the true accent from her. When we have our Alliance Française banquet next month, I want to take you as my guest." She laughed her young, girlish laugh. "We'll get new dresses and make a party of it."

The Belford living room and dining room were separated only by the smallest archway, so that they were like one big room. As Kathleen walked back into it, she smelled the strong, brown coffee percolating in the kitchen and felt the letdown relief of everyone over the visitors' departure.

Mother looked up at Kathleen's tight face and burst out, "The least she could do would be to phone us that she's coming. Do *we* go barging in on *her* at all hours, whether it's convenient or not?"

Liz said in a wondering tone, "Lemon with her tea! Sure, I never heard of that before."

"Everybody else but us takes lemon with their tea," Kathleen said.

Stacy stared ruefully at the leather-bound notebook

and pen in her lap. "I wish she'd given me the money they cost instead—"

Kathleen turned on her and said what she would have liked to say to Uncle Brian, "You ought to be ashamed!"

"I'm not—not a bit. Because my gym shorts—I've had them since I was in sixth—are practically worn through. Someday when I'm shooting a basket, they'll bust right out and expose my rear."

Uncle Brian wove his unsteady way out to the piano in the hall and began playing one of his Sir Tom's melodies—"The Minstrel Boy," Kathleen thought. Mother called her into the kitchen to hand her a cup of coffee. "Take this in to Brian. And see that he drinks it."

Uncle Brian looked up at Kathleen and the steaming cup, and went right on playing. She stood there holding it. "You needn't glower so," he said at last. "I wouldn't have hammed it up, if I'd known you had company. How was I to know? Creeping up as she did on her cat's feet, and coming in the front door?"

"You could have been more polite to her."

"Not without an effort." He softly rippled the keys with his long fingers and said in a mimicking voice, " 'Michael Parnell talked at our Alliance Française, and I gave a party in his honor. He autographed a copy of his book for me.' Thah!" He played a minute longer. "Your grandfather is a fine, old gentleman. Quality.

I'd like to go visiting him if I didn't have to get past the prima donna.''

"Here, drink your coffee.''

His hands crashed on the keys, and he leaped to his feet. "So I shamed you in front of your idol. And you want me out of the house.''

Mother caught his arm as he reached the door. "Sit down, Brian, and drink your coffee. We'll have supper ready in no time at all. Don't go now—the traffic's at its worst,'' she pleaded. "Wait, Brian—please wait.''

"Wait till I'm in better condition, you mean.'' He laughed recklessly. "I might be in worse—who knows?'' He bent from his tall height and kissed her, and banged out the door.

He backed his car with a roar, swung it about with wheels spinning, and zoomed away as though he were on a country road. Mother breathed, "Dear God, look after him.''

Liz murmured, "Now why did he go rushing off all of a sudden?''

Guilt prickled down Kathleen's spine. Home-going traffic was at its peak. If anything happened to him, it would be her fault.

Lying in bed that night, she wished she had answered, "No, I don't want you out of the house.'' She heard Ben come in from work. She wakened when Mother came up the stairs long after midnight. If anything *had* happened to Uncle Brian, would they bring him here? Toward morning she wakened with a start of terror, hearing the front door open and voices in the hall. She jerked up in bed. For one awful moment she imagined a limp body was being carried up the stairs.

It was only the twins and little Brian scurrying up and down the steps, and folding the papers they would load into bicycle bags and deliver.

Other mornings she never even heard them.

Five

❀

IMAGINE KATHLEEN being uneasy about the impression her zombie from Mexico would make at Adams High! Imagine her thinking that his showing up there with peeling nose, goose egg on head, grandpa shoes and shirt, and those weather-beaten khakis would cause Harmony Heights students to snub him.

She should have realized that the open-hearted grin which had so won her the morning he sniffed her cookies through the screen door and asked for a handout would work the same wonders with others. Well, to be honest, it was what was behind his grin—his readiness to listen to, or do for anyone.

The school called him Miguel from Mexico, and was

both delighted and awed at the way he casually sprinkled foreign words into his conversation.

He was in French II with Kathleen and Jeanie. *And* Rita Flood, who had taken French I at St. Jude's with Kathleen. And how Madame Miller—Mee-lair, she pronounced it—fell for *Michel,* and how they rattled off French together about Paris and environs!

She told him, "Michel, you must read that lovely book, *France, Yesterday and Today.* Even to read it makes me homesick."

He had already read it, he said. Yes, he liked it too.

And Kathleen's family fell for him. She came home from school one afternoon to find him sitting at the table with Liz, wolfing down her Irish bread while she watched with doting eyes. Stacy had shortened her Mugell to Mug, and he called her his *petit chou,* French for "little cabbage," though the small Belfords thought he was calling her "petty shoe."

By the time Kathleen got home that day, Miguel was calling Mother *mamacita* and Liz *acushla,* which was Irish for "pulse of my heart."

He also heard about the Belford half-a-bath fund that afternoon. It was when the littles came trooping in from school and Brian, who seemed to do the worrying for all three, said, "Mom, Sister Ursula says tomorrow is the last day for us to bring our money for the Korean orphans."

"I might know, I might know. Hand down the half-a-bath, and we'll take it out," she said.

Miguel listened with great concern while everyone explained about the up-and-down fund in the sugar bowl. "When it gets to be a hundred," Kathleen said, "Mom can call the plumber."

"But it's like the frog taking one jump out of the well and falling back two," Mother admitted with a resigned laugh.

The next morning, Liz, who was helping with the school lunches, said, "Kathleen, I'm putting in a bit extra for the boyeen. I worry about his getting enough to eat. You'll be seeing him at noon, won't you?"

Kathleen nodded. "Our lunch period is right after fourth-hour French, so some of the class just drift down to the lunchroom together."

Jeanie, with her crinkly smile, was the drawing card, as Kathleen knew. Many of the Adams students had gone through the nearby junior high with her, and the boys who knew her liked to linger near the locker she shared with Kathleen.

Two boys in French II, named John and Tom, had known her the year before. They looked enough alike with their lank, ginger-colored hair, dark-rimmed glasses, and identical white T-shirts to be brothers, though they were no relation; just close friends with a consuming interest in stock car races, and joint ownership in a stock car.

John and Tom sat in class with the absorbed attention of pointer dogs. They explained that to Kathleen at lunch. "You have to cultivate it. If a teacher thinks

· *69* ·

you're hanging on every word he or she lets fall, he or she does better by you. Try it."

Madame Mee-lair called them both John-Tom. "I have trouble with names," she explained to Miguel and Kathleen after class one day, "but even so I tag each one in my own mind. You, Michel, I think of as the very, very helpful one."

Kathleen asked shyly, "Do you tag me too?"

Madame laughed. "But yes. 'The one with violet eyes and your heart showing through.'" She put her hand on Kathleen's shoulder, and added kindly, "But, *ma cherie,* it is better—at certain times, you understand—for a woman to veil her eyes."

I must remember that, Kathleen thought.

The two girls who shared the locker next to Kathleen's and Jeanie's were also old schoolmates of Jeanie's. June and Deetsy.

June was a pretty, pretty blonde, and she knew it. The boys liked her—and she knew that too—so she wore a complacent little Mona Lisa smile along with her stunning clothes.

Deetsy was the gusher. She was always wildly excited over losing her chem notes, or forgetting her lunch, or what a new rinse did to her hair. She worked on it to make it as blond as June's. She had violent crushes on boys. Jeanie said she got charley horses from carrying torches. June and Deetsy were in French, and by the end of the first week drifted on to the lunchroom with Kathleen, Miguel, Jeanie, and the John-Toms.

The following Monday, when a quiet, polite boy from the Philippines (also in French II) came in alone and looked shyly about, Miguel called, "Over here, George." Jeanie added, "Yes, join us—we'd like to have you."

He bowed to them all and sat down, murmuring, "Thank you, thank you very much."

Kathleen looked at Miguel and Jeanie with something like envy. They were so sure of themselves. She wasn't. Ben called her snobbish. Could it be that all snobs were shaky and unsure inside?

That noontime, with the extra sandwich and apple tart in her sack for Miguel, she fell into step with him in the noisy stampede to the lunchroom. "Liz worries about your not getting enough to eat, Miguel."

"I'm not suffering. So far I haven't slighted Oscar on his cat salmon, though sometimes I'm tempted to dip into it."

His grandparents, he explained, were paying the neighbor across the alley fifteen dollars a month to care for the cat and their yard. The neighbor had turned the chores—and money—over to Miguel. "And I've still got the storm-window job. Just think! I got it on my own and I'm keeping it on my own."

"I should think your grandparents would cut their visit short when they know you're here and living in the basement."

"They don't know it. I don't want them to. I don't want them to come hurrying back. Because this trip is a big event in their lives. They wrote the neighbor across the alley that some in-law has a big fishing boat, and they're thinking of going on an ocean cruise. I can make out till October first and then I'll get a check from Pop.''

''Be sure and buy some clothes when you do,'' she advised him.

No, she needn't have worried about her zombie. Without even trying, he was a somebody at Johnny Q. And Kathleen Belford wasn't.

Those first weeks at school, other girls stood out because of their accomplishments, or just sheer good looks or personality. Sometimes in the hall, Jeanie would nudge her, ''Look quick, Kathleen—that girl in the white skirt! Isn't she a doll? She was Teen Queen when they opened the University Hills shopping center last June.'' In sixth-hour lit everyone looked with awe on a tanned girl, her dark hair almost a crewcut, who had won a high-diving meet in the summer.

This lit class, which was Kathleen's last except on gym and swimming days, was the highlight of her day. To think that Bruce Seerie, a *junior*, was in it with her! She had to look past two of his fellow football players to see his dark, shorn, curly hair, the pleasing line of his cheek, and his broad shoulders.

The first week, as she came in the door each day, he greeted her with his dazzling smile and, ''Hi, Kathleen, how's it going?'' The second week, after parting from

Jeanie outside math and while Jeanie went on to journalism, Kathleen raced down the halls to be early for American lit. She had learned that the football boys never lingered *after* class. The minute the bell rang, they were out the door and making for the practice field behind the school.

And she planned and dreamed that she would say to Bruce, "I don't see you in the lunchroom. You must have second period. We have a swell gang at our table." And he would answer, "I'll juggle my schedule around so I can join you." She even dreamed further that she would make pecan tarts—her foods class had made them—and bring him one.

But during those precious minutes before class, Bruce talked football. Coach really cracked the whip over them. The team called itself the chain gang. "He makes us eat lunch with him in a little room off the gym."

There went her dream of sitting next to him at their crowded table. "I think that's terrible. Why does he?"

"So he can supervise our intake of thick hamburgers, milk, and carrots. He's great on rabbit food. And so we don't sneak in pie, cake, or candy bars."

There went her pecan tart offering.

Money, money! When Kathleen first talked of changing to John Quincy Adams, her mother worried. "There may be a lot more expenses than at St. Jude's."

Kathleen had said, "But you won't have to bother about that. I can save my baby-sitting money this summer."

A week after school had started she was broke. And her current baby-sitting pay could barely keep her abreast.

It galled her, this being *poor*. She wished she could buy lunches as many did, or at least a dessert and drink. She wished she had more changes of costume as June and Deetsy had. She wore the coral-colored cotton, but it was a little dressy for school. She wore the new slip-over and plaid skirt, but when the day turned warm, the sweater was too warm.

Mother said, "Lovey, why don't you wear that frilly blouse and red skirt I got you?"

But she had got them at St. Jude's rummage sale. "I hate wearing clothes that somebody else has worn, especially somebody I don't know," Kathleen said unhappily. Nor was that all. All South Denver contributed to the sale, for parishioners solicited clothes from friends and neighbors. Suppose some girl at Adams High recognized the white frilly blouse or the red skirt!

It wouldn't have bothered Stacy. Even if a girl had said to her, "That used to be my blouse," she could laugh and say, "It did! Mom paid thirty cents for it at St. Jude's." But the very thought made Kathleen wince.

Nor would her pride ever let her say, "I haven't got the money."

The athletic tickets went on sale at school with much fanfare, much stressing of school spirit over the loudspeaker. The price was seven dollars for all football, basketball, and baseball games.

Deetsy had volunteered as a sophomore salesman, and that was all she could talk about at lunch. She and June already had their triple cards fitted into their billfolds. The John-Toms, as well as George, the boy from the Philippines, counted out their money to her. Jeanie didn't. "I'll pay as I go," she said, "because two Saturdays of every month I work in Dad's office helping his receptionist get out the bills. I'm the envelope-addresser."

Miguel could answer Deetsy's insistence with a bland, "I haven't got the dough, *ma cherie.*"

Kathleen said lamely, "I'll have to—to wait—and see."

She didn't have to wait long, for Ben waylaid her on the corner of Hubbell that afternoon after school. "I just wanted to tell you—if you haven't got your own money for an athletic ticket, don't go pestering Mom because—"

"How could I have my own money? All I saved had to go for book fees and lab fees, and the dollar for towels in swimming; and the gym suit alone cost four dollars, besides—"

"You needn't tell me," he interjected wearily.

"Ben, if you lend me the money, I'll pay you back. I don't want them thinking the Belfords haven't any school spirit."

"School spirit's one thing, and seven bucks on the nailhead's another. I haven't got it. Not after paying some on getting that impacted wisdom tooth pulled last week and losing a night's work. I promised to pay the dentist five a week." He reminded her that September was always a bad time, and it was worse this year with a repair job on the refrigerator. "And we're just coddling the car battery along, wondering how long it'll last. Mom's worried enough without your sulking over an athletic ticket, you hear?"

"Yes, I hear."

She saw only the grim set to his jaw. She had no way of knowing that he was thinking; I wish I could give it to you. I wish I didn't always have to say no when you want something so bad.

September was drawing to a close when Madame Mee-lair detained Miguel after class. Lunch period was almost over and Kathleen was putting her wadded-up sack in the trash container when he came hurrying up to her. She said, "Here's the sandwich Liz put in for you."

He took a hungry bite of it, before asking, "How'd you like to make ten bucks, Petunia?"

How would she! To be able to say to Deetsy, "I'll take my athletic ticket now." To be able to say to Bruce,

· 76 ·

"I was so excited when you caught that forward pass."

A lunchroom supervisor started toward Miguel to remind him that all eating of lunches was to be done at a table. He finished it before she could reach him. She smiled indulgently and shook her head.

"How Miguel? How could I make ten bucks?"

"You ever waited table?"

"Oh yes. Stacy and I always do at St. Jude's when they put on their suppers."

Madame, he said, had told him about a banquet where they wanted waiters and waitresses who could speak French—

"Ten dollars—wonderbar! You think I'm good enough, Miguel?"

"You can bluff it through. You know, 'Would Madame like coffee?' and such. Stick close to me and I'll help you. Ben said I could borrow one of his white jackets for it. It's the first Saturday in October."

"The first Saturday in October?" she repeated. "Not the Alliance Française? Because if it is, Aunt Eustace asked me to go to it with her."

He consulted a card as the bell rang, and they moved toward the door. "That's it. Alliance Française at the Country Club. Want half my Hershey bar? We're to be there at six, though the banquet—"

"It starts at seven," she said heavily. "Oh, Miguel, I—well, Aunt Eustace is one of the charter members. No, you eat your candy bar. She's a past president— she was awarded the *palmes de critique*—"

"Whatever that is. Just tell her you'll be there in white apron and cap, *merci beaucouping* your way about."

"I wish I could. But—don't you see? I just couldn't. She'll be at the head table with the notables. She said the speaker is an educator from France, and the superintendent of all the schools will be there—and the governor—and she—she wouldn't like to have her niece waiting table—"

"So what? Ten bucks is not to be sneezed at."

"I'm not sneezing." She was closer to crying.

He looked at her, puzzled. "*Guten Nacht*, Petunia, what are you trying to prove anyway?"

She blew her nose tearfully, angrily. "That's a silly thing to ask. What is anybody trying to prove?"

"Ask me what I am."

"All right, what are *you* trying to prove? That you're a free spirit, I suppose, by living in a basement on quince preserves?"

"Not a free spirit—just *me,* Miguel. I want to prove that I don't have to ride along on somebody else's coat-tails." He started off on his loose-limbed flapping trot, but turned back to call, "Don't forget the white coat."

The first edition of the school paper came out that very afternoon. Kathleen and Jeanie walked out of school reading it.

On the first line was a boxed,

Two Spanish exchange students from Venezuela were welcomed. So was the short-haired girl in Kathleen's lit class because of her high diving. Also a girl who had done a dance number in *La Bohème* in the open-air opera, and another boy because of his winning an American Legion essay contest. *And* "Miguel Barnett, linguist and traveler in many lands, but the most democratic American of us all."

It seemed that only Mr. Knight, the principal, revered the name of Belford.

Kathleen and Jeanie walked to the Boulevard and Downey's Drug. Jeanie was looking for a watertight swim cap, and Kathleen needed graph paper for math.

Because of Uncle Brian she hadn't yet invited Jeanie to walk home with her. She never knew when his red car with its battered fenders would be sitting at their curb, or when the strong smell of coffee, and his playing the piano would meet her when she opened the door. Sometimes he was in a dark, untalkative mood; again in a boisterous, devil-may-care one. Once when Stacy grumbled that there were songs about Kathleen Mavorneen, and Rose of Tralee, but never one about Stacy, he thumped out and sang,

> *Stacy, Stacy, give me your answer true,*
> *I'm half-crazy over the love of you.*

Yesterday morning they came downstairs to find him

on the living-room couch, his long legs twisted in the afghan Mother had spread over him in the night when he came in.

"Why does he keep coming to Denver?" Kathleen had asked Ben.

"He's looking for a job."

"He could get one in Bannon, couldn't he?"

"No, and that's the pity of it. When he came back from Korea he had his pick of them. Not because he was the town hero or because everyone loved him, but he was good. The fellow at the TV and hi-fi shop would have made him a partner if he'd stuck with it. But he's been fired from job after job because of his binges. He's good at building, and Grandda gives him work—but it's the same old story."

"Remember, Ben, the song he sang to Colleen? About her holding his heart in her two little hands?" Kathleen mused.

"Maybe she still does. Mom says no one can even mention her name to him."

From Johnny Q to Downey's was a long trek, and Kathleen and Jeanie were so tired and thirsty they would have liked to sit at the fountain and order a Coke. But their purchases had taken every cent they had, except four cents between them.

They were starting for the door, when who should come striding in with his cocky walk and red hair gleaming in the afternoon sun, but Uncle Brian! For a minute Kathleen's heart stood still, wondering how many stops he had made between Bannon and Denver. Not too many, she decided gratefully. "Mavourneen, my own," he greeted her.

She introduced Jeanie, and he put his wide arms around the two girls and herded them toward the tall stools at the fountain. "You little honey bears look tuckered out. Just sit down here and have a sundae or whatever your little hearts desire. Downey, these beautifuls are my guests, so treat them right."

Their little hearts desired chocolate sodas.

Jeanie twinkled up at him, "You'll join us, won't you, Uncle Brian?"

He looked with distaste at the brown, bubbly mixture Downey set before them. "I would, sweetheart, if I didn't have to watch my figure. And I promised Downey to see why his TV reception is blurry."

He took off the back panel of the set and tinkered with it until every station came in clear. And when Kathleen and Jeanie pushed back their empty glasses, he wouldn't hear of their walking home. Gallantly, he handed them both into his dusty red car. He dropped off Jeanie first.

When he stopped at the side of their house but made no move to get out, Kathleen asked, "Aren't you coming in, Uncle Brian?"

"Not this time, Mavourneen," he said restively. "Not this time." He was racing down the street before she opened the side gate.

In the next few days Jeanie would ask, "How's your handsome, adorable Uncle Brian?"

"He hasn't been in from Bannon since we saw him," Kathleen answered.

He hadn't, because that very night he had been in a barroom brawl in Bannon, during which he had been hit over the head with a bottle and then rushed to the hospital to have the cut sewed up.

Gran O'Byrne, crying so she could hardly talk, had phoned Mother from Bannon to tell her. But Kathleen couldn't tell Jeanie. Let her go on thinking of him as handsome, adorable Uncle Brian.

Six

❀

OCTOBER CAME. And so did Miguel's check from his father in Alaska. The next day he drove into the school parking lot in a very old and battered Mercedes Benz. He called it Mercy Be, and said it was held together by spit and a prayer. But it was still a foreign sports car, and that sent his stock even higher at Johnny Q.

He bought an athletic ticket from Deetsy. He bought clothes. Now he walked from French to the lunchroom in shirts and shoes which had not been packed away by his grandfather. Kathleen didn't think much of his choice. Plaid and checked woolen shirts. Bruce Seerie wore solid-color blue, white, or black T-shirts. And

Miguel now wore *colored* socks. Other boys in the know, like Bruce, always wore white ones with their loafers.

New clothes or no, Miguel could still look rumpled and thrown together. And he was the kind who always had to be tucking in his shirttails.

The high-school football season was under way. On October's first Monday, Bruce Seerie appeared in lit with a slight limp and a bruise on his jaw.

"Bruce, did you get hurt playing football?" Kathleen asked.

"Oh no. Just worked over a little bit. I guess you saw that two-hundred pounder I was up against Saturday."

She couldn't tell him that she hadn't seen the game because she couldn't raise seven dollars for the athletic ticket. "I just—well, I couldn't make it—something came up at the last minute."

"Next week when we tie into Harkness is going to be dog eat dog. Don't miss *it* whatever you do."

Some afternoons Miguel took Kathleen home in Mercy Be. Once he drove her past the brick bungalow on the edge of Harmony Heights where he lived in the basement. He wanted her to see how lavishly his grandmother's golden glow was blooming under his care. Often Jeanie would sit on her lap in the bucket seat, and they would drop her off first. If only Uncle Brian didn't lurk in the background she could ask Jeanie home for tea.

In the Belford dinette on Hubbell Street, Liz would keep filling Miguel's cup and plying him with her Irish bread, while he helped Kathleen with her French vocabulary, and she drilled him on American history. Imagine a sixteen-year-old boy not knowing Abe Lincoln grew up in a log cabin!

Stacy and Miguel had worked out a telephone signal system. His grandparents' phone was in the locked upstairs where he couldn't get to it. But he could hear it ring in his basement. So Stacy would dial the number, let it ring twice, and then hang up. That always brought Miguel and his car to take her to a basketball game at St. Jude's.

Stacy gloated, "All the kids' eyes get big as saucers when they see me riding up in that adorable little bug of his."

His history teacher had kept Miguel after school, when on a windy afternoon Kathleen came home to see a Bannon car parked at the side of their house. Not Uncle Brian's, but Grandda's. She remembered then that Liz had finished her treatment for high or low blood pressure, and was waiting to get a ride home.

Inside the gate, Kathleen stopped short. Stacy was huddled over on a bench in the back yard, her arms gripped across her middle.

"What's the matter, Stacy?" Crazy Stacy, as the littles called her, always got sick at her stomach when anything upset her.

She lifted a grayish green face and nodded toward the dinette porch that jutted out from the house. "I listened to Gran and Grandda—and all at once—I had to come out because—"

"Is Uncle Brian worse?"

She shook her head. No—no, he's going to be released—any day now." She had to swallow hard a few times. "There's a new doctor—at the hospital—and he's a psychi—chi—"

"Psychiatrist? What did he do or say about Uncle Brian?"

Tears rolled down Stacy's pale cheeks. "He told Gran and Grandda—they mustn't let Uncle Brian come home when he's drinking. He told them he—he had to realize himself he—was at the end of the road. I can't bear to think of—of their locking—him out."

Kathleen patted her shoulders, and felt a little sick at her own stomach.

"You go in, Katie Rose. Just let me sit here."

She walked into the porch dinette where Mother sat with Gran and Grandda. You'd have thought it was a wake. She could taste the salt of Gran's tears on her cheek when she kissed her. Grandda's calloused hand gripped hers hard.

When Grandda O'Byrne was young, he had been one of the Abbey players in Dublin. His big frame had no stoop or sag, and his eyes were surprisingly blue in his weathered face under shaggy, bleached-out eyebrows.

He was very vain of his great thatch of red hair without a sprinkle of gray in it.

Gran O'Byrne was a perky little brown robin of a woman, not much taller than Jill. The dresses she bought and wore were always too long for her, and whenever she came in her daughter Rose would say, "Look at you in that gawky dress. Slip it off while I turn up the hem."

She was doing that now while Gran sat at the table in a sweater over her slip. There was nothing perky about her today.

Liz, dressed for the trip to Bannon, brought a pot of tea to the table, and said to Kathleen, "Here, dear one, it's fresh made."

Their talk went on in sorrowful spurts as she drank it. She heard about the new doctor at the Bannon hospital who'd taken care of Uncle Brian and the cut on his head. "He's made a study of—of drinkers," Gran murmured. (No one used the word "alcoholic" when speaking of Uncle Brian.)

Gran and Grandda, Kathleen learned, were going to close their house in Bannon and go back to Nebraska to visit their oldest daughter, Mary. Gran's lips twisted, "If I was home, I could never lock the door against him."

Liz's face too sagged with grief. She burst out, "He's bleeding from the heart over that empty-headed little trollop."

Kathleen had to ask it, "Hasn't he ever seen her since he got back from Korea?"

"Never once," said Gran. "I wish he could. She's put on weight. I saw her when she came back to Bannon to her uncle's funeral. His *bluebell*!" she added bitterly. "She's more of a fullblown cabbage."

Mother asked, "How long will you stay back in Nebraska at Mary's?"

Grandda looked unhappily into his cup of tea. "It depends. A month mayhaps. Building is slowing up now with cold weather coming on, and it costs so much to get there that we won't be going again for a long time."

"If your house is locked against him, he'll come here," Mother said, not lifting her eyes from the hem she was whipping in.

Grandda nodded. "He will, he will. That's what we told the doctor. When we're gone and our house is not available, he'll only head for Rose's. And he said to tell you you'd be doing the boy no lasting good to take him in. I know it seems cruel, but this doctor says it's the only way to bring him to his senses. He'll never straighten up, the doctor said, as long as his family— what was the word he used now?"

"Condoned," Gran said in a small voice.

"Condoned!" Mother flung out. "Condoning is one thing. But closing the door on your very own is another."

Gran bent her head, her face working. Grandda said

· 88 ·

in a desperate voice, "Wisha, Rose darlin', we've tried everything else. All our reasoning, our scolding, our threatening has come to naught. Mother here has all but gone on her knees to him. He has to be jolted into facing up to it himself, the doctor says."

In the end, Mother agreed to take a firm stand. Gran put on her shortened dress. Grandda unfolded himself stiffly from the breakfast nook bench he had built, and said as he always did, "We'd better be on our way, Mrs. O."

They all helped Liz load her "bits and pieces" into the car. The harp-shaped loom had the visible makings of a woven scarf in it. Liz said chokily, "I'm making it for the lad."

The car turned on to Hubbell and headed north with slow dejection.

The next day was swimming day. Kathleen and Jeanie were always the last to leave the dressing room. What with some forty girls and six hair driers, most of the swimmers merely dried off the drip, ran combs through their hair and, because the school day was over, went hurrying on their way.

But Jeanie always stood patiently with the hot air blowing through her thick brown hair, because she had promised her father never to leave the building until her hair was bone dry. "He worries about my catching cold, and my Eustachian tube acting up."

If Jeanie made a promise, she kept it.

She constantly surprised Kathleen. That first day of school when she found Jeanie was an only child, she had expected her to be spoiled by indulgent parents. She wasn't. It was June and Deetsy, who had brothers and sisters, who bragged about putting pressure on their parents to get whatever they wanted. And they wanted every new fad that came along.

This day they had been dressed in new boat-necked slip-ons with wide horizontal stripes, and showed every one the pouch bags they had to match. Kathleen had seen them advertised as "A Touch of Tahiti." There was much envious oh-ing and ah-ing from the other girls.

Deetsy had said, italicizing two words out of every three, "Did I ever have a time prying the charge-a-plate out of old tight Mom! But Dad's the softy. Tears —that's all it takes. I just turn on the faucet, and I've got it made."

Kathleen had asked June, "Do you turn on the tears too?"

She gave them all her Mona Lisa smile. "Not me. I sulk."

When the other girls were gone, Jeanie said in her forthright way, "Honestly, Kathleen, it sort of turns my stomach to hear June and Deetsy talk like that. Feel the back of my hair now, will you? If that cap I bought is watertight, I'm a kangaroo. I'd be humiliated to *work* Mom or Dad even if I could, which I couldn't."

Kathleen said slowly, "Any one of us could work Mom for anything she's got. She's that kind. It's Ben who cracks the whip over us." Then, because this little time at the end of school with Jeanie was an honest, opening-up time of confidences, she added, "Mom plays the piano five nights a week at Guido's Gay Nineties."

She waited for Jeanie's reaction. She pushed her hair back from her flushed face and said, "Oh, that's fine. That's a lot better than being away from home all day like so many working mothers. She sounds wonderful."

In sudden relief that Jeanie *knew* and even thought it wonderful, Kathleen spilled out, "We never have enough money. At first what Mom made sounded like a lot, but it isn't when there's so many, and our house is old and there's always, always something going haywire—like the refrigerator or the water heater, or the laundry drain gets stuffed up. And the three littles— golly, Jeanie they're supposed to make some on their paper route, but there again their crazy bicycles always need something, and once they threw a paper and broke a customer's glass door. Oh, I don't know, but we never have enough to go around."

There was silence for a moment except for the swish and hum of the wall drier. Jeanie ran her hands through her hair and gave Kathleen a sober smile. "I guess no one is ever satisfied. I have times of wishing I wasn't an *only*—and even wondering about my being adopted. We don't even have very visity relatives. Gee, I'd give anything to have a wonderful, loving, adorable Uncle Brian like you.''

At that moment a girl came dashing back for a school book she had forgotten. And Jeanie was wriggling into her sweater, and saying, ''It's later than I thought. This is Mom's afternoon at Mount Carmel nursery, and I'm supposed to start dinner.''

This was no time for Kathleen to confide to Jeanie that there were times when Uncle Brian was far from adorable.

Seven

THE FOLLOWING FRIDAY after school, Kathleen,
Jeanie, and Ben scampered through a gusty rain to the
parking lot and the Belford Chevy. Ben was taking his
sister and her overnight bag to the Belford mansion.

"Aunt Eustace wanted me to stay tonight," Kathleen
told Jeanie, "so she can take me shopping for a dress
to wear to the Alliance Française banquet. It's tomorrow night."

She was glad Jeanie was driving over with them. She
wanted her to know the lovely, fascinating, fairy-tale
Aunt Eustace. So when Ben stopped in front of the im-
posing gray stone house, and reached for the bag, Kathleen said, "I want you to go in, both of you."

Jeanie backed her up, "I want to. I've always wondered about those turrets at each end and if they were round rooms or—"

"The silos are where the winding stairs go up," Ben said. "All right, we'll go in. But let's get away before they serve tea. All the formality, and Mrs. Van pussy-footing around makes me nervous."

"Oh no, stay," Kathleen urged. As long as she hadn't asked Jeanie to her own home, she wanted her to bask in the luxury of tea served in the Belford mansion.

"If we're asked, let's do, Ben," Jeanie said, her eyes dancing. "Who knows. Our names might land in the society column."

To get into the Belford house, one didn't just turn off the sidewalk and take a few steps to the front door. First, there were heavy, blackish iron gates to pass through before following a winding brick wall past a lily pool and a bronze deer which a snarling wolf was trying to down. (Little Brian worried about that deer. Whenever Kathleen came home from the mansion, he always asked, "The wolf hasn't killed the deer yet, has it?")

"Everything but a moat and drawbridge," Ben said to Jeanie as they ran through the rain to the front door.

And when Mrs. Van opened the door for them they still weren't *in* the house proper. They were in a vestibule, and from it went into the tiled foyer. Doors opened into Grandfather Belford's study, a downstairs bath, a coat closet, and the wide archway into the living room, which could have swallowed up the living room and dining room on Hubbell, plus the hall.

While Grandfather greeted them in his kindly, distinguished way, Aunt Eustace came hurrying in, looking flushed and young in her leaf-brown tweed. She had just come from a fashion show. She included Ben and Jeanie in her fond welcome, "I'm so glad you came in, too. What could be nicer on such a drizzly day than company for tea!"

Mrs. Van glided in and out. Where else but at Aunt Eustace's was the silver tea service so impressive, or the cups so egg-shell thin? Where else would the lemon slices have cloves stuck in them?

Pixie little Jeanie sat demurely in her pleated skirt, ribbed slipover, and matching socks and sipped her tea, her eyes bright as a chipmunk's. Her glance rested on the huge painting of Aunt Eustace—the presented-at-court one—over the fireplace; and the newer one done when she was in London last spring. This portrait hung in the dining room over the sideboard.

Aunt Eustace, following her eyes, gave her gay, rippling laugh. "The same artist insisted on doing it. He said he had never known anyone the years had passed over so lightly."

"Take a handful of the sandwiches, Ben," Grandfather urged. "They're little bigger than dominoes."

Ben, looking less square-jawed than he did at home,

was too ill at ease to take more than one. And only one of the *petits fours*, though Kathleen knew he could have eaten the plateful.

When Jeanie and Ben stood up and said their thank-yous, Kathleen walked with them to the door. She couldn't wait to ask, "Don't you think she's beautiful, Jeanie? And isn't it true about the years passing lightly over her?"

Jeanie nodded. "Yes, she looks ten years younger than Mom—maybe twenty after Mom's had a hard go-around at the nursery."

Aunt Eustace went to her room to rest and dress for dinner, and Kathleen stayed with Grandfather. He was working a double-crostic in a book review magazine, and he asked her if she'd like to help him. She saw that his double-crostic was something like a crossword puzzle only so much harder that only a scholar could work one. Who else would know what "pyrrhotist" meant?

He chuckled. "It means what your mother, Uncle Brian, and Ben are: redheaded."

He filled it in, and let the magazine lie on his lap. "I wish I could see more of your mother, Kathleen. She's a heart-warming person. Now that I'm feeling stronger, maybe she could go to a movie with me some evening."

Oh heavens! What could she say that wouldn't give away Mother's working at Giddy's because of that insurance—or rather, the lack of it. Mother always warned her when she went to visit at the Belford house, "Don't breathe a word about Dad's cashing in his insurance and putting it in the book store. I won't have that sweet old duck worrying about us."

"Some evenings she's busy, Grandfather, because— well, she plays accompaniments at—places." She looked over his shoulder at the double-crostic and asked quickly, "Do you know the next word, that 'A sense of well-being and buoyancy'?"

"Yes. *Euphoria*. Fill it in."

"It's a pretty word—euphoria." And then she began telling him about Ben and his getting straight A's in chem at Johnny Q.

All the while she could hear Mrs. Van moving quietly about in the nether regions, and could whiff vague but appetizing cooking smells. It wasn't the kind of a house that ever smelled of cabbage or onions.

Dinner was always an event at the Belford mansion. Service plates under the soup; Grandfather carving the roast at the sideboard. Aunt Eustace apologized prettily for wearing her velvet hostess gown which was the same tawny yellow as the chrysanthemums in the centerpiece. She carried the conversation, describing the fashion show. "Kathleen, I thought of how pretty you'd look in a crimson taffeta they showed." She always made Kathleen feel like *somebody*.

And so was going up to her rose and silver room at night an event. The draperies were drawn and the covers on the bed turned back. The bed light cast a soft glow on her gown and robe laid across a slipper chair. A far cry from the little room at home, and the double bed she shared with noisy, messy Stacy. She felt *euphoria*.

She felt it in the morning when Mrs. Van brought a tray of breakfast to her and said, "Just ring if you want anything more."

As though she could want anything more than hot chocolate, a half-grapefruit with a *green* maraschino cherry in the middle, muffins, and an individual omelet in a warmed dish.

Yesterday's rain had turned to sleet when Aunt Eustace took her shopping. The sleet didn't touch them, for at the Belford mansion one could step from the garden room into the garage and waiting car. And when Emil stopped in front of Madeline's, the awning to the curb sheltered them.

Madeline's was the kind of shop where only one dress or suit, with accessories to match, was shown in the window. Nor did customers paw over clothing on sales tables. (Mother would be lost here.) Aunt Eustace and Kathleen were ushered into a salon, and her favorite saleslady, Mrs. Neff, came promptly to ask what she could show them.

"Something very pretty and glamorous for Kathleen," Aunt Eustace said gaily. While they waited, she told Kathleen that she had thought of asking Mr. and

Mrs. Seerie and Bruce as her guests at the banquet to-night. "I didn't because we'll be at the speaker's table. But I want to have you over some evening for a little dinner party with them. Wouldn't you like that?"

Kathleen felt her cheeks flush. "Oh yes. Bruce is—he's always so nice. He's in lit with me."

Aunt Eustace laughed knowingly. "You two must get to know each other better. He's a charming boy, and his family has background."

The something pretty and glamorous, which Kathleen loved the minute Mrs. Neff showed it, was a silverish blue brocade with what Aunt Eustace called a portrait neckline. Kathleen looked at herself in the long mirrors in the dressing room; she could think only of how Bruce would see her when Aunt Eustace gave her little dinner party. She wanted him to see how slim her midriff was under the bodice, and to hear the whispery rustle of the skirt.

"One of our Stardust dresses," Mrs. Neff murmured. "They all have that short tulip sleeve. Do you have silver pumps to wear with it?" she asked Kathleen.

Even while she was answering that she had black ones that would do, Aunt Eustace said, "Bring us in some pretty silver ones for her to choose from, Mrs. Neff."

She chose a pair that twinkled in the light, and felt danceable on her feet.

Mrs. Neff glanced at the chalky gray trench coat which had gone through the washer many times, and asked, "Could I show you one of the little wraps all the girls are wearing for evening?" and Kathleen's aunt said, "Yes, do."

"Oh no, Aunt Eustace, you mustn't buy me anything more. I mean, the dress and pumps are so much and I—" And without knowing why, she thought of her mother and the velvet cape that was so inadequate for cold nights. And Stacy! She didn't mind lording it over her with a dress and slippers, but a new wrap—

"Hush, my dear," Aunt Eustace laughed. "These aren't expensive. I saw them the other day, and I wished I were sixteen again."

The short evening wrap looked like fur and was eiderdown light. It was called "Prom Night." Again Kathleen surveyed herself in the mirror, and thought only of Bruce tucking it around her shoulders and smiling worshipfully at her.

Aunt Eustace had already bought a dress of frosty, pale pink lace for the banquet. Mrs. Neff brought it from "alterations," and complimented Aunt Eustace as she tried it on, "It isn't everyone who can wear that shell pink."

Strange how when a girl steps out of brand-new splendor and puts on her old clothes again they seem even more tacky and down-at-the-heels! Kathleen's old trench coat looked as though it had wiped up the floor.

Well, it had. Last year at St. Jude's it was always sliding off the coat rack to lie in a heap beneath it.

So she hugged her boxes of clothes to her in ec-stacy, as Stacy would say, and shook her head when Emil offered to carry them.

At dusk, Aunt Eustace and Kathleen set out for the Alliance Française banquet. A wet-cotton snow was falling when again Emil opened the car door for them. He spread a robe over Aunt Eustace's pink lace and Kathleen's brocade, and drove through the clogging snow to the Country Club.

"Hope is the thing with feathers that perches in the soul."

If only it would stay *perched*. But no, it had to sprout wing feathers and soar. It did this night. Press photographers would be at the banquet. And of course their cameras would be focused on the speaker's table. Kathleen visualized Aunt Eustace and herself seated between the honored guest from France and the governor, engaged in spritely conversation, while the flash bulbs went off around them.

There was a bulletin board in the main hall at Johnny Q. The idiot board, everyone called it. Whenever a student or one of the faculty had a write-up in the paper— a girl winning a ribbon in a horse show, or the math teacher elected president of the Schoolmasters' Guild— it was stuck up there for the whole school to see. And that person was suddenly a *somebody*; others stopped to congratulate her, and to point her out in the lunch-room.

By the time Emil stopped at the Country Club entrance, Kathleen was seeing her picture—she hoped it would be her profile—on the idiot board, and hearing admiring comments. And she was saying to a boy with dark, curly hair, and teeth so perfect they looked like a toothpaste ad, "It was a fabulous banquet," while he looked at her with new admiration, and said, "Gosh Kathleen, I wish I could have been there."

Inside the club, they checked their wraps and wove their way through a babble of talk and men and women in black ties and evening dresses. Everyone was drifting toward the huge table set up in the form of a U.

And that's when the thing with feathers dropped with a heavy plop. For the flustered program chairman caught Aunt Eustace's arm and launched into an apology. The speaker from France had brought his daughter *and* son-in-law. The French consul and his aide had both accepted at the *last* minute, and the governor had brought his wife— "We simply couldn't make room for the past presidents at the head table."

Aunt Eustace and her guest were crowded in at a table down in front. Kathleen glanced at the mikes and flowers, and notables at the head table. And the first person she saw was Miguel in the white jacket she had ironed for him yesterday morning. He was serving jellied consomme and looking quite at home.

It wasn't fair. Aunt Eustace belonged with the guests of honor. She was always entertaining the board at her house. She had been the one who brought the renowned writer, Michael Parnell, as a speaker. She didn't blame her aunt for feeling aggrieved, and sitting there, aloof and cold to all the chatterers (in French) around them.

Kathleen ate what the French menu told her was *canards aux poires* and blinked as flashbulbs flared at the head table. *Good-by, eye-catching picture of Kathleen Belford on the idiot board at Johnny Q.*

They had scarcely finshed their *babas au rhum* when the speaker was introduced. He gave his speech in French. Judging from the blank faces, the few laughs and nods, Kathleen thought there must be others besides herself who could catch only a phrase or two. But everyone gave him a great ovation. Everyone stood up when the musicians played the "Marseillaise."

There was the usual stampede to meet the speaker. Aunt Eustace, looking suddenly tired and wilted in her pink lace, said she didn't want to join the crush. "I'll have one of the waiters tell Emil we're ready to leave."

They were pushing their way through the crowd when someone tugged at Kathleen's elbow, and a familiar voice said, "Look, Petunia. Just look at the tip I got to add to your half-a-bath fund."

It was Miguel, and her first thought was that the red *rhum* spots on the jacket would have to be soaked out in Clorox. He kept thrusting the bill at her, and saying, "Here, take it. It's a tip."

She looked in amazement at the number on the bill. "Five dollars! You got a five-dollar tip?"

"From the gov himself, if you please. His French was practically nil, so I interpreted for him and *le docteur* from France all through the banquet."

Aunt Eustace looked at him, and at the money in his hand, and Kathleen felt her stiffen. But Miguel went right on, "Or, Petunia, how about going home with me in Mercy Be? Then we can chuck it in the old sugar bowl together. And we can count it, and see how much closer it is to the hundred mark. How about it?"

Aunt Eustace said haughtily, "My niece came with me, and I'll take her home. And it's very poor taste for you to be flouting your tip and trying to give it to her." She evidently remembered then the rule of not speaking English at a club gathering, for she ordered him in French to have her car brought to the door.

Miguel studied her a brief moment, and then broke into voluble French which Kathleen couldn't follow and neither, she realized, could Aunt Eustace.

She repeated more sharply her order to have their car brought to the door.

He bowed and said, *"Mais oui,* Madame," and took himself off.

"He's in my French class at school," Kathleen explained. "Madame Miller thinks—well, he is her best pupil."

"His French is excellent, but his manners are atrocious."

"Aunt Eustace, he didn't mean to be—I mean he's just Miguel."

A disappointing evening and a disappointing ride home. She couldn't help regretting the ten dollars she might have earned. She knew Aunt Eustace was unhappy over not being with the notables. She wished Miguel hadn't put her at a disadvantage with his glib French. She tried to explain about the half-a-bath fun, and Miguel's interest in it. But she couldn't say much, because she had to shy away from any mention of the tips her mother made at Giddy's.

Aunt Eustace patted her hand. "I wish it could have been a happier, gayer evening for you. I keep wishing you could have the life I had at your age. Well, we'll have other parties, Kathleen."

Emil raised an umbrella and held it over her Stardust dress and white fluffy wrap, as he carried her overnight case and walked her through the heavy, clinging snow to the front door.

Eight

❁

HOME AGAIN!

In the hall Kathleen stumbled over so many overshoes the littles had left there, you'd have thought they
were centipedes. She carried her overnight bag upstairs.

No Stacy was curled up in the double bed. She must
have a late baby-sitting job. Kathleen wished she were
home so she could show off her finery and see Stacy's
green eyes widen with admiration.

What a shambles she had left their room! The closet
door gaped open showing a fearful disarray of shoes.
She must have pawed through the whole closet looking
for her snow boots before going out. She had washed a

sweater and rolled it in a towel and left it on the foot of the bed. Kathleen picked it up and felt the damp spot she'd have to avoid during the night. Dresser drawers were open. One of Aunt Eustace's pictures was toppled over, and the other was misted over with the bath powder Stacy always dusted on herself so generously.

She glanced in Ben's room to see if he were awake. She'd like him to see her new clothes. Even if he looked past her and said to his invisible ally, "I wish you'd look at the Duchess of Belford!" it would be better than nothing. But he was only a long lump in one of the two beds in his room, and dead to the world.

She went downstairs still wearing her white wrap. The kitchen clock said twelve-thirty; the banquet, music, and speeches had taken so long.

The Belfords too had an idiot board. Theirs was a big slate that hung on a cupboard door in the kitchen. On it Ben had written: "Mom, I brought you some brown crunchy ribs." The littles had scribbled a message too: "Dont anyboddy take the wire off gate becas Cully will go to Novaks and his foot is sore." And under that, one from Stacy which started out in large print and, because of space, ended in small, abbreviated writing: "TO WHOM IT MAY CONCERN: I WON'T BE HOME TO-NITE acct of Mr. & Mrs. Novak staying allnite where they are acct of slippery rds."

So Stacy was baby-sitting at the Novaks' across the street. It was Mr. Novak who always sang out *Oh, you beautiful doll* when Mother walked to the car in her Gay Nineties costume.

Cully ran limping and whimpering to the front door to welcome Mother, who came in. She too had to stumble through the overshoes, and Kathleen heard her muttering imprecations against the littles for leaving them there.

As Kathleen came into the hall, she was holding on to the newel post and shaking snow out of her pointed slippers. "Oh, it's you lovey! Did you ever see such a storm? And only the first week in October." She shivered. "When we passed the Shamrock on the Boul, I thought I saw Brian's red car. I couldn't tell for sure—"

Kathleen stepped into the light. "I left on the new outfit Aunt Eustace got me, so you could see it. The jacket's what they call brushed mohair."

Mother blinked snow off her lashes and looked at her for a long minute. She lowered her head and brushed off the melted snow. Kathleen realized she was crying— or rather trying not to—for she mumbled something about being chilled to the bone and wanting a cup of tea, and hurried into the kitchen.

Kathleen took the teakettle out of her hand and set it on the gas burner. "What are you crying for, Mom?"

"I—don't know," she said thickly. "Except that— that I'd like to get you pretty clothes. And I can't—and I'm just mean enough to hate her because—*she* can."

She was pulling off her lace mitts, and flexing her fingers that had raced over piano keys for hours. Kathleen wished she could say, "I don't care because we can't afford pretty clothes," but she did care. And right now she cared so hurtingly because she wanted Bruce Seerie's attention.

The kitchen felt chill. Mother lit the gas oven and her cigarette with the same match. She sat on the high stool with her stocking feet on the door, clutching her velvet cape around her. Kathleen poured boiling water onto the tea leaves. Mother reached out and warmed her hands on the big earthenware pot, and said, "You look pretty as springtime, honey."

After the first cup of tea the warm color came back in her cheeks. She let the cape drop off her shoulders. She was wearing the dress with the most frills and furbelows of any of her costumes. It was cream color with purple satin stripes. The overskirt was much ruffled, and caught up over the skirt of solid purple.

"You tore the ruffle on your overskirt," Kathleen said.

"This fool thing. It's so old, I think the thread is rotten, and I'm forever ripping the ruffles. Tonight they caught on the handle of the car door." She looked up and read Ben's message on the slate. "Let's have the ribs. I didn't know I was hungry till now. Take off your jacket, and tie an apron around your neck so's to protect your new dress."

Kathleen found she was hungry too. They both sat gnawing on the crusty ribs and dropping the bones to Cully. Mother said surprisingly, "You know, hon, when I was your age, I was so ashamed of my mother."

Kathleen set down her cup in amazement. For now Mother and Gran were so easy with each other, so devoted. "You were! What about?"

"The what-abouts would fill a book. The way she wore her hair in a bun instead of having it cut. The way she insisted on white lace curtains, when everyone else had colored and flowered draperies. But in Ireland, it seems, there were shanty Irish and lace-curtain Irish, so I suppose those awful lacy ones were a symbol to her."

Was Mother telling her this because she knew the what-abouts Kathleen was ashamed of would fill a book too?

"Did Gran know you were ashamed of her and the lace curtains?"

Mother chuckled, 'She'd have had to be an awful stupe not to."

Kathleen had given so little thought to her mother's once being young and unhappy and maybe, even as she, ashamed of being ashamed. She wanted to know more about that girl in Bannon. "Was there anything else about Gran that got your goat?"

"Oh yes. The thing I was the most ashamed of was

the way she *cried* at the drop of a hat. Gladness, sadness—it didn't matter—the tears rained down. I'd grit my teeth in rage. 'You don't *have* to cry,' I'd scold her.''

"What did she say?"

"She'd say, 'Ah, childeen, some people have tighter puckerin' strings to their hearts than others.' And I vowed that when I grew up, I'd be the poised, self-contained type—you know, the kind that people say about, 'She keeps her feelings to herself.' ''

They laughed together. For that was one thing Mother never did.

She went on with a rueful smile, ''And I always saw myself as a different kind of mother than I am. Ah, I was going to be a tower of strength and a fountain of wisdom who never once lifted her voice to her children.'' She heard Kathleen's giggle, and said defensively, ''Go ahead, laugh! You'll find out yourself that you are what you *are*, and not what you'd like to be.''

Kathleen untied the apron around her neck and folded it. But she was like the Belfords, and they had tighter puckerin' strings to their hearts than the sentimental, quick-tempered O'Byrnes.

There was something so both soothing and exciting about having mother open her heart here in the kitchen, with the snow coating the windows and the clock pointing to after one. Kathleen said, ''Jeanie's mother was telling us about your and Dad's romance on the campus. She said it was like the song—he took one look at you and then his heart stood still.''

Mother's eyes turned luminous. "So did mine," she said softly.

Maybe Kathleen could say, "So did mine when I looked at Bruce. Only my tongue didn't stand still. Did you gush-gush to Dad without being able to stop? Did you ache for fear he wouldn't like you?''

They were startled by Cully's sudden yelp, his scrabbling to the front door. Almost simultaneously, the door knocker sounded. Mother whispered fearfully, "Who do you suppose—? It wouldn't be Brian. He never comes to the front.''

Kathleen nodded toward the slate. "Maybe he tried the side gate. The littles wired it shut because of Cully.''

The color drained from Mother's face. "Then it was his car I saw at the Shamrock. Who else could it be at this hour of the night?''

The dining room was dark except for the light from the hall. Kathleen went on stealthy feet and looked out its window. Yes, there was a dark blotch of car at the curb at the side. You couldn't call it parked. Even through the snow she could see the rear end sticking far out in the street.

The door knocker clanged louder. Ben came racing down the stairs in his bare feet. His reddish hair was touseled, and he was looping the belt of his faded terry cloth robe about him.

Mother turned stricken eyes from the **door to** Ben. "It's Brian—" The bangety-bang of the knocker was deafening. She put her hands up to her face and moaned into them, "They told me not to let him in. But he'll be cold—and soaked to the skin."

Ben slapped at the excited Cully. "Keep still, you fool mutt."

They heard the rattle of the door knob, and saw it turn. Mother had evidently forgot to spring the night latch, for the door opened wide. Uncle Brian's wild and weaving figure stood silhouetted in the light and against the snow. His hair was coated with melting snow that dripped onto his face. His brown leather jacket was open, and his tie awry. He fumbled his hand onto the door jab to steady himself, while he looked at the three standing there in the hall.

He laughed boisterously for a minute, before he said, with what he intended as a sweeping bow—except that he lost his balance and couldn't finish it, "My dear own —my verry dearr own—" His voice was thick and burry with brogue. "I hope you'll excuse the intrusion. I'm setting a record tonight. I've been kicked out of three places already. This will make four. So you, Rose, you wired the gate shut against a sodden drunk contam —taminating your house and innocent children. But

· *113* ·

you forgot to lock the door. But don't worry now—don't wo*rrry* at all—because I'm going. A ve*rrry* good evening to you all—''

He turned on stumbling feet toward the steps. Kathleen heard her own voice cry out, ''No, Uncle Brian—don't go.'' Even as she said it, he slipped in the slushy snow. Ben, quick as a cat, was at his side and caught him before he fell. Kathleen darted out to help hold him on his feet.

Mother joined them, sobbing out, ''Brian—oh Brian, we could never close the door on you. Come in now out of the snow.''

He fought to pull away from them. He knew when he wasn't wanted, he shouted; he wasn't like the Irishman who had to be kicked down the stairs to take a hint. In the struggle, Mother's ruffles were ripped wider. Kathleen picked up the keys he dropped.

A belligerent, mocking man. ''Let me lie in the gutter,'' he challenged, as they guided him inside, through the hall and toward the couch. By the time he reached it, the fight was gone out of him, and he dropped down like a leaden weight.

Kathleen brought a towel and wiped his wet face and hair. While Ben took off his soggy shoes and socks, she helped her mother pull off his leather coat. One side of it sagged with a pint bottle in the big slit pocket. He was mumbling incoherently as Mother eased a cushion under his head. She warmed his cold hands in hers, saying, "Hush now—hush," as though he were one of the littles.

At last he "conked out" as Ben said. He went upstairs for his own shoes, took Uncle Brian's keys, and went out to repark the red car. Mother said to Kathleen, "You go on to bed, lovey. It's late. He'll sleep now."

In her and Stacy's room, Kathleen took off the new Stardust dress and hung it in the closet; slowly she put the white furry wrap in a clothes bag. It seemed as though another, untroubled, Kathleen, on another, untroubled, planet had walked out of Madeline's this morning.

Ben came up the stairs. She heard him go in and wake one of the littles—Jill, she thought—and say, "When you get up in the morning, you three, don't be yelling and clattering about when you fold the papers. Because Uncle Brian is asleep on the couch. You hear now! Don't wake him, whatever you do."

She kept listening for Mother to come up the stairs. The house had an unfinished feeling with her still down there. Kathleen went down.

Mother was kneeling beside Uncle Brian in her disheveled purple-striped dress with its torn ruffles. The afghan wasn't long enough to cover him, so she had added her velvet cape. Her fingers were smoothing back his hair, carefully skirting an inch of white bandage that showed in it. And she was crooning Brahm's

Lullaby about bright angels around my darling shall stand—

And guard thee from harm—and guard thee—

"I thought maybe I could make him coffee," Kathleen said.

Mother shook her head. "He's too far gone for it now. . . . When he was little, I used to sing this to him to put him to sleep. . . . That new-fangled doctor in Bannon said not to take him in." She lifted tear-rimmed eyes. "But what could we do, Katie Rose? He's still my baby brother."

Deep inside Kathleen, the Belford side reminded her that life would be so much smoother without Uncle Brian and his drinking. But the O'Byrne side of her answered, "Gosh, Mom, there wasn't anything else we could do."

Nine

E V E R Y S U N D A Y M O R N I N G, Kathleen, Ben, and Stacy sang in the choir at St. Jude's nine-thirty Mass. Mother played the organ. Ben had scolded her about it. "Baby Doll, you ought to have *one* morning of sleeping late."

But she had scolded back, "Now, now, Ben! Some people pray their way into heaven. Maybe I can play mine in."

In nice weather they could walk to St. Jude's. But this morning when a bright sun melted the snow into deep slush, Ben got out the car.

Uncle Brian had slept on the couch through all the hubbub of the littles getting off on their paper route and tramping in again in sudsy wet overshoes, of all the running up and downstairs getting ready for church.

St. Jude's choir would be minus a contralto this morning, because what with Mother *having* to play the organ, Ben having to drive the car, and Stacy *having* to stay at the Novaks until the parents returned, it fell to Kathleen to stay home with Uncle Brian. "He'll sleep till we get back, I'm sure," Mother whispered from the doorway. "But keep the coffee hot, in case he does wake up."

They were no sooner gone and Kathleen was upstairs, when she heard a racketing about in the kitchen. Hurrying down, she found Uncle Brian, fumbling through the cupboard for a cup. He turned, holding it in shaking hands. And a sad sight he was, with his rumpled hair and clothes, and the reddish stubble over his chin.

"Sit down, Uncle Brian, and I'll pour your coffee."

"Yes, I guess you'd better," he admitted.

He swished cold water over his face, dried it, and walked laboredly to the dinette table and sat down. He sat, studying the cup of coffee she put before him for a minute or two, before he lifted his bloodshot blue eyes. "I guess I made a holy show of myself last night. Too bad you and Ben rushed out and caught me as I fell. You should have let me go down the stone steps. With a little luck I might have bashed my head in."

It hurt her to see his shakiness and hangdog air. "I'll fix you a good, hot breakfast, Uncle Brian. What would you like?"

He didn't seem to hear her. "They told Rose not to let me in, didn't they? To bang the door in my face if I showed up, didn't they?"

"The new doctor at the hospital told Gran and Grandda to. It nearly broke their hearts to do it—to close up their house and go to Nebraska."

"I know. I know. God knows I'm not blaming them. They should have done it long before." He stirred his coffee moodily. "You, Mavourneen, you don't like having a drunken bum for an uncle, I know. But wasn't it you that called out to me last night not to go away?"

She answered around the lump in her throat, "Yes."

Silence fell, and lasted until he asked, "Did I dream it, or did your mother stay by me a good part of the night singing low?"

"Yes, she did. About bright angels guarding you from harm. She said she used to sing it to you when you were little. She said you were still her baby brother."

A wincing of pain passed over his face. He sat at the table staring into the depths of his cup of coffee for what seemed a long time. He got up then with a set look on his face and went into the living room.

"What are you looking for, Uncle Brian?"

"I'm looking for that part of a pint I had in my pocket last night."

Her heart dropped like a stone. Here we go again, she thought sickly.

He came into the kitchen with the flat bottle. She watched him unscrewing the cap, and wondered what would happen if she grabbed it out of his hand. She would probably have to pick herself up off the floor.

And then—she couldn't believe her eyes—he stepped over to the sink and poured it down. When the last drop dribbled out, he thoughtfully, almost gently, tossed the bottle into the wastebasket.

He turned to her, and she saw the resolute set to his jaws. "I'm through," he said solemnly. "By the hollow of heaven, I'm through with the stuff. If it was jolting —ah, and facing reality they wanted for me— It jolts and shames me to my soul to think of all of you taking me in last night—blithering sot that I was—and of Rose hovering over me—" he stopped, and clamped his jaw still tighter.

Such a sudden rush of love came over her that she reached for his hand. "I believe you, Uncle Brian. I believe you can, when you look like that. And I'll help— just anyway I can."

He gripped her hand tight in his. "Keep on believing, Mavourneen. I'll need it. I'll need your help. You asked me if I'd like breakfast. Yes, I'd like anything you can cook up. Mother of Moses, I'm starved for food. Fry up something while I go up and shave."

He ate like a famished man, and drank the coffeepot dry. He found the Sunday *Call* and pored over the Help Wanted columns. He made phone calls. He put on his leather coat, saying, "They're in need of a man at a warehouse down under the viaduct. Loading, unloading, and uncrating TV's and hi-fi's. I'm setting out for an interview."

"On Sunday?"

"He'll be there till eleven, he said."

The church-goers were home when he came back and said he was to start work the next morning. Mother's whole body went slack with relief, when he added, "I'm off the bottle, Rose." Probably all the while she played *Kyrie eleison* on the organ at St. Jude's, she was praying, "God have mercy on Brian."

He took Kathleen and Stacy to noon Mass, and then drove on to Mac's garage on the Boulevard to have his car checked.

Miguel came over that afternoon, bringing the spattered white jacket, and the governor's tip. Mother expostulated that he should keep it himself, but he wouldn't listen. That brought on the rite of counting the half-a-bath fund again. It was still a far cry from the hundred-dollar mark.

"Only fifty-seven dollars," Jill lamented. "Remember, once it was up to sixty-one dollars and forty cents? How come?"

"It isn't the how *come*, it's the how *go*," Ben said.

Miguel went down in the basement with Kathleen to help her wash the white jacket. "We'll soak it in a bleach before we put it in hot suds," she said.

He leaned against the laundry tubs and talked about the night before. Had Kathleen seen Madame Mee-lair all decked out in red velvet, and kissing everyone on both cheeks?

She hadn't seen her. She tried not to sound wistful. "I had on a new dress, but I guess you didn't notice. Hardly anyone did."

"You always look pretty, Petunia. Your aunt didn't give me time to notice much."

"Why did you rattle off all that French to Aunt Eustace?"

An impish light showed in his eyes. "Just to take her down a notch or two. Her acting so high-and-mighty sort of brought out the beast in me."

They were putting the two white jackets in the washing machine when Uncle Brian came down the steps. "I want to talk to you, Mavourneen—and you too, Miguel."

He reached into his pants pocket and pulled out a few wadded-up dollar bills and some silver. "Last night I sold my movie camera for fifteen bucks, and that's what's left—"

"Not your movie camera that cost over a hundred!" Kathleen exclaimed.

"Did you hock it?" Miguel asked. "If you did, you can get it back."

"No, I sold it to some joe in a bar—I don't even know which bar." He pressed the money in Kathleen's hand. "I want you to keep it. I've been thinking I'll be a lot better off without money in my pocket to reach for. I told the fellow that hired me I wanted the check made out in your name, Kathleen Belford—"

"In my name?" she gasped.

"That's right, girleen. And then you can cash it at Downey's Drug, and pay your mother for my board—"

"You know Mom won't want you to *pay*."

"You see that she takes it. I want to pay my own way for my own self-respect."

"You'll be driving to work and back," Miguel said. "What about money for gas?"

"I've my credit card for that. And I've credit at Downey's for any extras I need. You, Mavourneen, will be taking care of those bills for me too. And what money is left, I want you to hide where I can't get my hands on it. Hide it where only you and God know where it is."

Miguel said with his understanding grin, "Days when you're working won't be so hard, Uncle Brian. It's the holidays and the weekends. Pop and I had a friend in Mexico who went on the wagon, and he made

Pop promise that when the urge came on him, he would drive him far out of town and put him out of the car so he'd have a long, hard tramp home. So he'd be so tired, he'd fall into bed.''

"You know then what a man goes through," Uncle Brian said gravely. "And did this friend of yours get the best of the battle?''

"He did. Though once or twice Pop and I were afraid he couldn't stick it out. He said the first month or two were the hardest.''

They stood a few minutes with the old washing machine huffing and swishing beside them, before Uncle Brian said, "Ah, I know it's one thing for a man to say on a morning when his head is fair splitting with a hangover that he's through with the stuff. And quite another to live up to it. So, Mavourneen, you'll have to stick by me. When the thirst is on me, don't give me a dime. Even if I beg or threaten—''

"Why me?" she asked in something like panic. "Why not Mom—or Ben?''

"Your mother's an O'Byrne, and the whole lot of us have spinal columns of corn-meal mush where the ones we love are concerned. Not Ben either. I've a feeling I could even browbeat him. But you, Kathleen, you've got more Belford in you, and consequently more stubbornness. So it's you I'm counting on to be my bright angel to guard me from harm.'' He reached out his hand to her.

She held it and promised solemnly, "All right, Uncle Brian. I'll guard your money and you," and felt both elation and a strange humility.

Kathleen's and Stacy's bedroom was next to the bath. A joint of water pipe was directly under their clothes closet. Once the plumber had to cut out a small square of floor in it to fix a leak. He hadn't nailed it down because he said it would be easier to get to another time.

She found a pink plastic soap box and put in it the few bills and silver Uncle Brian had given her. She pried up the square of floor in the corner of the closet, and fitted the soap box in under the joint, and put the cover back on. There now, with shoes sitting on top of it, only she and God would know what was underneath.

They would now have another early riser at the Belfords' on Hubbell Street. Uncle Brian would get up at five when the littles did, in order to be at the warehouse under the viaduct by a quarter to seven. Kathleen and Stacy would now be making sandwiches and finding sacks for seven instead of six.

Later that evening when Kathleen called Stacy to help fix lunches, she came dancing into the kitchen carrying part of their Sunday *Call*. "Lookit! Here's Mug's picture on page thirteen, and all about your however-you-pronounce-it party last night."

The write-up of the Alliance Française banquet was brief. The picture showed the guest speaker and the governor talking together at the table, with Miguel standing behind their chairs. The caption under it gave the Frenchman's name with all his honorary titles, and then, "Miguel Barnett, student at John Quincy Adams, helps our governor over conversational hurdles."

Madame Mee-lair would proudly clip that up on the idiot board at school. Students would look at it and say with a proud chuckle, "That's our boy, Miguel." It did seem almost uncanny the way the things Kathleen longed for always came Miguel's way.

And without his caring a hoot.

Ten

KATHLEEN AND BRUCE met at the door of their lit class the next day. He said, "Hey, wasn't that a beaut of a pass Darby caught on the twenty-yard line? I thought for a minute I wasn't going to pull my man down."

It seemed to her that his face dropped when she told him she hadn't seen the game. "I guess I expect everybody to be as interested in football as I am," he said. "These postmortems bore Jeanie to death."

That same afternoon when she and Jeanie were alone during their hair-drying time, Kathleen asked, "Has Bruce dated you lately?"

Jeanie shook her head. "He's pretty tied up with

football these days. He stopped by one Sunday and asked me to go for a Coke at the Robin. And I was given a complete rehash of the game the day before.''

''He thinks it bores you when he talks football.''

''He thinks right,'' Jeanie admitted on a sigh. ''I can't help it. It's not that I'm lacking in school spirit. I'm hoping to get on the school paper, and if I do I'll work—work like an army mule to make good. But I've suffered through too many earaches from going to football games to be a rah-rah girl.''

And that's when Kathleen vowed: I'm going to the football games if it kills me. If she could talk *passes* and *pulling out his man* to Bruce it would give them a common bond, and—and maybe he would start asking her out for a Coke and the postmortems that bored Jeanie to death. It wasn't as though she were cutting in on her best friend's date. Not when Jeanie had said that very first day that she wasn't passionately fond of him. Maybe Bruce craved a girl to share his consuming interest.

Yessir, even if she couldn't scrape up the seven dollars for the athletic ticket, she could and would pay the dollar admission to each Saturday game out of her baby-sitting money.

Every evening that week she hoped for a call from one of her regulars; the McHargs with their two little girls, the Bartons with an arthritic grandma they never liked to leave alone.

No one phoned until Thursday at six, and then it was Mrs. Purdum. Kathleen dared not say no, though the four unmanageable, undisciplined, and overly energetic Purdum boys, ranging from the year-old baby to a first-grader, always meant an exhausting evening.

Stacy had once taken Kathleen's place only to announce, "I'll never go there any more. Those four little monsters make our littles seem like saints with helloes." (She meant "halos.") And this evening when Mr. Purdum sounded his horn for Kathleen at six-fifteen, Stacy enjoined, "Now you tell them you don't baby-sit *anyplace* for less than fifty an hour."

But Kathleen had gone to the Purdums' two years ago when she was glad enough to get thirty-five cents an hour. (There had been only three little Purdums then.)

Mrs. Purdum greeted her in her usual breathless and harassed manner, "Oh goodness, Katie Rose, I didn't get a minute to clean up the dishes—and you won't mind bringing in the baby's nighties off the line—dry them on the oven door if they seem damp—because he won't need his bedtime bottle till seven-thirty. And whatever you do, don't let Winnie out—because like everybody says, a beagle just never comes back on his own. You'd better give the baby his bottle on the couch because lately he's got the worst habit of pulling the nipple off it if you give it to him in his crib."

She ran back from the car to say, "Donnie and Kim

can have Wheaties if they want, because I only had time to scramble them eggs—and you put a spoonful of this brownish vitamin in the baby's bottle.''

The evening started out with the second little boy spilling milk on one of Kathleen's white sneakers. She put it on the oven door to dry, along with the baby's nightclothes.

She was giving the baby his bottle (and unknowingly sitting on a lump of banana on the couch) when a crash and scream sounded in the kitchen. The first-grader had climbed on the ladder stool for the package of Wheaties and both had tumbled to the floor. His screams lasted until she found a violet-colored disenfectant in the medicine cabinet, and smeared his knee well with it. While she was sweeping up the breakfast food the baby, as predicted, pulled the nipple off his bottle.

That meant a change of clothes for him, and the mixing of another feeding. She was warming the bottle when his brothers, hearing a siren in the distance, darted out the front door. Winnie saw her chance and took it.

When, at long last, the baby was in his high-sided crib, and the others were reasonably settled down, and she might have studied her math lesson, she felt conscience-bound to see if her milk-soaked sneaker was dry enough to put on so she could go out in search of Winnie.

She finally found a white sneaker in what was called the rumpus room. For a moment she couldn't believe it was hers. For at some time when her back was turned, one of the enterprising little Purdums had tried out his father's inked pad and signature stamp on its damp, white canvas, and it was well imprinted with "William J. Purdum. William J. Purdum. William J."

She made three sorties at intervals up and down the block, calling, "Winnie! Here, Winnie!" But no Winnie was in sight or sound, and she was still missing when the parents returned at ten-thirty.

Kathleen was in her own kitchen and close to tears, as she sponged the yellowish banana stain out of her skirt and soaked her tennis shoe in soapy water, when Ben came in.

"I thought you weren't going to the Purdums' any more," he said. "Wasn't it one of those kids that bit you on the ankle once?"

"On the thumb. It was Stacy's ankle they hacked with their dad's coping saw. I had to go tonight. I want the money for the football game Saturday."

"How much did you make?"

"A dollar forty for four hours."

"You mean you rode herd on those little hellions for thirty-five an hour? Why didn't you tell them to pay you fifty?"

The tears welled into her eyes as she scrubbed harder

to obliterate an almost indelible "William J. Purdum."

"I was going to, but they came home and gave me the dickens about the beagle getting out."

He stood thoughtfully beside her while she scrubbed on. "Is that all you've got—that dollar forty?"

"I've got fifty cents besides, and Stacy owes me forty-five for her half of a bottle of shampoo."

He took out a five-dollar bill and laid it on the sink beside the cleanser she was using so diligently. "Put that with what you've got, and buy an athletic ticket. It's cheaper than paying for each game each Saturday."

She smoothed back her dark disarray of hair with a wet, soapy hand. "But, Ben, you said—I mean, what about paying the dentist for your wisdom tooth?"

He smiled crookedly. "He won't have to close up if I let him wait a week for the five. You take it, Sis. I've been wanting to give you something for ironing my white jackets."

If only she could put into words the gratitude that churned up in her heart! She could only say, "Well, thanks—" and scrub harder on a capital W.

Neither could he say, "I want you to go to every game, and yell your head off without a care in the world like other girls." Instead, he said from the doorway in his old brusque way, "Don't be so darn mealy-mouthed with the Purdums. You tell them you won't put foot in that madhouse of theirs unless they pay you the regular fee, y'hear?"

The next day at lunch hour, she told Deetsy, "I'll get my athletic ticket now. I don't want to miss any more games."

"You got a way to go?" Miguel asked. "I'm on a storm-window job, and I might be late getting there or else—"

The John-Toms asked her how much she weighed and if she were a good prayer.

"A hundred and six," she said promptly, "and I can practice up on praying."

Okay, then they could crowd her in in their stripped-down stock car racer, they said. Adams was to play the ten-thirty game in the morning. She was to be out in front of her house at ten-fifteen, ready to leap in the car when it slowed.

"The old heap likes to run on a track, and she's sulked ever since we took off the smaller inside wheels and put on regular," one said, and the other defended loyally, "She's thirty-three years old. Maybe we'll be sulking too when we get that ancient."

Kathleen went to the game in the old car that huffed and puffed and had been painted a green so bright it would shame a shamrock. She followed every move Bruce Seerie, number nineteen, made. She yelled till she was hoarse when he kicked a field goal. And when

Adams lost by two points, no one grieved more than she.

She didn't have to wait till sixth hour to talk to him about it on Monday. She was coming out of math when she saw him at the second-floor lockers.

Oh, he had played a wonderful game, she told him— simply superb. *What was it about him that made her turn gushy?* She was telling him that everyone thought that if Coach hadn't taken him out fourth quarter, he might have kicked another—

An announcement over the speaker system interrupted. A special all-school assembly was being called for next hour.

Bruce said knowingly, "I'll bet it's about that Get-Acquainted party. Mr. Knight has been stewing about having to put it off till late in October. It's because the finish on the gym floor didn't stand up and had to be done over." He walked to the auditorium door with her, and then left to join his junior section.

Their principal announced that John Quincy Adams was having its delayed Get-Acquainted the following Friday evening in the gym. He gave a rousing come-one, come-all talk about it. Kathleen listened with her uneven Bruce Seerie thump of heart. Maybe—just maybe—

She and Jeanie left school together an hour later. They walked a block or two without a word until, to make conversation, Kathleen said, "Did you hear Mr. Knight say for everybody to come whether they had dates or not? But I wouldn't want to go without a date—"

"Shhh," Jeanie said, "I'm thinking and scheming." They walked another block before she asked in her startling way, "Are you still far gone on Bruce Seerie?"

She laughed when Kathleen stopped in her tracks and gulped for a breath. "Yes. But I suppose he'll take you to the Get-Acquainted."

"Yes, I suppose he will, just from force of habit, if I—if you and I—don't do some unladylike finagling. Feminine wiles, they're known as. You know who I have a terrific yearning to get acquainted with?"

"No. Who?"

"Your brother Ben."

"Ben? No kidding? He can be awful bossy."

"I like the bossy type. So look, Kathleen—"

"But won't Bruce be mad or hurt at you if you—I mean, after you've dated this summer?"

Jeanie's forehead wrinkled thoughtfully. "I don't think so. He isn't crazy about me—that is, he isn't the girl-crazy kind. Maybe I've told you how all summer he worked out at Coral Sands beach because he was nuts about water-skiing, and he wanted to show up good in their August meet. And then when some of the gang would whomp up a picnic or cookout, he'd need a date and he'd ask me."

Kathleen listened breathlessly as she went on,

"Bruce won't ask me right away because he doesn't like that pinned-down feeling. So in the meantime, how about your nudging Ben in my direction? Then when Bruce asks me, I'll say, "Golly, Bruce, I was afraid Coach might line up a practice game for the team that night, so when Ben Belford asked me I said yes.' Then I'll say, 'What about your asking Kathleen, and we can maybe make it a foursome?' ''

"But maybe there's someone else he'd rather take, Jeanie?''

"Not unless it's a secret passion, and Bruce doesn't go in for those. Okay, then? I'll work my end to line you up with Bruce, and you soften up Ben.'' She laughed excitedly. "We can't be hung for trying.''

"What'll I say to Ben?''

"How do I know, goose girl? Heaven will surely guide you. Just don't bust in on him and shove the idea down his throat.''

Kathleen laughed too. "I'll be sub-til, as Stacy says.''

"Stacy sounds swell. Does it upset her when you correct her for mispronouncing words?''

"Stacy isn't the upsettable kind. She really tries. But she no sooner gets one word straight than she comes up with another one. Yesterday she was telling about an oral at school and how she just sat there 'twinching' because she didn't know the answers.''

Jeanie chortled. "That's wonderful. It sounds like

wincing and cringing and twitching all rolled into one."

"Yes, but she gets all of us so confused that half the time we don't know whether we're saying it right or Stacy's way."

They came to the corner and the parting of their ways. "Be sure you catch Ben in a happy mood," Jeanie called after Kathleen.

Everyone at the Belford house was in not exactly a happy mood, but a watchful, hopeful one because Uncle Brian was still off the bottle. His day at the warehouse was finished at three-thirty, but he allowed himself no idle time. He had made friends with a fellow workman, Marve, who was building a garage and hoping to finish it before cold weather. So Uncle Brian went home with him and helped lay brick or mix cement. Often he stayed on and had supper with Marve and his wife.

A dog-tired Uncle Brian would come home late. He would send one of the littles to Downey's Drug for a paperback mystery and, after a bath, read till he fell asleep. "There's something so lulling about a nice, bloody murder," he said.

If this keeps on, Kathleen planned, I can ask Jeanie home with me.

That Monday afternoon she hurried through tea and ironed the white jacket Ben would wear that night. She hung it over the register in the dining room for the warm air to dry it out at the seams and, finding one of the buttons off, hunted for a matching one. She called Ben into the dining room to get him away from the family.

"Ben, this button I'm putting on isn't exactly the same but—"

"Sure, that'll do. And I thank you kindly, Kathleen." (She was never the Duchess of Belford when she ironed his jackets.)

Now was her time. "That Get-Acquainted Friday night sounds like fun. You're going, aren't you, Ben?"

"I've got to work."

"But you could get off. Remember once you worked an extra night for some fellow and he—?"

"Clyde. Yeah, Clyde owes me a night, but—"

"You ought to go. You like to dance, and you need something in your life besides just work, work, work." (Their mother always worried that Ben didn't have enough fun. "He'll be an old man before his time," she said.) Kathleen pressed her point, "You know, 'All work and no play. . . .' "

He twisted the quote with a rueful grin, " 'All work and no play *makes* Jack.' Oh, I don't know. I don't like to stag it. And I don't know any girl well enough to ask her."

"You know Jeanie. And you like her, don't you?"

"Ho. There're so many fellows that like her she has to stumble her way through them."

Maybe heaven did guide her, for she said swiftly,

"Yes, but her dad won't let her go out with a lot of them. He's Dr. Kincaid."

"I know. He comes into the Robin sometimes. If I'm not busy we talk about medical school and such. I told him I planned on being a pathologist if I could make it. He's a nice guy. He knew Dad at the U, he tells me."

"Yes, and they knew Mom too. So even though they're particular who she goes with, they'd let her go with you." He didn't answer, and she added hopefully, "Why don't I just tell Jeanie you'd like to take her to the Get-Acquainted?"

"I can make my own dates," he said shortly.

Uncle Brian brought home his pay check for two weeks' work that evening. Kathleen cashed it at Downey's Drug, paid his bill there, and the one for gas at Mac's filling station. Mother wouldn't take his board money until he told her he would move out if she didn't.

"You still have money left," she told Uncle Brian.

"Guard it with your life, bright angel," he said with a tired smile.

The next day when Kathleen, Jeanie, and Miguel were unwrapping sandwiches, and their table mates were in line for the plate lunch, Ben came hurrying up. He had a later lunch hour, so it was between classes for him. Without preamble, he asked, "Jeanie, if you aren't dated for the doings Friday night, will you go with me?"

Terrific yearning or no, Jeanie kept it casual. She

gave Ben her crinkly smile and said, "I'd like to go with you, Ben."

"I can be at your house by eight," he said. "That all right?"

"Right as rain," she nodded.

Ben went hurrying on to his next class.

And then Kathleen wished he had chosen a different time and place to ask her. Because Miguel said promptly, "Hey, Petunia, why can't you and I go to the party with them?"

She looked at him in his raucous plaid shirt. She looked helplessly at Jeanie, and then down at the dark soggy brownie that Stacy had baked. She swallowed twice, and said, "I've already got a date."

That was certainly setting a match to the bridges behind her. That was certainly putting herself far out on a limb that *might* be cut off, but she was gambling on heaven.

Miguel said in a shocked voice, "You've already got a date! But, Petunia, you're my girl."

"Oh, come now," she said airily. "You practically told me the first time I saw you that you fell in love with Stacy at Wetzel's—"

"Sure, I love her. I love your mother. I adore Liz. I love old lady Wetzel like a mother because she sells me a ham end real cheap when it gets to where it doesn't slice good. You dummkopf, don't you know the heart has a lot of rooms?"

"Imagine that! What room am I in in this large-sized hotel you're running?"

"You're in the heart-warmingest room—you know the one where there's a teakettle boiling—"

They were interrupted by the return of the lunch buyers, the pulling out of chairs, and Deetsy's chatter.

That was on Tuesday. Wednesday was a long, long day. But on Thursday Jeanie passed Kathleen a note in French class. "Bruce asked me, and I gave him the round-the-mullberry-bush bit. The ground is laid. Warning: He doesn't like a STICKY GIRL."

Madame Mee-lair was having the class take an imaginary walk along the Seine for the imaginary buying of books and pictures. Kathleen was engrossed in her own anguished thoughts—supposing, oh, supposing Bruce didn't ask her! She was suddenly startled to hear, *"Mademoiselle Belford, voudrais un livre?"*

She could only stammer out, *"Mais oui, Je voudrais un livre,"* like the repeat line in a primer. Because Mademoiselle Belford didn't want a book. All she wanted was for sixth-hour lit to come.

It came. And all the class discussion about Edgar Allan Poe didn't even go in one ear, much less out the other. The closing bell rang zingety-zong, but it sounded to her like, "It's now or never."

A sidelong glance told her Bruce had detached himself from his protective guard of football players and was coming toward her. His smile was beautiful. And his words were music. "I'd like to take you to the Get-Acquainted tomorrow night if you haven't got somebody else."

She clasped her prose and poetry book tight to her front so he wouldn't hear her heart pounding. But she remembered Jeanie and answered, "I'd like to go with you, Bruce."

That was certainly the understatement of the year. She would be enchanted. She would be forever grateful.

"Mom's already promised me the car," he said. "But I'd rather not double date, if that's all right with you. I'd rather just pick you up and take you home myself."

One of the football boys prodded from the doorway, "Snap it up, Seerie. We haven't got all night."

"Okay then with you, if we go by ourselves?" he asked anxiously.

"Oh yes, that'll be fine."

"I'll be by for you at seven-thirty."

"That'll be fine—just fine."

She was still saying, "That'll be fine," like a needle stuck on a record, when the same eager footballer grabbed Bruce's arm and said, "Save the getting acquainted for the Get-Acquainted, or Coach will be riding us all for holding up practice."

The boys went scuffling down the hall. Kathleen leaned weakly in the doorway. Bruce had said, "I'd rather not double date—" That didn't sound as though she were second choice, did it? That sounded as though maybe he had asked Jeanie because he thought she expected it, didn't it?

Walking down the hall to her locker wasn't walking. The thing with feathers wasn't perching, but soaring.

She passed Rita Flood standing in front of one of the Get-Acquainted posters and, numbed as she was by *ec-stacy*, smiled at her.

Rita promptly clutched her arm. "You going to this shindig?"

"Yes, I'm going with Bruce Seerie, one of the football players." She wanted the whole world to know it.

"What about Ben? I thought maybe if he don't know any of the girls here, he might—"

"He's got a date." Some of the world's rosy cast faded. That nervy Rita, thinking Ben would squire her to a school party.

Rita said, undaunted, "If I don't get a date I'm going anyway with some of the girls." She gave herself a preening twist. "But whatta you bet I don't pick up a date to go home with?"

"Good luck," was all Kathleen said, for she saw Jeanie at their locker, and she broke into a run.

"He asked me, Jeanie. He asked me. And you know what? He said he'd rather not double date. He said he'd rather just come for me in his car—and take me home himself."

"Whatta you know!" Jeanie said in unfeigned delight. "Maybe—" and she did a little transposing of the "Gypsy Love Song," and sang out,

> *He's traveled the whole world o'er,*
> *And you are the one, dear, that*
> *He has been looking for.*

One of Kathleen's fondest dreams had to go. Bruce wouldn't see her in the Stardust dress, or hold the luscious white wrap for her. She wouldn't be dancing with him in silver slippers.

Because all the next day at school the talk centered on what girls would wear to the Get-Acquainted. The matter was cinched when Kathleen and Jeanie spent their study hour to help decorate the gym. Boys were piling corn shocks in the corners; girls were cutting pumpkins into jack-o'-lanterns, and fitting candles in them. Definitely, in keeping with the corn-husker motif, it would be a sweater-and-skirt or blouse-and-skirt affair.

"Oh, Jeanie, won't anybody be dressed up? I'd like to wear the new brocade Aunt Eustace bought me."

"You'd look ridiculous in it. Save the glamor for another time."

But Kathleen refused to go all the way hillbilly. From school, she made the long trip to the Boulevard for mint-green tint. The white rummage-sale blouse, with its half-inch ruffles stitched down the front, *was* pretty and becoming. And no one would recognize a mint-green blouse topping her plaid skirt.

She washed her hair and put it up on rollers. Because Bruce would be calling for her, she cleaned the whole downstairs, threatening the littles to boil them in oil if they dirtied it up. She was afraid her hair wouldn't be dry in time so in between cleaning, dyeing, and ironing her blouse, she kept poking her head in the oven until she felt dizzy and slightly parboiled.

You'd think her family would realize that this was the turning point in her life, and that from this night on all Johnny Q would tag her as Bruce Seerie's girl. Hadn't he said, "I'd rather not double date"? She cherished those words like so many pearls.

You'd think they'd at least allow her time for a leisurely, foamy bath. But no, when Stacy asked if she could go shopping with the Novaks because the stores were open Friday night, Mother said yes. Only Jill was left to help Kathleen with the supper dishes. And while Jill was able to outfight any boy her size in South Denver, she was no Mother's Little Helper.

But Kathleen was dressed and waiting by seven-fifteen. She went through a time of jittery panic for fear Bruce might arrive before Ben left to take Mother to Giddy's. Why did they both have to dawdle so? She kept saying, "Hurry up, Mom, or you'll be late."

She meant, "Hurry and *go* before Bruce Seerie sees you in that outlandish costume."

Their old Chevy had barely pulled away from the curb at the side when Bruce Seerie stopped in the front of the house in his—at least, half his and half his mother's—cream-colored convertible. Kathleen, shaky with relief and giddy with anticipation of the evening ahead, opened the door for him.

Eleven

❀

WITH BRUCE's guiding hand on her arm, Kathleen had gone down the front steps to the Get-Acquainted on winged feet.

Her feet were leaden when he walked her up the steps a few minutes before ten-thirty. She had messed up all chances of another date with the boy she idolized. She had been slapped down. It was all her own fault, and that made it even harder to bear.

At the door Bruce, the well-brought-up boy, said all the usuals. It had been a swell evening and he thanked her for going with him. He even said from the bottom step, "Be seein' you."

Ha! As though she didn't know he was thinking, *From a distance, that is. I don't like a sticky girl.*

She opened the door and went in. She hoped none of the family was about. All she wanted was to crawl into bed with her shame and misery.

But Stacy greeted her. "I peeked out the window and saw your All-American hero, and his yummy car. I waited up to show you how the star forward at St. Jude's looks in her new white jersey and green shorts." She turned on the living room light, and leaped into the air as though she were tossing a basket. "Now I can put my whole soul into the game, and not worry about bustin' out all over like June."

"Sister Cabrina will never let you get by with such *short* shorts," Kathleen said around the pain under her ribs.

"But I'll try. If worst comes to worst, I can let out the hems. She'd like to see us all in bloomers below the knee. I didn't have enough money for the shorts after I bought my jersey and socks. But Mr. Novak bought them, because they appreciated me staying with their brood the night of the snow when they couldn't get home. He said it wasn't often he got a chance to buy pants for a pretty redhead."

"He's so corny."

"I know it, but I like corn. Tell me about the party."

As though she could tell a young sister the thing that hurt like a throbbing tooth. She said thinly, "Nothing was the way I thought it would be. I thought we'd just dance with the boy we came with. But you should have seen Mr. Knight bouncing all over the place with a portable mike, and having us do all this joining of hands and circling the gym, and then he'd yell out, 'Everybody dance with his partner on the right. This is a Get-Acquainted, boys and girls.' "

She hadn't wanted to get acquainted with anyone but Bruce. She had wanted everyone to know she was with him.

"Did they have girl-buttinskys? I think they're fun," Stacy said.

"Yes, girl-buttinskys and boy-buttinskys, and everybody-buttinskys. That was Mr. Knight's idea of Just One Big Happy Family. And the gym was jammed. More girls than boys too." She wondered, but with little concern, whether Rita had managed a date to go home with.

"Oh well," Stacy comforted, "there'll be other dances when your football hero can breathe sweet nothings in your ear when you dance together."

No there won't, she thought, and that's what hurts worse than any toothache I ever had.

"Did you dance with Mug? Did he have a date? Did he have fun?"

"We danced about three steps together. He didn't have a date, but if there was anyone he didn't get acquainted with, I don't know who. I'm going to bed."

Stacy said she'd wait up to show Ben her new basketball togs. "Or do you suppose he'll linger on when he takes Jeanie home?"

"He might," she muttered. Jeanie would never be the prize fool she had been. That was what hurt—unbearably.

In their room, Kathleen didn't turn on the light to undress by. She climbed into the double bed and lay on her side, tense and wide-eyed.

It had been a blouse-and-skirt affair. The few who wore dressy dresses looked self-conscious and apologetic. But the girls who were the *best*-dressed, and the envy of every other girl in the gym were the ten or twelve who were wearing yellow sweat shirts with a football player's name lettered on the back—Lane, Hyder, Detmyer.

On slim girls those bulky sweat shirts hung like gunny sacks, but that hadn't mattered—oh, not at all. For, like a fraternity pin in college, like a diamond on an engagement finger, they were symbols that announced to the world, "See, I'm a football player's girl!"

June wore one with McGaffey on it.

And every time Kathleen glimpsed a yellow sweater weaving through the mob, she coveted one with "Seerie" on it in black letters.

She had asked Bruce to let her wear his.

In the dark, her cheeks burned with shame. She should have remembered Jeanie's warning, "He doesn't like a sticky girl."

But he *had* acted so devoted, she defended herself to herself. He *had* breathed sweet nothings in her ear when they danced a brief length of the gym together. "I didn't know I was bringing a professional hoofer. I'll bet you've taken dancing lessons since you were five."

"No, just danced since I was five." Dancing was another thing Uncle Brian said came as natural to an O'Byrne as howling to a cat.

And when they'd be allemandeing left in Mr. Knight's circle, and Bruce would come to her, his face would light up. "Oh, there you are!" As though he *had* traveled the whole world o'er, and she was the one he had been looking for. Besides, he had said, "I'd rather not double date—I'd rather just pick you up and take you myself." The pearls she had cherished!

They had fought their way to the long refreshment tables for cider. There were also doughnuts and ginger cookies (made in foods class for the occasion), and Bruce had touched his paper cup of cider to hers, "Here's to us!" She sipped cider that was nectar. And then he asked, "Sure there isn't anything else you crave, Kathleen?"

Well, wouldn't any girl have said, "Bruce, I crave to wear your sweat shirt"? And wouldn't she have gushed further, "Haven't you noticed how many girls are wearing them tonight? And I think they're swell— they're just gorgeous—"

The second she said it, she wished she hadn't. For he took a backward step and looked at her out of jolted brown eyes. Then they dropped to the cider in his paper cup, and he studied it as though a fly were swimming around in it.

His smile when it came on again was confiding—almost gentle. "You know, Kathleen, all that football gear is school property. It burns Coach to a nub for the players to let the girls wear their sweats. Cripes, you should hear the way he chews them out if they don't have them when they're on the bench."

She supposed it was what Aunt Eustace called *background*, that kept him from saying, "I don't want you wearing my sweat shirt."

She couldn't remember whether she answered or just stood there like the goose girl Jeanie called her. But she would never, never forget his looking at the clock high on the gym wall and comparing it to his wrist watch and muttering that it was curfew time for the guys who would be playing against West High the next morning. "The chain gang has to be home by ten-thirty."

It was then she understood why he hadn't wanted to double date. Her last solace was taken from her.

In the double bed on Hubbell Street she buried her head in the pillow and sobbed.

She heard Cully's wlecoming bark when Ben came in. She heard him and Stacy laughing together. Imagine anyone being in ec-stacy over green basketball shorts. They came upstairs together.

Neither did Stacy turn on the light, but undressed in the scant light that came from the hall, whistling softly through her teeth. Kathleen could follow her movements. She was getting into her short, red-checked nightgown that she kept on wearing even though it was so worn the bottom was more fringe than hem. She was folding her new shorts and jersey lovingly.

She thumped herself down beside Kathleen. She lay for a minute before she said in a surprised voice, "Aren't you asleep yet?"

Kathleen intended only a brief, "No," but a hiccoughing sob came out with it.

"Katie Rose, what in the world are you crying about?"

"Noth-nothing."

"Nothing, my eye. Wasn't that bozo nice to you?"

"Of course—he was. Bruce is—is always nice."

"You mean you're gaga over him?" she pursued. "Well, that's nothing to wail about."

"You don't—understand. I—I made such a sap of myself."

"Can't you unmake yourself a sap?"

"No-o," Kathleen choked. "He'll never like me—not now."

Stacy reached out to her and patted her hand, and said in a mothering voice, "Katie—I mean Kathleen— why do you take things to heart so? What do you care if he never looks your way again? Golly sakes, there're hundreds and hundreds of boys at Adams. You just pick out one and give him the glad eye. You just forget old big-stuff Bruce whatever-his-name-is.'' After a minute she added, ''You stay in bed in the morning. I'll wash and iron Ben's jackets for you.''

She meant well, but how could she understand? Life is so simple when you're fourteen.

''Thanks,'' Kathleen gulped out.

But long after Stacy slept, the pain throbbed on— and on.

Twelve

THE NEXT DAY was Halloween, and Trick or Treat night for the three youngest Belfords. They had bought ghost masks at the dime store, and were so eager to don the skeleton suits they had worn in a St. Jude entertainment that they could scarcely eat their supper.

Kathleen could scarcely eat hers, but for reasons she kept to herself. Jeanie had phoned early this morning, and Kathleen had thought: I can't tell her I asked Bruce for his sweat shirt.

Jeanie's giggle had something of shyness in it. "I'm just dying to know if Ben said anything about his date last night."

"Not Ben. Not to me. He's the close-mouthed kind."

"I had a hunch he was. And I'm dying to know how you and Bruce got along."

Kathleen evaded her. "I only caught fleeting glimpses of him—courtesy of Mr. Knight."

"I know. What a free-for-all! I wasn't sure what color Ben's eyes were until he came in for a sandwich afterwards. I tried to find you and Bruce when it broke up at eleven to ask you to come too, but—"

"He had to get home early because of Coach's orders." She said—and even saying it was like touching the sore tooth, "That's why he didn't want to double date."

"For heaven's sake, why didn't I think of that? I should have known the coach's slightest word is law to him. Weren't we the conclusion-jumpers? I'm helping with the bills at Dad's office today. I suppose you're going to the game."

"Not today. Stacy wanted to use my ticket."

But she had been the one to press her ticket onto Stacy. Kathleen had no heart for watching number nineteen in all his padded-shoulder glory. Besides, Deetsy would be sure to push up and say, "So Bruce dated you last night. Is he taking you home after the game?"

At the supper table Mother, who was in a tired, nervous state, nudged her. "Eat your supper, Kathleen. Mr. McHarg will be coming for you any minute." And to Jill she snapped, "Will you stop smelling your food? You'd think we were poisoning you."

For some unaccountable reason, Jill was going through a phase of sniffing at everything she picked up. "It's just a habit of hers lately," little Brian said soberly.

Stacy interrupted with, "I always had more fun going out Trick or Treating. I just loved those little packets of candy corn. Do you suppose I'm too old to—"

"You certainly are, you big lug," Ben said firmly.

"You ought to see some of the great big, biggety boys that go out," Jill said.

"Yeh, and a lot of people don't give to them because they're too big," said her twin. "And that makes them mad because we get our sacks full and they don't, and they're mean as mean."

"They're no-goodniks and they're just spoilin' for trouble," Ben said. "So don't go starting anything with them, y'hear?"

"We dodge up alleys when we see 'em," they all assured him.

They were off with their big paper sacks in which to bring home their loot. Brian turned back to say, "Stacy, I'll save you all the candy corn I get. And you can have all the black jelly beans, Katie Ro—I mean Kathleen."

The McHargs, who lived at the edge of Harmony Heights, were going to a dinner dance that evening while Kathleen stayed with their small Diane and

Debbie. The little girls too were all agog about going out for Trick or Treat, and were already dressed in angel costumes of tulle which Mrs. McHarg had made them for a Christmas play.

Diane wasn't six yet, and chubby little Debbie was only four. Their father thought they were too young for such carryings on, but Mrs. McHarg said, "They've heard all the other children talking about it, and they've set their hearts on going. Kathleen can take them out for a little while. It's childish disappointments that give them inhibitions later on."

(Mrs. McHarg read all the books on child psychology that the Belford mother never bothered to.)

So with the smaller Debbie clinging tight to Kathleen with one hand and to her sack with the other, and with Diane scampering ahead, they set out in the strong, chilling wind. The little girls couldn't reach door bells. Kathleen would ring for them and step aside while the man or woman of the house answered, made a pleased to-do over golden-haired angels with wings coming to their door, before dropping candy bars or cookies into their sacks.

Diane proved to be a stubborn angel. Every time Kathleen said, "There, that's enough—we'd better go home," she insisted, "Oh no, we want to go to a lot more houses." Debbie would add, "Only five or seven or three more."

Up and down the streets, knots of children with rattly sacks scurried swiftly. Four older boys roughly crowded Kathleen and the little girls off the sidewalk. They were all at least sixteen, and weren't in costume except for eye masks. One jeered at her, "Where's your mask, baby? Or don't you need one?"

She hustled the little girls past them.

She had thought when they started that it would be fun to pound on Miguel's basement door. His grandparents' house must be in this block and close by. She remembered the house was only about six blocks from Hubbell Street, and that great clumps of golden glow grew in front. But was it the second or third house from the corner?

The three Belford skeletons who were across the street saw them and came streaming over. They pushed their masks high on their heads because Diane and Debbie were frightened of them, and showed how nearly full their sacks were.

The four toughs who had pushed Kathleen off the walk appeared again. The Belford group drew closer together, waiting for the boys to pass. The corner light showed up their sloppy jackets and tight, tight jeans. They, too, carried sacks, but the sacks looked empty.

They didn't go past, but stopped to light cigarettes and survey them insolently—the Belford littles, the small blond girls, and Kathleen. One said, "Hi again, baby. Are you following us?" and they all guffawed uproariously.

Kathleen suddenly felt far from home and unprotected.

The biggest of them, and probably the ringleader, stepped up to her. She could see a scab on his ear, and smell his sweaty unwashed clothes. "Looks like you little girl midgets did better'n us. We had pretty poor pickin's. People don't go for us."

Jill, who could always say the wrong thing at the wrong time, said, "You're too big to be going out for Trick'r Treat, that's why."

"Well, look at half-pint tellin' us off," one said. Again they all guffawed at such amazing wit.

The boy with the scabbed ear bent over and peered into Diane's sack. "Hmm-mm. Candy kisses. Nobody gave us candy kisses. So I'll just take your bag and you take this damn' near empty one of mine."

He yanked it from her tight fingers, and she let out an agonized shriek. Kathleen grabbed him by the arm. "You give that back, you big bully. You ought to be ashamed."

He threw her hand off his arm, his strong fingers hurting her wrist as he gripped it. She had never known what a *leer* was until he brought his face close to hers, and she saw his lips curl and the moist look in his eyes. "You don't want me to have any candy kisses, huh? Then how's about a real one?"

He was showing off what a sharp guy he was to his pals. In her fear and fury, she kicked him on the shins, screaming at him, "Get away! Get away!" and to the world at large, "Help—Help!"

He called her a hell-cat and twisted her wrist.

Pandemonium broke loose. A skeleton dove at him like a football player making a tackle. (It was Jill, she found out afterward.) Diane screamed on as though all her teeth were being pulled. Masks and sacks fell. Kathleen's ugly leerer had her pinioned against the tree, while the littles fought like tigers—kicking, clawing, even biting at the hands that reached for them. Kathleen too was screaming like a banshee.

Suddenly a tall, lanky figure seemed to drop from heaven. His hard fist landed on the scabby ear of the boy twisting her arm. It was Miguel, and his fist kept flailing in all directions.

Doors across the street were opening. A man in his shirt sleeves was running toward the fracas. The young hoodlums took to fast heels. One minute they were there. The next, there was only the pounding of their feet as they raced toward the alley and darkness.

"Petunia, did that roughneck hurt you?" Miguel panted. "If he did, I'll chase him till I get my hands on him."

"No—no. Just my wrist—but it'll be all right."

They all stood, disheveled and breathing hard, in a welter of torn sacks, stepped-on masks, spilled apples and lollypops. The man across the street muttered that if it would do any good, he would call the police. "But they're far and away by now." He said he'd send his wife back with a flashlight so they could gather up the spoilage.

She came in a sweater over a housecoat, and shivered all the while she flicked the light over the ground, and the skeletons gathered everything up. Diane was wailing, "I want my very own sack back." The smaller Debbie, who had never made a sound through it all, stood rooted to the spot hugging her untouched bag.

Jill said, "Those old meanies didn't even take their own bags with them. They haven't got much, but we'll keep whatever it is."

"Come on inside, Petunia," Miguel said. "You kids just scoop up your treats and bring it all into the basement and we'll see what's still edible. We'll fix up your very own sack, Diane."

Kathleen pushed back her dark, wind-ruffled hair. "I thought you lived near here, but I wasn't sure which house—"

"This is my dungeon."

He took her arm, and picked up little Debbie. The others trailed behind them on the walk that led around the bungalow and to the back door. They went down steps into a laundry room, and walked through it to what was called a recreation room when the house was built thirty years earlier.

He cleared a fluffy yellow cat out of the one comfortable chair, and pulled it in front of the fireplace for Kathleen. Now that the sudden onslaught was over, her knees were shaking and her teeth chattering. He examined her red wrist, muttering, "That slob—that stinkin' slob." He went to the laundry room and came back with a washcloth wrung out with hot water, and wrapped it loosely around it. "In a minute I'll change it to cold."

He spread a newspaper on the floor. "Okay, kids, dump all the scrambled loot together and sort it out. Good thing most everything comes wrapped these days."

It was calming to sit in front of the fire and listen to the twins' businesslike, "Here's a red apple for Debbie," and have licorice jelly beans and suckers dropped into her lap. She said absently, "Jill, stop sniffing at every candy bar."

Miguel took off the now lukewarm cloth and put on a cold one. "Did you have fun at the Get-Acquainted last night?" he asked.

She hedged by asking, "Did you?"

"I sure did. I guess everybody did. If he didn't, it was his own stupid fault."

Or *her* stupid fault. But like someone wriggling a hurting tooth with his tongue, she said, "I went with Bruce Seerie. Maybe you know him?"

"Yeah, I know him. He and a couple of boys on the team are having it tough in Spanish. And you know how every player has to be signed up in three academics before he can play? So I help them with translations now and then. I noticed you dancing with him. Wish I could dance that good. He's good at everything. You ought to see him dive."

He was even good at putting a girl in her place, she thought bleakly.

The five sacks were now divided evenly, though the Belford three, being experienced Trick-or-Treaters, had collected far more than the angels Kathleen had rung doorbells for. And then she saw the three heads, the color of cornflakes, bent together in conference. They could hold one with a minimum of mumbles and nods, and then come out with a decision. All three of them stood in front of her, and Jill said, "You won't tell about the fight, will you?"

"You mean at home? Why?"

Matthew shrugged. "We never tell about things like that at home. Last Sunday when I was coming home from church, a kid threw a pumpkin at me, and almost put out my eye. Grown-ups always worry."

Brian contributed, "If Ben knew, he mightn't let us go out next year. I said I was sure you wouldn't tell."

She noticed the bump on Jill's forehead, and Matthew's swollen underlip. Brian was sucking at a cut on his hand. In her behalf, they had certainly leaped valiantly into what would have been a losing battle if Miguel hadn't appeared when he had.

She had always thought of them merely as three pesterers to complicate her life. She had always lumped them together. But at that moment, she saw them as three separate individuals: Matt, the tough strutter; Jill, the spokesman; Brian, with his shy sweet smile, the worrier, the conscience for the three of them.

"Don't worry. I won't say a word at home." She felt a queer, fluttery pride to be in a secret with them.

Miguel threw more wood on the fire. Firewood was stacked in a corner. His school books were scattered over the table. A bedroll was lumped on a couch, and shirts and socks hung on a drying line.

Kathleen pried a jelly bean off the roof of her mouth, and asked, "Haven't you heard yet when your grandparents are coming home?"

"Nope. As far as the fellow across the alley and I can figure, they're still on their cruise in the tuna boat."

"But I should think you could open the door to the upstairs, and have a real kitchen, and a bedroom with a bed. You could answer the telephone, instead of listening for Stacy's two rings."

"*Your* two rings too if you should need me. Sure, Petunia, I could get a locksmith but gosh, that's grandma's domain, and I'd feel like a trespasser. I'm doing fine down here. They left the gas furnace set at sixty so when the weather got cold nothing would freeze up. All I need is this fire in the fireplace to keep warm. I have a hunch they'll be home about Thanksgiving."

"Doesn't your father know yet that they're away and you're living here on your own?"

"No, I haven't told him. He'll send another check the first. That's tomorrow. He sends plenty for me to get by on. No, he's got a job to do, and I don't want him feeling like he should rush down here and rescue me." Again his urchin grin. "Grown-ups always worry."

"I worry, Miguel, about your transcript." She was curious too, wondering often what grade he had changed.

"It's beginning to scare me too. Maybe I'll come yelling to you for help."

"I'll come running if you do."

He crunched on a flattened popcorn ball thoughtfully for a moment. "Seems like it's in the stars, Petunia, that when one of us needs help, the other comes to the rescue. That first day when I was hollow clear down to my heels, you fed me. You were my savior. So I have a feeling that whichever one of us is in a jam, the other will come running."

No one was so easy to talk to as Miguel. She told him about Uncle Brian. "He's working so hard, what with his job and helping a fellow named Marve build a garage, that he's losing weight. But he hasn't touched a drop."

"Keeping busy is a lifesaver," he said.

Miguel not only took her and her small charges home, but he packed the three littles in Mercy Be as well. Matthew argued, "Gee, it's just a little ways to our house," but Miguel insisted, "Pile in. I wouldn't put it past our scrappy little pals to be layin' for you."

Back in the McHargs' quiet house, Kathleen dropped into the first chair feeling limp and drained. But Diane breathed a rapturous sigh. "This has been the most wonderful time I ever had in my whole, whole life, Kathleen. Can't you hardly wait for next Halloween?"

Thirteen

ON MONDAY AFTERNOON, Kathleen walked slowly down the hall to American lit, clasping her prose and poetry book tight. This time it was to cover her heart's thumpety-thump of shame and humiliation. How could she ever face Bruce? How could she ever sit in the same room with him? She saw him outside the door, and stopped in sudden cowardice. She'd go to the office and say she had a headache and get excused. But there was always tomorrow. She dragged on.

He greeted her with his same bright smile and "Hi, Kathleen, how's it going?" In grateful relief, she groped her way to her desk.

The next day he even lingered to ask her what was

the shortest length Mr. Jacoby, their teacher, would accept for a book report. But she sensed a certain wariness about him that all but said, "So far and no further, Kathleen, shalt thou go."

If only she could undo her blunder at the Get-Acquainted!

November's first blizzard greeted the students when they pushed through the wide glass door that afternoon.

The Belford family fell to scurrying up mittens, scarves, sweaters, and storm boots. The half-a-bath fund had to be tapped for knitted ear bands for the paper carriers, weather stripping for the back door, and mittens for Stacy. (She was always losing hers.)

The bitter cold affected the Chevy's ailing battery, so St. Jude and Adams students fanned out to school afoot in cold winds and crunchy snow.

Kathleen looked long and longingly at the store ads picturing fleece-lined coats with attached hoods, also fleece-lined. "The Weatherwise. Warm, lovely, flattering." But she didn't dare mention one, because by now Ben had decided a new battery for the car was a must, and that was a severe dent in the half-a-bath.

So she and Stacy zipped the plaid wool linings in their old trench coats. The coats had shrunk from washing; with the lining still unshrunk, there was a bundly look around hem and front.

Kathleen couldn't be as blithely philosophic as Stacy, who figured just how long it would take her to save her baby-sitting money for a new Weatherwise. But her arithmetic was as haphazard as her pronouncing of words.

November's blizzard brought out a flowering of these coats at Adams High. Leave it to June and Deetsy to be the first.

June chose black gabardine lined in pale blue fur which she thought, and rightly, did well by her blond hair. Deetsy, who went in for startling effects, had a white one lined with scarlet.

On these bitter cold days, Uncle Brian came home from his job about the time the children did from school. When Jill asked him if Marve's garage was finished, he snapped, "No, it's far from finished. But we're not damfool enough to mix cement in zero weather."

Mother's eyes turned harried, as she tried to think up some carpentering or painting job around the house to keep him busy. And Kathleen decided, I'd better not ask Jeanie to come—not yet.

Bruce's book report must have been far too short. For Mr. Jacoby handed it back, saying, "A six-year-old could have found more meat—or fish—in *The Old Man and the Sea* than you did. Or did you realize there was a theme in it? Suppose you take your mind off football long enough to try it again."

Kathleen saw the confused, helpless look on Bruce's face.

Mr. Jacoby was a youngish, sallow-faced man who wore startling sport shirts, and liked to mention authors he knew. On a snowy afternoon when the class-room smelled of wet wool, and a few students sucked on cough drops, he asked, "Have any of you read, or even heard, of Katherine Anne Porter?"

Kathleen's hand went up. She had read *Pale Horse, Pale Rider.* (Thank heaven for her summer of intensive reading!)

It delighted him.

Mr. Jacoby also went on what the class called a poetry binge. He walked up and down in front of the room, his eyes glowing, his hand gesturing, as he read excerpts of poems from their *Prose and Poetry.* The football players would slouch lower and lower in their seats, till their booted feet stuck far out in front of their desks.

But Kathleen felt right at home. For a brief while she wouldn't glance Bruce's way, because she was see-ing her father with a cup of tea in one hand and a book in the other. And she knew that Mr. Jacoby in his driven way was, like Father, saying, "A poet is only a person who is able to say what is in all our hearts. We can't say it, so he says it for us."

On another day Mr. Jacoby, looking bored and weary, suddenly flung out, "I know it isn't on our supplement-ary reading list, but have any of you—just on an off chance—read *Don Quixote?*"

He pretended to be overcome when Kathleen put up her hand.

They discussed the book—the symbolism of the windmills, and Cervantes' writing it to ridicule other books of romantic chivalry.

The boy behind her grumbled, "Teacher's pet." But, looking across at Bruce, she thought she saw wonder and new respect in his eyes. And that's when dormant hope began scrabbling for its perch again.

Bruce needed Mr. Jacoby's okay on the slip to turn into Coach before each game. Why couldn't he, recognizing her grasp of literature, turn to her for help in lit just as he did to Miguel in Spanish?

Jeanie was out of school with a cold, so Kathleen walked home through a fine, sleety snow, and her dreams took over again. . . . Bruce was saying, "Did you find a theme in that story about the old man going out and catching a fish, and then having it gnawed to the bone before he got back?"

"Oh yes, Bruce. His catching the biggest fish in the sea is allegorical." (Her father had explained that to her.)

"Well, how about us having a Coke at Downey's, and your going into this allegory bit?". . .

At home, her mother poured tea for Kathleen out of the big earthenware pot. Uncle Brian was there, restless and moody, and impatient.

She was looking through the bookshelves for their

copy of Hemingway's *The Old Man and the Sea* when her mother said, ''Brian, why don't you go out and visit Grandfather Belford again? He phoned me today to ask if we were getting along all right in this cold weather. He can't go out, and it must be lonely for him.''

Often when Uncle Brian had time on his hands, he drove out to the Belford mansion and visited with Grandfather. Before going the first time, he had said, ''Call up out there, Mavourneen, and find out if your aunt Eustace is home.''

''Why?''

''Because I'd like to hobnob with the old gent, but I'd be more at ease if she weren't about.''

''Why would you?''

''Because she doesn't like me. And I'll let you in on a secret, bright angel; she doesn't, because I don't play up to her. Go ahead and phone.''

''She'd think it was crazy if I just called up and asked her if she was home.''

''Then change your voice and pretend you're selling something.''

''I wouldn't lower myself to.''

But Stacy would, and did. She'd pretend she was calling from the Murray Dance Studio or taking a TV poll. She would ask for the lady of the house, and if Mrs. Van said she was not in, Stacy would say, ''Thank you very much,'' and report gleefully to Uncle Brian, ''The coast is clear.''

This snowy day Uncle Brian, being in a devilish mood, phoned himself, and asked for Miss Belford. He put on a thick Scotch accent, and asked if he could show her some hand-knit sweaters he had just brought from Edinburgh.

Kathleen glowered at Stacy for giggling.

He replaced the phone, and reported in a mimicking voice, "Miss Belford is not interested. She is dressing for a dinner engagement, after which she is attending the symphony."

He put on his leather coat, very prancy and pleased with himself. He called good-by from the doorway, but Kathleen didn't look up from the book in her hand. Mother lit a cigarette, and the first puff of smoke came on a sigh of relief. "I'm glad he'll be spending the evening there. It worries me to see him jumpy from craving a drink. He always comes back more at peace with the world. I'm so glad he and Grandfather hit it off so well."

Kathleen didn't answer. She was furious with them all for making a game out of his trips to the Belford mansion.

The November days sped on. And still Bruce had not turned to her for literary help. Maybe he was waiting for her to offer it. Maybe, with the final Thanksgiving game coming up, he was desperate about getting Mr. Jacoby's name on his slip.

On the Monday before Thanksgiving, and after her

rehearsing over the weekend, "Bruce, I just happened to read *The Old Man and the Sea,* and it's all fresh in my mind—and Mr. Jacoby does go all out for what he calls the depth charge in a story—" Bruce was not in class. Neither were the other two players.

Kathleen couldn't ask it, but the boy behind her did, "What happened to Seerie and McGaffey and Darby?"

Nothing, Mr. Jacoby said drily, except that the coach had asked him to take them in his morning class so the team could have more time to work on signals for the big game.

The irony of fate again!

She walked home with Jeanie that afternoon to listen to Conversational French records. They kicked off storm boots and sat cross-legged on Jeanie's bed rubbing their cold toes, while in the room across the hall Mrs. Kincaid ran her electric sewing machine. Jeanie sorted through the stack of records, and bent over double to put one on the portable player on the floor. She bent over sideways to reach a plate of fudge on her dressing table.

"It's grainy because after Ben and I drove down to see if there was skating on the park lake, we had to cook it fast to get it done before he went to work."

"It's good though," Kathleen murmured. Three weeks and three days since the Get-Acquainted, but it could still hurt that Ben had carried on from that night, and her date had not.

She knew by the concern in Jeanie's eyes that her

next question would be, "Hasn't Bruce asked you for another date yet?" And it was.

"The answer is N-O, no."

Jeanie crinkled her nose as she always did when she was puzzled. "Funny. He likes you. He thinks you're a heavenly dancer. I can't understand it."

Kathleen blurted out—for, after all, she couldn't go through life with Jeanie asking her if Bruce had dated her, "He's scared of me. He keeps me at arm's length because the night of the Get-Acquainted, I asked him for his sweat shirt."

Jeanie turned startled eyes on her. She might have reproached, "Didn't I warn you, goose girl?" but the very misery in Kathleen's eyes and woebegone face checked it. Jeanie only sat, scratching her big toe with the edge of a record. She mused, "I guess we both got carried away by his wanting to take you alone instead of double dating. What'd he say when you asked him for his precious sweat?"

"He looked as if I'd hit him in the stomach. And then he said that Coach chewed out the fellows that didn't have their—"

"Coach wasn't the only one that would have chewed him out. So would his parents. Mom is a friend of his mother, and she's so afraid of his getting involved with some greedy little number—or one that's too serious. Oh, I know Bruce acts like an independent soul, but don't ever think he doesn't like to keep in his folks' good graces. So he can flash around in his mother's car for one thing."

"Maybe if they—knew me," Kathleen said painfully. "I mean—Aunt Eustace knows them real well—and she talks about having me to dinner—"

"They'd have to know you had no designs on him." Jeanie's forehead as well as her nose puckered in deep thought as the French voices on the record discussed pictures at the Louvre. "Look, Kathleen, Miguel said a mouthful when he said the heart has a lot of different rooms. So why don't you—as long as you can't keep from putting Bruce on a pedestal—just shove him off into a storeroom for future reference? And then go about business as usual? Open up to Miguel. And the John-Toms are nice kids. Then there's that cute Freddy in math—I heard him telling you he'd like to teach you all the angles."

The sewing machine across the hall was silent, and Jeanie's mother called out good-naturedly, "Why don't you try listening to the records? Or are you hoping to get it by osmosis?"

"We're talking about our cruel parents," Jeanie called back.

The sewing machine started again. "I wish I could," Kathleen admitted. "But from the first minute I saw him—" And she told Jeanie about the drab and boring afternoon when she felt that life had passed her by, and how she had opened the door to see Bruce standing in the glow of the sunset. "And he seemed like—just like—"

"A gift from the gods?" Jeanie sighed.

When the last record clicked off, and the plate of fudge was empty, Kathleen slid her feet into clammy storm boots. Jeanie walked to the end of the block with her. A car with Johnny Q students came to such a sudden stop in the snowy street that their faces were sprayed with snow crystals. Deetsy leaned out a window to scream joyfully, "We've just come from the park. They're scraping part of the lake for skating. And stringing up lights. Whoopee!"

The next morning when Kathleen and Jeanie were at their locker, and Deetsy and June at theirs, Jeanie announced that she was having a skating party Thanksgiving night. Thanksgiving was the day after tomorrow. She said, "So, June, if you see McGaffey before I do, you ask him. I'll see the John-Toms in French—"

Deetsy broke in in her breathless burble, "Can I tell Miguel? Let me tell him, Jeanie."

Jeanie laughed, and said okay. She answered the puzzled look on Kathleen's face as they walked up the stairs to second floor and their first class, "Don't tell me you haven't noticed Deetsy buddying up to Miguel in French, and gushing over him at lunch? He is her present pulse beat, though I don't think he knows it yet."

"For gosh sakes."

Jeanie went on, "Thanksgiving isn't the best night for a party, what with the wind-up football games and family dinners. It'll be kind of a scrambled affair. I mean it won't be like the ark where all the couples come in two by two."

"I think Ben has to work."

"But he tells me he can manage to get off early—earlier than eleven. I told him if he couldn't make it to the lake for skating, to come on over to the house in time for pizza and dancing to the hi-fi. And I phoned Bruce last evening."

Kathleen halted as though the steps were suddenly steep. "What'd he say?"

"He's thrilled to be your date. But he wanted me to tell you, in case he didn't see you, that they're having a late family dinner, and his folks will expect him to drive some of the antiquated relatives home. So I told him to head for the park when his chores are done."

Kathleen said in a small voice, "Sounds as if he's playing it safe."

"No, I'm sure the relative gag is bona fide. As I say, he does have to keep on the good side of his folks so he can use the car. I'll be dateless too till Ben gets off. Dad will take me to the park, and we'll pick you up on our way. About eight."

"Jeanie, are you having this party to help me out?"

"Maybe. Maybe to help us all out." They had reached the door of their foods laboratory where this morning they would discuss table settings. "And this time, Kathleen—"

"I won't cling, I promise."

"You know that untroubled—even smug—way June has around boys. Her smile practically says, 'I'm not worried about your liking me because there are plenty of others who do.' Maybe you could take a leaf out of her book, Kathleen."

"I'll take the whole book."

At their lockers that afternoon, Deetsy looked a little dashed. "I asked Miguel," she told Jeanie. "But I couldn't seem to get it across that he's to be my date. He said sure, he'd come—that it sounded like fun—"

"Since when have words failed you?" June wanted to know.

Jeanie said, "Don't worry. I'll mention it to him."

Kathleen came home from school to find the littles and Stacy in the hall, excitedly gathering up shoe skates. They too had heard that the park lake was ready for use.

They ate an early supper and Ben loaded them all into the car. Kathleen's reason for going was to practice up for Thanksgiving night when she would be skating with Bruce. And also to see what the best-dressed girl skaters were wearing.

Some wore the usual slacks and jeans with heavy plaid shirts or padded jackets. Some wore scarves over their heads. But the *best*-dressed ones were in ribbed leotards the color of their heavy slip-overs, *and* a very fetching something new in caps. They were like toboggans only made of suede and, instead of tassels at the end, had bells that jingled. They wore mittens to match.

A girl from St. Jude's told Stacy they were called Pierrot caps, and also what the set cost at Madame Simone's on the Boulevard. Stacy gave a low whistle. "It'd take a long, long night of baby-sitting," she said.

The next day Kathleen plunged. She took all the baby-sitting money she had been saving toward a Weatherwise coat to school with her. After school, she and Jeanie walked to Madame Simone's. Jeanie bought a red Pierrot set. Kathleen chose a blue that almost matched her turquoise sweater. She bought the leotards she needed too, although she had to borrow sixty cents from Jeanie to complete her purchases.

When she got home she tried them all on in front of the mirror in her room. She also tried on June's unconcerned little half-smile.

Fourteen

WOULD Thanksgiving night never come?

Kathleen had gone to the game and thumped her fists and stomped her feet to keep warm. She had watched every play so that she could discuss it intelligently with Bruce that evening. Adams won the game, putting them in fourth place in the city league in which eight high schools competed.

She had gone with the John-Toms, but the green stock car refused to budge at the game's end. Miguel walked home with her. His Mercy Be was also laid up with a frozen radiator.

He was their only guest for the turkey dinner at one. Ordinarily, Gran and Grandda drove in from Bannon.

They had returned from their visit in Nebraska, but the roads were bad, and the weatherman predicted the temperature would drop below zero by night.

All afternoon Kathleen counted the hours until eight, and whipped up a hem in her plaid skirt to make it into a short, skating one, and prayed the prayer she read every Sunday in her missal, "Set a watch, O Lord, about my lips." Let them not gush. Let them only smile as coolly and serenely as June's.

She didn't mention to Miguel that Jeanie and her father were taking her to the skating party for fear he'd say, "I'll just stay and ride over with you." He still seemed blissfully unaware that Deetsy was sharpening her claws for him. When he mentioned going home to go over a history outline, Kathleen didn't say, "Stay." Neither did Stacy because she was baby-sitting that evening.

What with being so absorbed in her own plans, it wasn't until late afternoon that Kathleen realized what a desperate mood Uncle Brian was in. He paced the floor, looking out one window and then another. He muttered about the cold weather holding up his work on Marve's garage. He turned the pages of the paper, and then hurled it across the room.

Mother said, "Brian, there's a good show on TV—channel four."

"Is there?" he said in a dead voice.

"Look, Brian, I ran next door for a minute, and they

lent me these murder mysteries. Mickey Spillanes."

"Thanks."

Stacy too. "Hey, Uncle Brian, how'd you like some fudge? I feel the urge to whip up some."

"I can't think of anything I'd rather *not* have."

They had tea and turkey sandwiches at six. Uncle Brian didn't want a sandwich *or* cranberries, *or* pumpkin pie. "Here, Brian, I made fresh tea," Mother said. "Let me give you—"

"No," he shouted. "For the love of Moses, no. My gullet is sickened from swilling down that thin brew." He moved in to the piano in the hall. He played one Irish ballad after another without ever finishing one.

"God help us!" Mother breathed. Her hands shook as she cut the pumpkin pie and put pieces on their plates. Jill, sitting next to her, said, "I didn't say I wanted any," and Mother said shortly, "Oh, eat it, and hush."

Jill, the obtuse! She argued on, "I don't like ginger, and if it's got ginger in it—" She bent her head, sniffing audibly at the piece in front of her.

It was purely reflex on Mother's part. Her hand shot out and gave Jill's head a vehement push downward until her nose was buried in the brown custard of the pie. "Get a good smell while you're at it," she muttered.

They all laughed. They couldn't help it when they saw the coating on Jill's nose and the shocked look on her face as her head came up. Mother looked as surprised as Jill. It was she who reached out with a paper napkin and cleaned her face. "It drives me wild the way you're forever smelling at food."

Again Brian defended her, "It's just a habit she's got."

Jill was made of tough fiber. There was only that first startled second when she looked as though she would cry, and then she said valiantly, "It did smell gingery," and managed to laugh with the others.

Uncle Brian's playing went on while Stacy pelted up and down stairs, waited at the door, and was picked up by the folks she would baby-sit for; while Ben got into his white jacket, and Mother hurriedly dressed in her corn-colored *peau de soie* and came down ready for her evening at Giddy's. She carried her overshoes into the kitchen. Ben knelt and put them on for her.

She said in a low, troubled voice, "Kathleen, I'd give anything—anything—if I didn't have to go out there tonight. But the place will be full and running over with football crowds wanting all those Hail, Hail to old whatever."

"I tried to get Clyde," Ben said, "to take my place tonight. He isn't home. And there's no one else—no one." He took the sugar bowl with the half-a-bath fund and put it in the oven. "Just in case it might be a temptation to him."

The three stood while the frenzied playing in the hall beat at their ears. Mother turned appealing eyes to

Kathleen, "Could you stay home with him, lovey, just till he—?"

"You mean miss Jeanie's skating party? They're coming after me at eight."

"We can't leave him alone," Mother said. "All day the thirst has been building up in him. Couldn't you just stay till he gets to bed? That's why I got him the Mickey Spillanes. Couldn't you call Jeanie, and tell her you'll be a little late getting over to the park?"

"And how'll I get there?" she hurled out in disappointment. "Just go walking all the way over there in the dark by myself?"

"You won't have to," Ben said swiftly. "Let him keep on playing there at the piano. Then surely he'll go to bed because of having to get up in the morning. Soon as he does, give me a ring. I can leave the Robin for fifteen, twenty minutes and drive you to the lake."

Mother murmured again, "If it wasn't such a festive night out there, I could ask Giddy— Oh, Katie Rose, it's my job."

"I know. You two go on. I'll stay till it's all right to leave."

Uncle Brian wouldn't look up from the keyboard to answer their good-bys as they went out the door. Kathleen pulled the phone into the kitchen, and dialed Jeanie. "Don't stop for me. Something's come up and— and I don't know when I can get away."

A pause at Jeanie's end while she waited for her to

say more. She added lamely, "Uncle Brian's sick but—but I'll see if—"

She replaced the phone hurriedly for the music stopped on a discordant crash. Uncle Brian went into the living room, and bellowed to the three littles to turn down the TV. He paced about the house, until Kathleen asked, "Do you want something to read?"

"No, I'm sick of books and all the words in them. I'll tell you what I want, Mavourneen. I want a few dollars of the money I entrusted to you."

"No. No, I can't give it to you."

"Why can't you now?"

"I promised you I wouldn't."

"Ah that," he discounted. "Well, I'm *un*promising your promise as of now. Just a few dollars is all I'm asking."

She wished she weren't here alone with him except for the littles, who would be no help at all. She shook her head. "No, Uncle Brian."

He gave her his winning smile. "Can't you understand, my own? A man can take just so much being cooped up with women and kids, and then he craves to get out and hear man-talk."

"You mean at the Shamrock? But if you went there, you'd start drinking."

His voice was more wheedling. "God love you, girleen, just dole me out a dollar then. No one can get polluted on a buck's worth of watered-down drinks."

It would be so easy for her to run upstairs, unearth the pink plastic soap box and slide just *one* dollar bill off the sizable roll there. But she kept shaking her head. He wheedled on, "I'll tell you what, sweetheart, give me that one measly dollar—that's all I ask—and you can keep all the rest yourself. Every red cent of it. Use it to buy any fancy furbelows dear to your heart, and it'll be between the two of us. No one need know, and no harm done."

A Weatherwise coat dangled itself in front of her eyes. But something kept her shaking her head. "No, Uncle Brian. No."

He went into an ugly rage. He had worked like a slave for that money, and what right had she to refuse him? Cully yelped in alarm about them, and he gave the dog a cuff that sent him whimpering behind the piano.

He pushed Kathleen aside roughly and went into the kitchen, saying, "Rose wouldn't begrudge me a bit out of that sugar-bowl fund of hers, and I'll be paying it back—" She listened to his opening and banging cupboard doors, his rattling of china. But there was no sound of the oven door being opened or shut. It evidently dawned on him that the sugar bowl was well hidden, and his fury mounted.

Again he brushed her aside and made for the stairs. "So you're all in league. I never thought I'd see the day when I had to cadge drinks, but God knows I've bought enough for those hangers-on at the Shamrock." He turned on the second step to bellow out, "Keep the money and be damned to the whole lot of you. You'll not be making a tabby cat out of me. I'm going."

He would, too. What—or who—could stop him? In her desperation, she thought of Miguel and his saying about Stacy's signaling him by phone, "*Your* two rings if you ever need me."

She snatched up the phone, dialed, and waited to hear the two buzzes. Even as she hung up, she heard the vicious thumps overhead that was Uncle Brian stamping his feet down in his heavy boots.

She waited helplessly as he clopped down the steps, ransacked through the closet under the stairs for his leather coat. She was thankful for the time he spent hunting for his car keys.

At last he found them. As he started for the door, she pleaded, "Wait, Uncle Brian. Miguel is coming over and—" Despair put the words on her tongue, "—we thought maybe you'd let us take your car—his is frozen up—and all the kids are going skating."

It worked. An O'Byrne could never refuse a favor. "Sure, you can use the car," he said grandly. "Only I can't be waiting around the whole evening for him to show up."

Never was a step on the porch, never was the opening of the door more welcome. Miguel must have run all the way. He was panting for breath, and his thin face was purple with cold. Kathleen said swiftly, "I told

Uncle Brian we'd like to take his car to go skating.''

"Provided you drop me off on the Boulevard as you go,'' Uncle Brian amended, his hand on the door.

Miguel had pulled off his mittens, and was blowing on his hands, but his eyes took in Uncle Brian's wild restlessness. "You're craving a drink, is that it?'' he asked.

"Yes, I'm craving a drink. You've heard someone say he'd cut off his right arm for one. Well, I'd hack mine off with a kitchen knife for just one. Get your skates, Kathleen, and come on.''

There was no time to rig herself out in the new leotards and shortened skirt. No time to adjust the Pierrot cap to a becoming slant. She reached for her trench coat and skates. "Here, Miguel, you can take Ben's,'' she said.

Uncle Brian went out the door, letting in a blast of bitter cold air while Miguel thoughtfully adjusted the skates over his shoulder, and walked beside Kathleen to the car.

Uncle Brian was already behind the wheel. Miguel opened the door for Kathleen, and then went around to the driver's side. "How about my driving, so I can get the hang of it while you're with us?''

Uncle Brian obediently but impatiently shoved himself over in the middle of the front seat, and Miguel took the wheel. He started off slowly, talking all the while about the difference in shifts between this car and his old Mercedes. He was still talking when they reached the Boulevard, and Uncle Brian ordered, "Turn here."

He didn't turn, but kept on the street that led to the park. He said, "Let's all go skating first. You can wear Ben's skates, Uncle Brian, because I can't skate for sour apples anyway."

"Let me out," Uncle Brian thundered.

He might have jumped out of the car, if he could have without pushing either Miguel or Kathleen out first. He might have reached out and turned off the motor, if they hadn't been in a lane of traffic.

It was a bad time. Uncle Brian threatened them and threshed about between them. But Miguel drove ahead, and Kathleen talked loudly, "Remember, Uncle Brian, when you taught us all to skate on the lake at Bannon? They've got music here so the fancy skaters can waltz." She even lied through her teeth, "I'd like my friends to see what a swell skater you are."

The one thing she did *not* want was for her friends to see her uncle in the driven mood he was in.

No answer from Uncle Brian.

Miguel drove through the park, and as close as he could to the lake's edge. He got out; Kathleen got out. For what seemed a long minute, Uncle Brian sat in the car. And then he flung himself out, and stood surveying the skaters caught in the bright flood lights while the music filled the cold air. What he was thinking, Kathleen didn't know, for all he said was, "Not much more room than a flooded barn lot."

In a kind of reckless bravado, he walked with them to the benches where skaters put on and took off skates. Jerkily, he tugged off his boots and put on Ben's skates. Before she could lace hers up, he stood up and clomped away. "I'm hoping he can skate it off," Miguel said.

Kathleen minced down to the frozen lake, her eyes searching over the skaters. None of Jeanie's party crowd was there yet; it was a little early for them. Uncle Brian was already racing on choppy strokes in and out of the crowd.

The park lake was huge. But only a small part had been scraped smooth and lighted. Rifts of icy snow marked off the skating space from the rest of the dark lake. Uncle Brian plowed right through the barrier and onto the bigger area. "Is it all right for him to skate out there?" she asked Miguel.

"There's no danger. It's just that it's bubbly and rough from the ice melting through the day and freezing over again."

She skated about uneasily, watching, waiting. A group of husky college boys were joining hands for a crack-the-whip. There was the usual disclaiming of, "I'm not going to be the whip-end—not me!" Because everyone knew that the last man—even the last two or three—were due for a nasty spill. That was the whole idea.

Uncle Brian skated back into the bright lights in the thick of the argument. Someone asked him to be end man, and he said sure, why not. She tried to call to him that he'd only be thrown, but he paid no attention. The whip started with a lot of the smaller children and fumbling skaters scurrying out of its way.

Miguel, without skates, stood at the ice's edge, and she moved over to him. They both watched, noticing how the leaders started out fairly easy in working up speed, and how the ones on the end were skating with all their might, hoping to escape the final snap and hard tumble.

Uncle Brian, the last in line, was skating as unconcernedly as though he couldn't care less what happened. It came! The whip cracked, and though some of the tail ones managed to keep their feet, Uncle Brian and the man next to him skithered over the ice in a tangle of arms, legs, and skates, with caps and gloves littering the ice.

She skated toward Uncle Brian, but he was on his feet before she could reach him. The slit pocket of his leather coat was ripped and hanging. One of the gloves she picked up was his, and she shouted after him. But by then he was stumbling through the drift surrounding the skating area, and plunging on into the unlighted expanse of rough ice as though bloodhounds were baying at his heels.

Two people pushed up to her as she stood watching—

Miguel without skates, and Jeanie Kincaid, teetering on hers. Kathleen didn't know she was crying until Miguel said softly, "Don't cry, Petunia. It'll do him good to wear himself out."

Jeanie touched her arm. "It's Uncle Brian. Why did you say he was sick?"

"He's wild for want of a drink," she confessed. "I didn't tell you before because—because you thought he was wonderful—and adorable."

"I still think he is," Jeanie said staunchly, and she stood on with them watching. Sometimes they lost track of him when the trees around the lake cast shadows. Sometimes they saw him hit an extra rough spot and fall. Jeanie murmured, "They're cartons and sacks and stuff like that frozen in the ice."

He came into the smooth, lighted section again. Jeanie skated up to him. "Hi, Uncle Brian. Remember me? I'm Jeanie."

He was panting for breath, and a bruise near his eyes was swelling, but blarney never forsook him. "How could I ever forget you, my darlin' honey bear? Haven't I thought of you every wakin' minute?"

"You're a wonderful skater. Why don't you skate with Kathleen and me?"

He crossed arms with them and skated for a while. He dropped their hands. "There now, my beauties, it's too crowded here. I'm afraid I'll bump into some fat mama or knock over a little codger." And again he was off.

Jeanie skated with a boy she knew. Freddy, in Kathleen's math class, asked her to skate with him. Then she, Miguel, and Jeanie gravitated together and looked out over the lake to where that lone figure raced with his shadow. They winced each time he fell. Each time he staggered to his feet, and raced on. He came close enough to their part of the lake for the floodlights to catch the red of his upstanding hair.

Jeanie murmured, "It's like that song about the tall boy, walking far apart—only he's skating. 'Tall boy, bleeding from the heart.' "

He was more unsteady on his feet. He fell oftener and got up more slowly. Miguel said, "I think he's about had it. I'll drive around to that side of the lake and get him in the car."

"I'll go with you," Kathleen said.

She had to sort through the shoes under and around the bench to find hers and Uncle Brian's before she followed Miguel. Jeanie came running after them. "It looks as if he's limping. You want me to help?"

"No, you've got your party," Kathleen said. "Look, there's a carload now from Adams." No one could miss Deetsy in her white parka with its furry, flame-red lining. Well, she'd have quite a look to find Miguel among the skaters. "And, Jeanie, I don't know what time I'll show up at your house."

"Oh, Kathleen, there'll be other parties. Take Uncle Brian home and see him through."

Kathleen was beside Miguel when he backed Uncle

Brian's red car out of the melee of cars. Ah, there was that unmistakable cream-colored convertible being maneuvered into a space. The driver climbed out, shoved his toboggan cap more snugly over his dark, curly hair. His knobby, turtle-necked sweater looked two inches thick. So Bruce had done right by his antiquated relatives, and was now joining the party. Just when Kathleen Belford was leaving.

They reached the far side of the lake and called to Uncle Brian. He kept on skating. By now he was like a bird with a hurt wing that circles on and on, with its circles gradually narrowing. They waited and waited in the bitter cold until Kathleen's feet were like lumps of cement. Uncle Brian had to fall once more. They walked over to where he half sat, half sprawled, winded and spent.

"Ready to go home, Uncle Brian?" Kathleen asked.

"Yes, take me home," he said heavily.

He was docile as a child while they knelt beside him and took off his shoe skates and put on his boots. He hobbled wearily to the car. He sat there between them on the drive home without a sound except for his breath rasping in his throat.

They had to help him out of the car, through the side gate, and into the house. He clung to the newel post at the foot of the stairs. "I'd better settle for the couch tonight," he muttered.

"No," Miguel said, "we'll help you up the stairs.

You'd better get a hot bath, or you'll be like a ham-strung mule tomorrow. Here, you hang on to the banister, Uncle Brian, and I'll boost you along.''

It was a labored climb up stairs that had never seemed so long to Kathleen. She steadied Uncle Brian from behind. Once he lost his balance, swayed and dropped back a step, with his boot heel coming down hard on her foot. Her toes were too numb to feel it.

The telephone was ringing, but they could only let it ring. It had stopped by the time they reached the head of the stairs. They guided him to the bathroom, and Kathleen turned on the water in the tub.

''I guess the two of you got more than you bargained for when you took me skating,'' Uncle Brian said with a flick of a smile.

Miguel grinned back at him. ''You sure were a glutton for punishment. You, Petunia, go down and make some hot cocoa. We could all stand to have our innards warmed.''

The cocoa she made was filmed over before the hot water finally stopped running in the tub. The pungent smell of liniment seeped down the stairs. When she heard Miguel helping Uncle Brian in to his bed, she skimmed off the cocoa, reheated it, and took a mug of it up to him.

He held it between his two shaking, bruised hands, and gulped it down as though it were medicine. Kathleen pushed back his wet, touseled hair and noticed that the bruise near his eye was darkening. He touched her hand. "Ah, bright angel, I never hated anyone as much as I did you this evening. And never loved anyone more than you at this moment. Now I've another favor to be asking the two of you. Don't be spreading the word about what an unmanageable scut I was tonight."

"We won't," they both promised. "We'll just say you went skating with us."

His eyes closed. He fell into exhausted sleep before they left the room.

Fifteen

❀

THE PHONE RANG AGAIN as they came down the
stairs. It was Ben at the Ragged Robin. He had been
calling home all evening, and could only get Jill, who
said Uncle Brian "had carried on terrible" and that
Kathleen and Miguel had gone out with him. "Did he
head straight for the Shamrock, Kathleen?"

"No, we took him skating with us. He's had a hot
bath and now he's in bed, sound asleep."

She heard Ben's long-drawn breath of relief. "Sis,
you're wonderful. I don't know anyone else that could
have handled him. You're the Rock of Gibraltar." It
came to her as a shock. It was the first heartfelt compli-
ment her older brother had ever paid her. He went on,

"Mom's been in a stew all evening. I'll call her right away and tell her. Hey, how about the party at Jeanie's? Want me to swing by for you?"

It came as another jolt that right then she felt *older* than old bossy Ben and that, like Mother, she wanted him to have fun instead of all work and worry. "No, you go on, Ben. Jeanie will be expecting you. Miguel and I are having some cocoa—and then we'll see."

She had no sooner hung up the phone than she realized that Jill, in her striped boy's pajamas, was crouched on the stairs.

"For heaven's sake, Jill, aren't you kids asleep yet?"

"So you managed to keep Uncle Brian away from the Shamrock?"

"Yes, we did. Is that what you waited up for?"

She shook her head. "Matt's sick. There's lots of three-day measles at St. Jude's. We want you to look at him."

She and Miguel went back upstairs and into the room that always smelled of the two white mice in their cage, and the turtle in stagnant water they kept forgetting to change. Matthew was hunched up in his bottom bunk, the covers pulled tight under his chin, while little Brian hung over the top one, big-eyed with concern.

"Show them your spots, Matt," Jill ordered.

His cheeks were flushed, his lips dry, but he tried to brave it out. "I'm not sick. My head just kinda aches, and it kinda hurts to swallow."

"A while ago he was shaking all over," his younger brother said. "And tell them about Joey that sits right next to you at school having to go home with the measles."

The rash on his chest and behind his ears looked like measles to Kathleen. "We'll all get them," Jill said philosophically. "Have you ever had three-day measles, Miguel?"

"Yep. I've had every kind of measles in every different language."

Matthew took to shivering again. Kathleen gave him an aspirin, and found another blanket to tuck around him. Jill said for him, "He'd like some of the lemonade like you make so good."

She had learned to make it from the efficient Mrs. McHarg, mother of Diane and Debbie. Instead of merely squeezing out the juice, she sliced the lemons thin, rind and all, added sugar, and then muddled the juice out with a pestle so that, as she explained, you got the special lemony flavor from the outer skin.

Kathleen used a wooden spoon for a pestle, and made it with hot water because of Matt's chills. He drank it thirstily, while Jill and Brian were telling him to stay in bed when the alarm went off in the morning. "We can work the paper route by our ownselves."

The kitchen clock said ten-thirty when again she skimmed and heated the cocoa. She felt so chilled that, like Mother, she lit the gas oven, and opened its door to rest her feet on. Ah, there was the sugar bowl and contents Ben had put in for safe-keeping. She set it back on the shelf.

Miguel pulled up a chair and found room for his booted feet on the oven door, too. "Just like old married folks," he said with a grin.

As her feet warmed, her toes ached from Uncle Brian's boot heel grinding down on them. She sipped her cocoa and said, "I don't think I'll go to the party." She had no heart for scrubbing up and dressing up, and making merry in Jeanie's house in Harmony Heights. "But it isn't too late for you to go, Miguel. Deetsy will be looking for you."

"Deetsy? Oh yeah, I'm supposed to pair off with her." His impish grin again. "Well, I don't think she'll wither away without me. But maybe Bruce will without you."

She gave only a rueful grunt. Fat chance of Bruce withering away without her!

"He's a good joe," Miguel said. "I had dinner the other night at his house."

"At the Seeries'! Dinner? Were you helping Bruce with Spanish?"

He said around a yawn, "No, they asked me because they're going to Mexico, and they wanted the lowdown on Acapulco and Cuernavaca and such. I'll bet they never had a guest that ate so much."

"What are they like?" she asked breathlessly. "What is Bruce's mother like? Is she—nice?"

· *200* ·

A pause. Miguel, she realized, seldom spoke ill of anyone. "She's a—well, a no-nonsense sort of person. Compared to your mother, she's got a hard chromium finish."

Oh dear! She was afraid to hear any more about Bruce's mother. She changed the subject. "I told Ben to go on to the party. And guess what? He called me a Rock of Gibraltar."

"You are, you know, whether you want to be or not."

No, she had never wanted to be. She had wanted to be glamorous and sought-after like Aunt Eustace. Lately, to impress Bruce, she had aspired to be a literary light. But tonight—"I feel so much older," she murmured, "just years and years *older* than when Ben put the half-a-bath fund in the oven this evening."

He turned that over in his mind. "It isn't the months or years on a calendar that make us older. It's what happens to us. You know, Petunia, it seems to me that I stayed about thirteen, maybe fourteen, until I came to Denver. Not that Pop coddled me—he couldn't when we were always on the move. I couldn't help seeing a lot of life in the raw, but still, Pop is such a dynamic character. I was always shadowed by him, though he didn't even know it. He wanted to drive up here with me. Yes, and he would have, except that a friend of his needed a ride as far as Santa Fe, and it was only a day's drive farther for me alone." He shook his head wonderingly. "I'm glad he didn't. Everything would have been so—so different."

Her head was nodding with drowsiness. He set down his mug, and said on a wider yawn, "I will now slip and slide my way back to my old dugout and my four-footed friend, Oscar."

Even while she was thanking him for all his help with Uncle Brian, he was out the side door. After a minute, he opened it a crack to say, "Now don't go sneaking off to the party when my back is turned," and closed it again.

Jeanie phoned Kathleen early the next morning to ask about Uncle Brian.

"He's all right, I guess. He was gone to work when we got up. Mom is worrying about his not wearing his torn leather jacket."

"It's warming up for a change." She talked then about her party. "Deetsy is consumed with jealousy. She thinks because you and Miguel were both absent that you have designs on him. And are you wondering if your handsome hero wondered why you didn't show up, and what I—"

"What did you tell him?"

"I simply tossed off that something had come up at the last minute you thought more important."

"Oh, golly, Jeanie, supposing he thinks—"

"It won't hurt him to think there's competition. That, too, comes under feminine wiles."

"Yes, I know," Kathleen said halfheartedly.

Jeanie added on a laugh, "Deetsy was feeling so frustrated about Miguel last night she wants to whomp up a sort of get-together for this evening. It seems her aunt Clare has a cabin about thirty miles up in the mountains. But you know Deetsy's harebrained ideas, and besides there's that little problem of transportation. Oh-oh, there's someone at the door."

Last night Kathleen had been too buffeted, chilled, and weary to feel sharp disappointment over missing Jeanie's party. But hearing of their gay time, she suddenly felt left out and cheated. Jeanie had told of their pushing back the furniture and dancing. To think that she might have been there dancing with Bruce!

Her desolation grew when, in her room, she saw the Pierrot cap, leotards, and shortened plaid skirt she had planned to wear—along with her practiced June-Kathleen smile. Now she had only the dreary job of *un*shortening the skirt for school. Bleakly she ripped out the stitches.

She listlessly washed Ben's jacket in the basement, and made more lemonade for Matthew in the kitchen. By now every square inch of him was covered with a red rash. "He feels better since he broke out," said spokesman Jill.

The phone kept ringing and ringing that morning, but the calls were all for Ben. Kathleen heard only unrelated bits of his conversation. . . ." No, I don't take Mom to work Friday nights." . . . "Yeah, I can drive up and talk to him. Oughtn't to take too long with a blow torch." . . . "Good lord, does she have to take the dog?"

Ben and Mother would hold a low-voiced conference, and then he would go driving off. On his return, there would be more murmured consultations. Kathleen saw her mother tap the half-a-bath fund, and hand Ben some bills. Then Mother happily stirred up a double batch of Irish bread, while Ben struggled up the basement steps with a long sled.

She was just asking, "What's all this about?" when a phone call came for her. It was Bruce. He said, "Things are shaping up for our trip to Deetsy's aunt's cabin. But I thought I'd better find out first if you had anything else on for this evening."

She said, around her heart that pushed up past her tonsils, "No, I haven't a thing for this evening."

"Well, fine, because I'm counting on you for my date." She listened to his apology about not being able to get their car; his mother needed it to take herself and friends to a lecture. "I guess Ben will let you know when Miguel's car will be ready."

"Miguel's Mercy Be? But it's frozen up. He said he had to wait till December first for money to—"

"It's his radiator, and Ben pushed him to the garage on the Boul, and it's being thawed out now," Bruce said. "So just as soon as everything and everybody is gathered up, I'll be seein' you."

"I'll be seein' you," she echoed.

She stood with her hand on the phone and called out, "Mom, what's all this you and Ben have cooked up?"

Mother laughed joyfully. "We waited till we were sure we could swing it. We didn't want you disappointed again. This Deetsy talked her aunt into going up to her mountain cabin to check it over—"

"That Deetsy! She brags about twisting her folks around her little finger."

Mother chuckled at that. "Well, she didn't twist her all the way. The aunt grudgingly consented to go up, only she would *not* drive her car. But there was no reason in the world why Ben couldn't take ours."

"And you gave him the money to give Miguel for thawing out his radiator?"

"Loaned it. Miguel insisted on giving his IOU to the half-a-bath. But, heaven help us, two couples in that little wheelbarrow of his!"

"Who else besides Deetsy with Miguel?"

"Deetsy's friend with a football player named Mc-something."

"June and McGaffey."

"That's right. It sounds like fun, honey, and maybe it'll make up for your missing out on your skating party last night."

So scatterbrain Deetsy had launched a plan, and Mother and Ben—yes, and Miguel—had carried on with it to give Kathleen a happy evening. Why, oh why couldn't she ever tell her folks how grateful she was? Why wouldn't the words come? But perhaps, as Madame Miller said, her heart showed in her violet-blue eyes, for her mother gave her a playful whack and said, "Get along now, and put on the warmest clothes you can find. Ben thought they'd be ready to go about three."

She was waiting in the hall in leotards and Pierrot cap by three. She was still waiting when Uncle Brian came home at a quarter to four. His colored glasses almost hid the dark bruise around his eye. He looked graver and thinner and older in his dark suit with a V-necked sweater under his coat.

She could feel the roughness of his skinned knuckles as he took her hand. "In case I didn't thank you last night, Mavourneen, I'm thanking you now." And with a twisted smile, "The first chance you get, would you be dippin' into our money and buying me a pair of gloves?"

Mother said, "Oh, Brian, praise God it wasn't so cold today. I sewed up your leather jacket, worrying all the while about your being outside without it."

"You needn't have, Rose darlin'. Cold or no, I wasn't out in it. The boss promoted me to an inside job today."

With that a great uproar of barking dogs met their ears. Their faded Chevy at the side was hardly recognizable with two toboggans roped to the top, and a strange boxer's head thrust out the window, yelping in frenzy at Cully, who leaped at him from the outside.

Kathleen snatched up her mittens and hurried out.

The disgruntled Aunt Clare was in the front seat between Ben and Jeanie. Bruce, in the back seat, was trying to dodge the boxer's scramblings.

Miguel's low beetle of a car was pulled up behind theirs, and he leaped out to collar Cully. Deetsy, snugged into the bucket seat, looked quite pleased with herself. June and McGaffey sat behind. In that space that was not meant for passengers but for luggage, they were sitting so low their knees were up to their chins.

Mother came running out with Irish bread in a sack. The O'Byrne in her, thought Kathleen. They all believed that, in accepting hospitality, you should never go "with one arm as long as the other."

Mother yelled to Deetsy's aunt over the barking din that maybe an extra loaf of bread would come in handy, and Aunt Clare yelled back, "Homemade? I'll say it will." She shouted that she was taking Bobo because he needed a run in the mountains, and she motioned Bruce to open the car door just wide enough for Kathleen to ease in.

"Is all of you in, Kathleen?" Ben asked. "Then we're off."

She and Bruce were crowded in the back with four glass jugs of water, a carton of food supplies with a strong smell of fish and onions, not to mention the pony-sized Bobo who lunged over them for a backward look at the outraged Cully. Aunt Clare alternated in reaching back to give her dog a clout, and turning to give Ben driving directions. Jeanie winked at Kathleen.

She took happiness with her, and everything Bruce said or did added to it. He muttered confidentially, "Auntie's a bit on the sour side because Deetsy horn-swoggled her into this, but everybody else is happy." She stifled her impulse to say, "I'm so happy I could pop," and instead, put on an imitation of June's little half-smile.

Up and up the Chevy climbed into the mountains, facing the sun that was starting to close up shop for the day. Behind them came the faithful beetle with Miguel at the wheel. He looked like a Russian in a fur cap that must have been his grandfather's.

Aunt Clare's cabin, set among snow and pine trees, was like something out of the brothers Grimm. There was all the bustle of starting fires, and the thumping of palms on shoulders to warm themselves, and seeing what dense fogs of breath they could blow. When the fire in the fireplace crackled and Bruce said, "Stand close, Kathleen, and get warm," she wanted to shout, "I'm not cold. I'm warm all the way through." But June, the self-possessed, wouldn't say that.

Woodcutting before tobogganing, said Aunt Clare. The boys took turns with the axe. Most of them wore heavy ski sweaters. Even Ben was in one of Liz's cable-stitched ones. But Miguel wore *three* grandpa flannel shirts, and all three shirttails were out before he had even picked up the axe. Bruce—ah, Bruce, the star athlete, was poetry in motion when he chopped wood.

Tobogganing down a white hill was like a roller-coaster ride, with the extra dividend of purple sunset and fine snow tingling on Kathleen's face, and Bruce's saying, "Hold on tight to me." She didn't hold as tight as she wanted to. This was her evening for playing it cool.

They sat on the floor and ate Aunt Clare's clam chowder. They danced. The others moaned about Aunt Clare's prehistoric Glen Miller records, but they were beautiful to Kathleen. She danced with Bruce, and hummed, and wanted to tell him that song writers, like poets, could set to words and music what was in the hearts of others. She looked at June, who was dancing with McGaffey with an indifferent—even slightly bored —smile. So Kathleen kept her thoughts to herself.

She was amazed when Aunt Clare said, "It's getting on toward ten. Time to gather up and head for home."

There were still only two littles, instead of three, at breakfast in the dinette the next morning. Matthew was there, his spots almost faded away, but Jill was in bed waiting for hers to reach their crimson peak.

Kathleen was there in the flesh, but in spirit she was still dancing with Bruce to "That Old Black Magic" and "Always in My Heart."

Mother asked, "Lovey, what did Aunt Clare put in her chowder?"

"Fish, I guess," was the vague answer.

Ben answered, "Clams and shrimp and celery, along with the potatoes and onions."

"How did everyone like the Irish bread?" Mother asked her again.

She only stared. She couldn't remember whether anyone ate bread or not.

"Every crumb disappeared," Ben said. "Aunt Clare was sore because she hoped there'd be some left for her to take home."

"We'll take her a loaf the first chance we get," Mother said.

Stacy asked, "How did that girl—what's her name now?—make out with Mug?"

Ben threw back his head and laughed so heartily that Cully jumped out from the table, all tail-wagging hysteria.

"Deetsy. She stuck like adhesive to the poor guy. You should have seen the help-help look in his eyes. He was the one that peeled the onions for Aunt Clare. He was the one that kept sprinting out to get more wood. He'd sit down to eat, and she'd start cooing at him—and he'd leap up to get something for somebody. I don't think he even sat still long enough to eat."

Ben could hardly finish the telling for his deep haw-haws. "But the thing Jeanie and I laughed about till we could hardly dance, was the way he worked up such a sweat dodging her that he had to keep peeling off one shirt after another—"

Mother laughed till the tears rolled down her cheeks. "Didn't you notice it, lovey?" she asked weakly.

"I sure did." But she didn't add, "She was the horrible example to me." Surely Bruce had noticed that Kathleen had neither gushed nor clung.

Her mother jogged her out of her trance to say, "Listen, all of you, while I tell you about Uncle Brian's new job. His promotion."

His job for the wholesalers under the viaduct was loading TV's and hi-fi's, trucking them to the warehouse, and uncrating them. Another man checked and adjusted them before they were sent out to dealers. But the adjuster wasn't at work yesterday, because he had been hurt in a car accident. Uncle Brian took his place, and the boss was so pleased with his work, he was keeping him on the job.

"I'll bet he's a hundred times better than the other fellow," Stacy said.

"Of course he is," Mother said. "So last night after he went to bed, I called Gran at Bannon and told her about it. She was so happy she cried. She said she was going right over to church and say prayers of thanksgiving."

"But Thanksgiving was the day before yesterday," Matthew said.

"You can have a day of thanksgiving, stupe," Ben said, "without turkey and pumpkin pie."

Yes, Kathleen thought dreamily, you could have Thanksgiving sitting on the floor eating clam chowder, if the boy next to you had dark, close-cropped hair, and kept asking, "You doing all right, Kathleen?"

Sixteen

THE ALL-SCHOOL ASSEMBLY, called for fifth-hour on Monday, opened with the Lowry Air Force band playing the national anthem. Kathleen was always so stirred, so churned-up by it. She was with her lunch-room crowd, and she impulsively reached out to Miguel and whispered, "Does it make you want to cry?"

"It makes me want to be nice to old ladies," he muttered back.

Mr. Knight stood behind the mike. He told them that their mayor, their governor, their President had all signed the proclamation, making this United Nations week.

Schools all over the city, he went on, would be having

exhibits and programs. But he had discussed with the faculty how John Quincy Adams could best bring the true meaning of this important week to every student. They had decided to be unique in their way of celebrating. He did not believe in anything that smacked of spectator sports. "As an old Spanish proverb says, 'He, who would bring back the wealth of the Indies, must take the wealth of the Indies with him.' " Which, he said, could be translated into *participation by all.*

Kathleen heard a low rumble of, "Oh no! Not that One Big Happy Family bit again."

Mr. Knight was now telling them that on his recent trip through Spain, France, and Italy—yes, and riding a bus in Ireland—he had been impressed at how other people were less inhibited about singing, dancing, and playing instruments.

"What is your origin? English, Swedish, Polish, African? Whatever it is, be proud of it, be willing to share with us, and let us be proud with you."

The long and short of it was that on Friday of this week every student was to come to school in costume. The student body would take over the gym during lunch hour for a United Nations plate lunch (price fifty cents) and an extemporaneous talent show.

Although laughs and moans went up from some, Miguel nudged Kathleen. "Sounds like a hootenanny," he beamed.

Mr. Knight, with his boyish, cheer-leader smile,

waited for the outburst to spend itself. He lifted his hand appealingly. "Please, students, this is very close to my heart. There's not enough to give and take, not enough sharing of ourselves. Don't hide your light under a bushel. If you need to be coaxed, consider yourselves coaxed. And I'll give you a little tip."

The little tip was that Miss Axelrod in the library was an expert pianist who would accompany where accompanying was needed. "Even though we're calling it extemporaneous, it wouldn't hurt if you whispered in her ear what you plan to sing, dance, yodel, or play on your bazooka."

They jostled their way out of assembly amid murmurs of "Friday morning, I aim to have the three-day measles." For measles were causing absences at Johnny Q as well as at St. Jude's.

Deetsy pushed close to Miguel, and asked coyly, "Are you hiding your light under a bushel?"

"I could hide my light under an egg cup. But I still wish those bozos hadn't swiped my guitar on the way up from Mexico."

Kathleen told at home Mr. Knight's enthusiasm over his talent show. "He says it's close to his heart."

"Oh, lovey, then you and Ben wear your Irish piper costumes," Mother said. "If that Miss Axelrod is any kind of player she can do 'The Irish Washerwoman' for you to jig to."

Kathleen decided to wear the costume. But the very

thought of getting up in front of those hundreds of students sent cold shuddders down her spine.

On Tuesday evening, Uncle Brian brought more news that gave the whole family a lift. He was now getting the ''bugs'' out of all the new TV sets the stores were stocking for their Christmas trade. One of the biggest dealers told him of a store he was opening in San Francisco the first of the year. He offered Uncle Brian the job of manager with a very good salary.

''Are you going to take it?'' Mother asked.

''I don't know. I'll have to think about it.'' He winked at Kathleen. ''I'm not sure yet whether I can get along without my bright angel guarding me from harm.''

Uncle Brian no sooner went to bed than again Mother was on the phone telling Gran and Grandda about him.

''It'll be all over Bannon by morning.'' Mother laughed in malicious glee. ''I know *one* family that will hear about it—if Gran has anything to do with it—and with a few fancy embellishments too.''

''Colleen's folks, you mean?'' Kathleen asked.

''You bet that's who I mean. Even though Colleen's never showed her face down there except for her uncle's funeral, she'll hear about it. Her, and her thinking she did so well to grab off Fred Kleim and his little one-horse garage.''

''Garages don't have horses,'' Jill corrected.

Again the littles were two instead of three. Brian was now in bed, and asking Kathleen to make him hot lemonade.

The next day Miguel appeared in French wearing a brand new Hawaiian sport shirt. In the lunchroom, when again all but he, Kathleen, and Jeanie, were at the counter, he asked archly, "Would either of you care for a chicken breast or a piece of angel food cake? Or perhaps a kumquat?"

"A kum-*what*?" Jeanie gasped.

"Your grandmother's back from California," Kathleen guessed.

Yes, his grandparents had arrived yesterday. "Sweet old Grandma is conscience-stricken, and trying to make up for all the meals she didn't cook me. Ask me what I had for breakfast."

Kathleen laughed. "Quince marmalade and mustard pickles?"

"First course, fresh pineapple. Then waffles, chinked in with sausage and eggs. Last night I slept in a first-floor bedroom under a down comforter, after first taking a bath in a tub. I'm a pampered darling. Please note, a crease in my pants."

They both laughed at that. There might have been one when he left his grandmother's, but there was none now. He wasn't the kind to hold a crease.

He said, apropos of nothing, "Neither Grandma or Gramps know Mr. Knight or any of the teachers here."

"Is that good or bad?" Jeanie asked.

He said soberly, "I wouldn't have slept a wink all night if they had."

Each afternoon, Kathleen walked hopefully into lit.

Each day, she saw only the empty seats where the football players had sat. She asked Mr. Jacoby after class, "Aren't the boys on the team coming back in this class? Because the football season was over on Thanksgiving."

His smile was even more caustic. "But now it's app gym. And if I'm not mistaken, basketball follows. The faculty must show the old school spirit by shortening their day in order to give them more time for athletics."

"Oh," was all that disappointment let her say.

But there was always the chance of running into Bruce in the halls. Since the evening in the mountains, he was less wary. He shared a tangerine with her one day. He relayed a message from Aunt Eustace: She had flown to New York to see some plays, and hadn't been able to reach Kathleen to tell her good-by. He walked with her from second floor to her locker on first.

Her cool, Mona Lisa mask was paying off. Madame Mee-lair couldn't say now that she wore her heart in her purple eyes.

On Friday morning the whole family on Hubbell Street was seeing that Kathleen and Ben were properly garbed as Irish dancers. Stacy pressed the lacy and ruffly blouse Kathleen would wear with green kilts. The littles polished the silver buckles on her and Ben's black pumps.

"I'll bet you'll be the prettiest girl there," little Brian said.

Mother draped the square of material from shoulder to shoulder on her, and pinned it with a heavy Tara brooch. "Now you tell them all at school that nuns in Connemara did all the heavy embroidery on this brat. And that the wool in your kilts is handwoven—"

"Oh, for heaven's sakes! I suppose you want me to walk in the door, and make a speech about the lace on my blouse being Limerick lace, and how the brooch is Connemara marble."

Ben, looking very self-conscious with his bony knees showing between ribbed socks and short green kilts, put his black velvet jacket on over his own frilled, white shirt. He laughed and ruffled Mother's hair. "Shall I tell them Grandda wore this jacket when he danced with the Abbey players?"

"Of course," she said, and tied a green ribbon round Kathleen's smoky black hair.

Stacy stood on tiptoe to fit Ben's beret at the right slant on his red head. "You're a handsome brute," she said.

But as they drove to school, Ben took it off and stuck it in his belt.

They needn't have felt conspicuous. Adams' halls were full of outlandish costumes. June and Deetsy were gypsies, with at least five pounds each of beads, brace-lets, and anklets—and loop earrings, the size of curtain rings. Deetsy squealed out at sight of Kathleen, "Are you going to dance?"

"No. I just wore this to please Mr. Knight."

"Everybody says the same thing. Everybody's scared to get up and show off. Everybody, except the girl that did a ballet dance in *La Bohème* last summer."

June raised her eyebrows and said, "Don't forget you've just been corrected," and Deetsy exploded, "Yes, I just happened to ask her if she'd be doing her ballet dance from *La Bohème*, and she put her nose in the air and said, 'There is no ballet in *La Bohème*. My ballet number is *based* on Puccini's *La Bohème*.'"

"Do tell!" Kathleen laughed.

Jeanie's ninety-eight pounds seemed weighted down by a maroon velvet dress with miles of heavy braid on what she thought were called "panniers," and a high, also heavy, headdress. "It's a Swedish court costume that belonged to a great-aunt of Mom's, and it took dozens of safety pins to make it small enough for me. It's so hot and scratchy," she sighed.

Someone asked her if she'd be doing the Swedish gavotte. "Thank you, no! I don't even know whether I can last till then."

Miguel came to fourth-hour French, needing only a donkey to look like a picture on a tourist folder of Mexico. His old hauraches flapped on his feet, a striped serape was folded over one shoulder, and he carried a raffia-covered jug. His straw sombrero was so wide it more than covered his desk.

Rita Flood was wearing a piper-player costume that was an imitation of Kathleen's, with kilts and brat made of sateen. In her shrill voice, she told the class, "Kathleen and I did an Irish dance together at St. Jude's last year, didn't we, Kathleen?"

Maybe if I were big of soul, Kathleen thought, I'd say, "Yes, we did." But it wasn't true. She, Ben, and Stacy had put on the dance, with Rita being one of about twenty as stage background. She didn't answer Rita.

The French class was in progress when Mr. Knight came into the room. His eyes searched over the class until they rested on Kathleen.

He said hurriedly, "I wanted to ask you about your mother. I remember her playing the piano for us all in the student union years ago. She was wonderful. She could play anything anyone asked for. Has she kept in practice, Kathleen? Would she be able to come and play accompaniments for our United Nations program?"

Kathleen gasped. "But I thought Miss Axelrod—"

Miss Axelrod, he explained, had some badly bruised fingers. Just fifteen minutes ago, a heavy card file had dropped on her hand in the library. "Time is short, but I couldn't help wondering if your mother—"

Kathleen sat silent, her thoughts jumbled. Of course

Mother was capable of playing any accompaniment. But suppose she appeared in one of her thrown-together outfits. Suppose some pupil or teacher, who had gone to Giddy's for their famed lasagne, recognized her as the redhead at the piano.

While she groped for an answer, her eyes met the spiteful gleam in Rita Flood's. She knew in that instant that, even were she close enough to nudge her and say, "Don't tell him Mom plays at Guido's," Rita would.

This was Rita's chance to get even for the times she, Kathleen, had eeled away from her—yes, and for not saying only a few minutes ago, "Yes, Rita and I put on a dance together at St. Jude's."

Mr. Knight asked again, "Has she kept her hand in, Kathleen?" and Rita answered promptly, "She sure has, Mr. Knight. She plays every night out at that Gay Nineties place on the Henderson Road. And, like she always told the Sisters at St. Jude's, she can play anything anybody can even hum."

I could strangle you with my bare hands, Rita Flood. The Aunt Eustace side of Kathleen thought: now what will Mr. Knight think about that revered name of Belford in educational circles?

Mr. Knight laughed in relief. "That's wonderful. She sounds like an answer to prayer." He fired questions at Kathleen. What was their address? On Hubbell. Why, Hubbell Street wasn't far. What class did her brother Ben have at this hour? He remarked that time was of the essence, and went hurrying out.

Now they knew. But the whole class seemed as happy about it as Mr. Knight. Miguel said, "Wait till you hear her play." Jeanie smiled at Kathleen, "Oh good, good. Now I'll get a chance to meet her. I've always wanted to." Madame too smiled at Kathleen, and said in French that a girl was fortunate—or was it *blessed?*—to live close to music.

For perhaps a full moment Kathleen sat there before relief—that was almost peace—filled her. What a snob she had been to think anyone at school cared whether her mother played at Guido's or in grand opera. Her relief was twofold: Rita had done her worst, and Kathleen need be uneasy no longer.

Madame rapped for order, and the class went on.

The passing bell rang, and they joined the traffic jam to the gym. As they inched their way along, piano music reached out and met them. Miguel nudged Kathleen. "It's *mamacita* all right. I recognize her happy thumpety-thump.

So did she. Next question: What was Mother wearing? At the door of the gym when others craned to see the tables set up and decorated with flags of every country, she looked toward the center. A low stage had been moved in, and a piano had been angled close to it.

One glance satisfied her. Mother wasn't wearing the

blouse with clowns and performing dogs. A white one topped a full flowered skirt. She might have worn a plain, dark one—but Kathleen wouldn't quibble about that.

The United Nations plate consisted of Mexican tamales, German potato salad, kosher dill pickles, French croissants, and Chinese fortune cookies. A bottle of Coke sat at each place. Jeanie, whose cheeks were red as apples, said, "If anybody can't drink all his Coke, have mercy on me. I'm smothering alive in this outfit."

Mr. Knight moved about from piano to tables, eager and anxious as a mother hen. Kathleen saw Rita Flood at the end of their long table next to a stoutish, blond girl in a Dutch costume. Deetsy pointed out the girl at the next table who had danced in a ballet version of *La Bohème*. "She's just bustin' to show off," she said acidly.

Where was Bruce? Did he know it was Mrs. Belford at the piano, playing a medley of everything from "Dixie" to "The Volga Boatman"?

About the time the last drop of Coke was being sizzled up through straws, Mr. Knight took his place behind the portable mike. He thanked them one and all for entering so magnificently into his participation program.

"On with the hootenanny," a boy's voice called out. Uneasy titters passed through the gym.

"Who's going to be our lead-off performer?" Mr. Knight asked.

No one made a move.

Everyone seemed to sit tighter and pull into himself. No one wanted to be first. There was dead silence except for the rippling piano music. Kathleen saw her mother look at Mr. Knight's tense face.

Still playing, she turned on the piano bench and searched over tables until she located Ben. Her eyes probed on until they found Kathleen. She played on with one hand, while she motioned them, and called out clearly, "Ben, and you, Katie Rose. Come on up here."

Ben reached the low platform before Kathleen did, because she went on weighted feet. "Somebody's got to break the ice," Mother whispered. "You two sing." And the very way she broke into "Cockles and Mussels" was like an order.

Uncle Brian had taught the three oldest Belfords to sing it when they were barely able to talk. They always sang it for Bannon relatives and at St. Jude entertainments; last St. Patrick's Day, they sang it at Guido's Gay Nineties.

Ben, like Uncle Brian, had a rich, true tenor. He led off, and Kathleen's quavering contralto soon followed firmly.

Through streets broad and narrow,
I push a wheelbarrow, singing
Cockles and mussels, alive, alive-o.

The tune was lilting and catchy and, before the first alive-o, hundreds of feet were stamping time to it. Ben and Stacy had always added an extra something to liven it. So when they came again to "I push a wheelbarrow," Ben said low, "Grab my feet," and threw himself down on his hands. Kathleen caught him by the ankles, and pushed him along. He could even make motions with his arms like a wheel's turning.

It brought down the house. Ben bowed, and Kathleen curtsied.

Always before, she had been a reluctant entertainer. But the stamping, the Coke bottles thumping tables, the cries of "More! More!" went to her head like wine. She suddenly loved being out in front and feeling every admiring eye on her.

She was the one who leaned over the piano and said, "Mom, play for us to do our jig."

Her mother crashed into "The Irish Washerwoman." Kathleen's feet had never felt so winged; her heels had never clicked so madly. Far back in the gym she saw Bruce Seerie. *You see, Bruce, how good everyone thinks I am.* She outdid Stacy in cutting loose. When Ben threw in a little ham by bumping her rear with his, she bumped back, and reveled in the loud guffaws and shrieks that went up.

The ice was broken. Maybe Deetsy was right about the ballet dancer being eager to show off, for she was the next to hurry up with some sheet music, and confer with the pianist.

No wonder their school paper had welcomed her with open arms. She was professional. Dressed as a Paris street waif in a tattered skirt, her bare feet danced a story of Bohemian love and cold and hunger.

No wonder she was heartily applauded when, at the finale, she went down limp as a rag doll, her long blond hair wiping up the floor. And no wonder that when she took her seat, there was another uneasy hush, and more hugging of chairs.

Heavens, who would think the ice would need to be broken again! But the ballet number was so perfect, so big-time, that Kathleen sensed everyone's thinking, I'm not good enough to follow *her.*''

Again a tense lull, with Mr. Knight urging, ''Who'll be our next performer?''

The second ice-smashing was done by none other than Miguel. He put on his sombrero, adjusted his striped serape, and strolled forward with a guitar he had evidently borrowed from someone. He lifted his foot to the edge of the piano bench and rested the guitar on his knee.

The first chord he twanged contained a sour note or two. He turned his shameless grin on the audience, and said, ''I'm a little out of practice.'' The school roared— not in derision, but in high spirits.

He sang about the Mexican cockroach—''La Cucaracha.'' The accompanist helped cover his poor playing. Her singing helped out his reedy voice. Everyone else joined in.

For everyone, even Mr. Knight, couldn't help realizing he had been willing to make a poor show of himself just to keep the hootenanny on its feet.

It was. No one had qualms about following *him*. The girl in the Dutch costume was bending down to put on her wooden shoes, and Rita Flood helped her pin on heavy flaxen braids. She did a clog dance to a Dutch folksong. A boy put on an act of a Swede trying to tell his girl how to marinate the herring he caught. Talent broke out all over the place. Tambourines clashed, and castanets clicked. A boy in a Swiss costume yodeled. Two Negro girls sang a spiritual.

The sixth-hour starting and ending bell rang and was ignored before the show ended. Mother sat, flushed and smiling, as faculty and students pressed around her, asking if she knew this song or that. But a beaming Mr. Knight helped her off the piano bench, and said they mustn't impose on her longer.

Ben was at hand to take her home, and Jeanie suddenly clutched Kathleen's arm. "Hey, let's ask Ben if he'll take us too."

Kathleen didn't want to go. She liked being thumped on the back and told what a sensation she had been. And she was watching Bruce working his way from the back of the gym. But Jeanie was saying, "Please, Kathleen, let's get out of here. My head's aching so I can hardly see."

Mr. Knight escorted them—Mother, Ben, Jeanie, and

Kathleen—to the car, still voicing his deep appreciation. While Ben drove to the white house with its pink tiled roof, Jeanie took off her headdress, and was working at the neck fastening of her dress. She was out the car door before Ben could open it for her, and was starting up her flagstone walk.

"You all right, Jeanie?" he called.

"Yes, I'm all right. I just can't wait to get out of this dress. It's so hot—and I'm so thirsty." She forced a smile, and added vaguely, "I'll—I'll be seeing you."

She wove her unsteady way and hurried through the pink door.

Seventeen

KATHLEEN COULDN'T WAIT to phone Jeanie the next morning, and gossip with her about the performance at school. Maybe—just maybe—she had gotten some word as to what Bruce thought of her part in it. And she wanted to tell Jeanie that Mr. Knight had sent Mother a box of roses with a card that read, "A very small thank you for coming to the rescue."

Mother, being Mother, had said, "We'll look at them and enjoy them all day and then, Ben, let's drop them off to Kitty on our way to work." Kitty, it seemed, worked at Giddy's, and was convalescing after an operation.

But when Kathleen telephoned, Mrs. Kincaid

answered. Jeanie was in bed with the three-day measles. "She's more spotted than a leopard. How about you, Kathleen? Have you had them?"

"We were all talking about who's had them and who hasn't. Stacy has, so I must have. Or else I'm immune, because the littles have been bobbing in and out of bed with them all week."

"You never know. So take care of yourself, honey. If you feel feverish or chilly or headachy, go right to bed."

She had been chilly all morning. But that was because it had turned bitter cold again in the night, and old fresh-air Stacy had opened their window. She was huddled close to the hot-air register when Ben and Mother set out to buy groceries.

Aunt Eustace telephoned. She was back from New York, and giving a little dinner party this evening. The Seeries were coming, and she thought it would be nice if Kathleen came, because she had asked them to bring Bruce.

Nice? It was heaven-sent. At last Bruce would see her in the Stardust dress and silver slippers.

Aunt Eustace laughed her gay, tinkly laugh. "I'm sure your coming will keep him from being bored. So look your prettiest. Seven-thirtyish. Will you have a ride? I'm afraid Emil won't be—"

"Yes, I can get a ride." She would even walk the eleven or twelve blocks, and gladly, if need be.

She hurried upstairs and shampooed her hair. A queer dizziness came over her when she stood up straight after bending over the washbowl. She had to feel her way to the laundry hamper and sit down hard. The bones under her scalp felt sore when she stuck pins into the rollers.

Mother and Ben returned when she was in the basement washing Ben's jackets. She ran outside to hang them on the line so the wind would whip them dry. Back in the kitchen, the warm, steamy smell of a hen stewing on the stove sent waves of nausea through her.

Mother said, "Lovey, you look sick. For the life of me, I can't remember whether you were at Bannon when Stacy had the measles or not."

"I am *not* coming down with the measles. Jeanie felt hot and thirsty all day yesterday before she did."

"Not Matt," said Jill. "He just shook and shook."

Mother cluck-clucked. "And running outdoors with your hair wet. You're shivering."

"For cryin' out loud! I'm shivering because it's cold, and I washed my hair because—"

But no, maybe this wasn't the time to tell her mother she was going to Aunt Eustace's to dinner. Nor was it the time, when in mid-afternoon, Mother answered the phone, and relayed to Kathleen, "That was Mrs. McHarg, wanting you to baby-sit tonight. But I told her you might be coming down with the measles, and asked if Stacy could come instead."

"And she said I could," Stacy rejoiced, "and I hope they stay out late-late-late, so my Weatherwise coat fund will grow-grow-grow."

Kathleen put on an extra sweater and took an aspirin. Her head didn't *ache*; the bones in it just didn't seem to fit together.

Nor was it any time to mention Aunt Eustace's dinner when Mother brought Ben's jackets in from the line, and ironed them herself.

And all the while she was planning: Mom and Ben will leave early because of taking the roses to Kitty. Then she would hurry and dress, and have Uncle Brian drive her to the Belford mansion. She would probably catch merry Ned for it, but an evening with Bruce would be worth it. Mother was just trying to *wish* the measles on her.

Kathleen waited through the usual bustle of Mother and Ben taking off. Her last words were, "Take a hot bath, lovey, and go to bed."

She took the hot bath, and soaked the chill out of her bones. But she didn't go to bed. She dressed in the blue brocade and silver pumps, and put her lipstick and comb in a small silk bag, all the while glancing out the window and listening for Uncle Brian to come home. What was keeping him?

It wasn't until she was waiting in the downstairs hall that she had a vague memory of his saying something about having the dents in his fenders ironed out.

Seven-twenty. She couldn't wait any longer. She would have to go on foot, as she had so often in nice weather.

Brr-rr! The door no sooner closed behind her, than the icy wind went through the fluffy wrap as though it were cheesecloth. It swooshed under the skirt of her dress. It stung tears out of her eyes, as she started up Hubbell Street. In the dark, it was hard to see the slivers of ice on the pavement, hard to keep from slipping in her high-heeled pumps. If only the wind didn't buffet her so!

She got as far as Wetzel's store. The tin sign that said AL FLOOD, BODY AND FENDER WORK whipped and clattered and started a roaring in her ears. Suddenly, her eyes and nose started running as though a faucet had been turned on. She stopped and leaned against a tree in the curbing, and groped in the shallow pockets of the jacket. Why hadn't she thought to put a handkerchief, or even a paper tissue, in her pocket; why hadn't she crowded one into the small vanity bag?

Now what? She couldn't backtrack five blocks home to get one. She was already late—and so winded. But she couldn't go walking in and greet Seerie parents and son, gushing like the fountain at the park in summer. She leaned against the tree, confused and helpless, and shivering convulsively. She pressed closer to it for support, for her knees felt as though they were coming unhinged.

The door of Wetzel's store opened, and a girl came hurrying down the steps, zipping up a boy's padded jacket as she ran. It was Rita Flood, and she stopped short at sight of Kathleen. For a minute neither spoke, then Rita said, "Well, look who's here, all dressed up fit to kill."

Kathleen, befuddled by the roaring in her head, the chattering of her teeth, and the tears running out of her eyes and freezing on her cheeks, wasn't capable of answering. Rita, misreading her silence, flung out, "It's all right with me, if you aren't speaking to me. I suppose you're sore because I told Mr. Knight about your mother."

She started on, but stopped to impart, "Your uncle Brian's in the shop. He's helping my old man pound out his fenders."

It even took a minute for those words to sink in. Uncle Brian—was—in—the shop. She couldn't remember what she had wanted him for. . . .

With Rita watching curiously, Kathleen left the tree's support and took stiff, uncertain steps to the shop's door. She tried to open it. Rita was at her side, saying, "You're pushing on it. It opens out, can't you see?" and gave it a wrenching pull.

The heat that met Kathleen was like a blast from Hades as she stepped in to the blinding glare of overhead lights, the smell of hot metal, and the hiss of an acetylene torch, shooting out stars like a Fourth of July sparkler. A greasy gnome of a man was holding it, and someone else was bent over pound-pounding—

The picture began to blur. A voice from a great distance boomed against her ears, "Mavourneen! Mother of Moses, what are you doing—?" And suddenly, she wasn't in a body and fender shop at all, but in a black tunnel where sounds roared and lights zigzagged crazily. The last thing she saw was Uncle Brian leaping toward her. The last thing she heard was Rita's scream, "She's fainting!" and felt her elbow hit something hard and hurting. The last thing she thought, as the tunnel walls closed in, was: This is the way it feels to die.

Afterward the littles told her of Uncle Brian carrying her from his car, through the side door and up the stairs, of his bellowing orders to them for aspirin, hot-water bottles, extra blankets. They said he phoned their doctor, and he phoned a prescription to Downey's Drug, and Matt went posthaste on his bicycle to pick it up.

All that horrible night, she fumbled her way through the black tunnel. She would feel a hand on her forehead, and open her eyes to see Ben leaning over her. Another stir in the room meant that Stacy was gathering up her belongings to sleep in the alcove off Mother's room. Another time she heard a rustling of silk, and voices, and was dimly aware of Mother wiping her eyes, and saying, "No, my little own—no, don't throw the covers off." Each time the tunnel pulled her back.

Once, a long time later, she opened her eyes and saw Uncle Brian sitting by her bed, and she cried out, "It's so black in there—and I'm so scared—"

"Musha, musha, what is there to be scared of," he scoffed, "with me right beside you?" His big hand tightened on hers.

The next day she didn't know when the family went to church, or when they came back. Someone brought the funnies and left them on the bed, because she remembered their sliding to the floor when she turned over. Someone—she thought it was toward evening— pushed her hair back, and announced, "Look. They're coming out. She'll be all right now."

Her three-day measles were five-day ones. She didn't sit up in bed until Wednesday noon when Mother brought up a large suit box with "Madeline's" lettered on it. "From Aunt Eustace," she said.

As yet her mother hadn't said a word about her setting off to the dinner party, when she had been told to go to bed. "I've been wondering about—I mean what Aunt Eustace thought when I didn't show up," Kathleen faltered.

"Uncle Brian told her. She phoned when he was getting you to bed that night."

Kathleen waited for the scolding, but all she said was, "A mother can paddle little kids when they do wrong. But when you get older, child, life has a way of paddling you even harder."

But life had paddled her unfairly. Why couldn't the measles have held off just *one* day? Why couldn't she have had one beautiful evening of being part of that intimate little Belford-Seerie circle?

Aunt Eustace's gift was a negligee ensemble. Mother shook out first a short, rose-colored gown trimmed in a froth of lace; and next, a matching peignor of soft challis, luxurious too, with ruffled lace covering the yoke, and satin ribbon ties.

"Dear heaven, how that woman always outdoes us," Mother sighed. "Ben and I planned to tap the half-a-bath when he came home from school, and buy you a robe. Only it wouldn't have held a candle to this. Put it on, sweetheart. There's nothing like something glamorous to lift female spirits."

And there was nothing like a get-well card in the mail from the boy in her life to lift spirits even higher. It wasn't only the roses and bluebirds on it, but the last two lines of the greeting verse,

> *And to say I think of you*
> *More often than you know.*

Bruce *must* have stood in Downey's Drug and read over dozens of cards before he found this very one. Hope wasn't dead after all. There came the rustle of wings again.

Kathleen was propped up in bed, noting idly how the setting sun turned the icicles outside her window into incandescent rose and lavender tapers, when Stacy came to the door. She said with a dubious look on her face, "Here's Rita Flood to see you."

Kathleen sat up straight as Rita stepped in, and said with belligerent dignity to Stacy, "I want to talk to Kathleen."

"Go ahead and talk," Stacy said in a voice that meant, "I don't want any part of it," and ducked out. (Two years ago Rita and Stacy had engaged in fisticuffs outside Wetzel's store, when Rita called her a red-headed Mick.)

And talk Rita did, without meeting Kathleen's eye, but standing stiffly in her brother's oversize padded jacket, "I noticed your white fuzzy jacket got grease on it when you fell on that dirty floor of our shop that night—oh, not very much—and so I got some of this naphtha out of the ten-gallon can Dad has there—and it's real good, even if it does smell to high heaven."

She thrust a pint jar of colorless liquid at Kathleen. As Kathleen took it, she said wonderingly, "Well— thanks, Rita."

Kathleen thought fleetingly of a talk that had been given to the students last year at St. Jude's. At the time, it had been only so many nice-sounding words. . . . A man who had been with the Underground in France told of being captured by the enemy, and sentenced to death. Only by a miracle had he escaped the firing squad. He was a changed man, he said. Because of his deep gratitude for life, things that had formerly irritated him left him untroubled. He had greater understanding and charity for all human beings. . . .

Perhaps Kathleen's own floundering through that suffocating, black tunnel had done something like that for her. Because she looked at Rita, and felt no desire at all to strangle her. It surprised her to realize that you could feel "understanding and charity" for someone you didn't like.

Rita stood there, her uneasy eyes still avoiding the girl in the bed. She evidently had more to say, and didn't know how to say it.

To relieve the tenseness, Kathleen said, "Your friend that did the wooden-shoe dance at the hootenanny was good, wasn't she?"

Rita's eyes lighted. "That's Gretchen. She never would've got up and done it—she was afraid someone would laugh at her for being fat—if I hadn't just made her. She's one of the girls I eat lunch with. There's four of us that are real good friends."

Another pause, and she blurted out, "What I thought was that maybe you'd be so mad at me for telling right out in French about your Mom—I mean, I thought maybe you'd tell the kids at school about my brother being sent up to the Industrial School. Or maybe you have already?"

You could feel *pity*, too, deep and hurting, for a feisty, bare-legged girl who worried about keeping the new friends she made at a new school. "I only mentioned it to Jeanie—but she never tells things. I won't say a word to anyone else. Yes, I was mad at you for telling about Mom—and then I was glad. I was a dope to think it mattered."

"That's a lot different from having a brother doing time."

The three young Belfords were clattering up the stairs, and into the room with lemonade *they* had made for Kathleen.

Rita said from the doorway, "Like I say, that naphtha cleaner sure smells at first, but you hang your coat outdoors for a whole day."

"I will. And thanks again, Rita."

And Kathleen wondered again about charity and understanding.

Eighteen

❁

TALK ABOUT COINCIDENCES! Just as Kathleen, in the new Aunt Eustace peignoir came downstairs the next afternoon to phone Jeanie about their lesson assignments, the door opened, and Ben ushered in Jeanie herself. Behind her was Mrs. Kincaid.

Jeanie said, "I invited myself home with Ben to see you. And when we stopped to tell Mom, she invited herself too."

Mother was delighted to have company for tea. So were Stacy and, of course, Ben. They all had tea and warm Irish bread in the dinette. The littles were busy in the kitchen, cleaning paintbrushes in a vicious-smelling liquid. They were forever scraping paint from spokes or handlebars, and putting new paint on.

Ben let down the bamboo curtain between dinette and kitchen.

"You sure took your time having the measles, Kathleen," Jeanie said. "I've been back in school two days."

"Oh, Katie Rose—I mean Kathleen—always has to do everything the hard way," Stacy answered.

Jeanie's dancing eyes turned to Kathleen. " I heard your mother call you Katie Rose that day at school. Why don't you want to be called that? I love it, and you seemed exactly like a Katie Rose when you cut loose and danced. I'm going to call you that from now on. Why, the whole school is swarming with Kathleens, and Kathies, and Kays, but not another Katie Rose."

"Oh, lovey," Mother said, "I'm sorry if I let the cat —or Katie Rose—out of the bag that day at school."

Former irritations certainly were slipping away from her, for she said, "It doesn't matter—not a bit." And when one of the littles called out, "Honest? Can we call you Katie Rose again?" she could laugh and say, "Sure. You always do anyway."

And so, between sips of tea, Kathleen became Katie Rose again.

So much to talk about while Jeanie gave her their lesson assignments! Especially Mr. Knight's hootenanny. "I was so woozy that day," Jeanie said, "I didn't tell you two what elegant performers you were. I didn't know you were a junior Caruso, Ben."

"Not Caruso. Didn't you know?—McCormack willed me his voice."

"And who else," Katie Rose said, "would get up and make a jackass out of himself—just to encourage others—but Miguel. I hope Mr. Knight appreciated it."

"Oh, he did," Stacy said. "Because when Mug told him about his guitar being stolen Mr. Knight hunted up an old one he found kicking around his basement, and gave it to him. It has to have new strings. Maybe he'll play it when we go out Christmas caroling. Because he can't sing for sour apples."

"Neither can I," Jeanie said. "But could I go caroling too?"

"Sure you can," Ben said. "You can be the lantern bearer."

Uncle Brian came in from work. That called for a fresh pot of tea. He called Jeanie his honey bear and his darlin' dear. She and her mother laughed at everything he said. He roared to the three in the kitchen, "You, limbs of Satan, can't we drink our tea, without its tasting of creosote?"

The teapot was drained when little Brian, the worrier, pushed back the rattly curtain. "Mom, you remember about Sister Cabrina wanting you and all of us to come today and plan the music and things for the Christmas play? And Ben has to come, to talk about lights."

"Yes, my dear own, I remember." And to Mrs. Kincaid and Jeanie, "If only I could put the fear of God in them the way the nuns can!"

They laughed at that too.

Uncle Brian said he'd take the Kincaids home, while Ben took the folks to St. Jude's. In all the to-do of good-bys, and Ben's rounding up the littles, and—wouldn't you know!—Mother giving their guests what was left of the Irish bread, Stacy turned back to say, "I forgot all about Ben's white coat for tonight."

Katie Rose said she would iron it, but Mother told her she ought to go back to bed. "I'll take care of it when—"

"Never mind, never mind," Uncle Brian put in. "I have to iron myself a white shirt, because I'm having dinner with Grandfather Belford. I'll whisk over Ben's jacket while I'm at it."

"Yes, go rest, Katie Rose," Jeanie said. "You look tuckered out, and I want you back in school tomorrow."

Alone in the quiet house, she dropped down at the dinette table, feeling suddenly spent and shaky. Rather than climb the stairs, she stretched out on the long cushioned seat where the littles always sat.

Now, after all her efforts to be called Kathleen, she was back to Katie Rose. It felt as warm and comfortable as an old coat. . . . And after all her uneasiness about Jeanie's coming home with her and finding Uncle Brian the worse for drink, Jeanie had come; and she and her mother had fitted right in. . . .

She heard Uncle Brian come into the kitchen, but she was too sleepy to call out to him. He was letting down the ironing board. She wondered drowsily if he were getting the best of what he called the raging thirst in his bones. She went to sleep to the thump of his iron and his soft whistling.

Cully's bark half roused her. Someone was rapping on the side door which was close to her head. She heard Uncle Brian open it, slapping down Cully as he did. She listened to a woman's breathless voice, "Brian! Oh, Brian, I had to see you." He must have stood there staring, for the caller added on a foolish laugh, "Don't you know me—Colleen?"

Colleen! Katie Rose's ears pricked up at that. She supposed Uncle Brian muttered that he was ironing— and maybe couldn't leave the iron on. For Katie Rose heard the click of high heels in the kitchen, and another clink of what she thought were bracelets. She caught a whiff of perfume that was *not* what Stacy would call sub-til.

Uncle Brian said, "Excuse me, for going on with the ironing. I'm after needing a white shirt to wear out this evening, and Ben has to have a white jacket for his making of sandwiches." He was rolling his *r*'s as he always did in a time of stress. "Rose and the kids were after going—"

"I saw them go. I saw you leave and then come back. I've been watching the place like a criminal." Again that foolish, or maybe coy, laugh. "But, Brian, I had to see you—I had to see you alone."

What could a girl behind the bamboo curtain do? She couldn't yell out and say, "Hey, I'm here," could she?

"Did you now?" he answered over the thump of the iron being upended and the soft swish of his shirt as he moved it on the board.

Colleen was nervous all right. She kept repeating that it had been so long since they had seen each other. "But you haven't changed a bit, Brian."

"I've changed. We've all changed in ten years' time, Colleen."

Katie Rose had to see this Colleen person that neither Uncle Brian nor any of them, except Gran, had seen since Uncle Brian went off to Korea. Without making a sound, she lifted her head and peered through the tiny slits of the bamboo curtain.

The caller was leaning against the refrigerator, and tapping one foot. She had on a tight bright blue dress and a fur stole. And a choker necklace that matched the bracelets which clinked with every move she made. No wonder she had to tell Uncle Brian who she was. She was a far cry—and a good thirty pounds—from the slim-waisted flower of a girl who had danced with him there in their living room. Ah, and held his heart in her two little hands!

Uncle Brian was ironing away as though his life depended on his finishing his white shirt.

"Do you ever think about the wonderful times we had together, Brian?"

"Yes, I think about them."

Katie Rose strained her ears to detect what else was in his voice. Love, or longing, or bitterness? But she could only tell that his brogue was more burry than ever.

"I've never forgotten them, Brian. Remember how we'd go to every dance we heard about—even if it was fifty miles from Bannon—and dance the whole night through? You told me I had a foot of shod air, and eyes that would shame the blue morning glories. Remember how you used to make up crazy love songs and sing them to me?"

"That was a long time ago. That was before you were Mrs. Kleim."

She moved so that the man at the ironing board couldn't help looking at her. "Maybe you're wondering why I came," she said.

"I am."

Her words came in a rush. Fred's uncle in Bannon had told them of Brian's offer of a fine job in San Francisco. She and Fred weren't happy—they never had been. She had been to no dances and to very few movies since she was married. All Fred did was work at the garage. She never knew when he'd be home, because if extra work came in, he'd work late. "Or just sit down there and go over his books—and get out his bills."

"I should think you'd be down there helping him.

Isn't that a wife's place to help her man get ahead?"

"I hate it. I hate the old, dirty, smelly place. And Fred's so stingy. I keep remembering how you were always giving me foolish little presents. I don't love him—I never have. Brian, don't you understand?"

"I understand a lot, Colleen. You married him because you were afraid of getting a poor broken reed of a man."

"But everybody in Bannon said you'd be coming home in a wheelchair, and—and—"

"—disfigured beyond recognition," he added.

"*Everybody* said it. And I—I hardly knew what I was doing. But it was you I loved, and you—you loved me—"

"Yes, I loved you. I could never have gone through what I did, but for the thought of you waiting at home for me. I could never have made the break from prison with guns sniping at me, and bolted through barbed wire like it was mosquito netting. Nor hid out in slimy ditches, till I was a delirious, babbling idiot when our men finally found me."

But he said it all without feeling. He put his shirt on a hanger and started on Ben's jacket. He said then, "You haven't said yet why you came here."

"I came to tell you that—that it isn't too late for us. I can get a divorce from Fred. When you go to San Francisco, I could join you there." She laid her hand on his arm. "We can start in where we left off. Please, Brian."

He didn't shake off her hand. Nor did he stop ironing. Katie Rose almost called out, "Tell her *no*. Tell her *no*."

He said in that same flat voice, "There can be no picking up—something—that's been trampled to bits. There's no going back, Colleen."

And still she stood, until he said almost gently, "You'd better be going now. Rose will be home any minute, and I won't answer for the reception she'd give you. Go now, and try being a decent wife to the man you married. Forget all that romantic stuff your head is so full of. Besides, I may go to San Francisco, and I may not."

He went to the side door with her. Katie Rose thought he said, "Thank you for coming, Colleen."

He came back to finish Ben's jacket. He put up the ironing board. Should the eavesdropper lie low and hope he wouldn't find her, or should she—?

She had no choice. He pushed through the bamboo curtain to hang the white coat over the register in the dinette. He stopped in amazement at sight of her there. All in one breath, she said, "I didn't go upstairs because I was so tired, and so I went to sleep here—you know how Mom always stretches out here when she takes a nap, and so I—"

"And so you heard all that went on in the kitchen?" he accused.

"I was half-asleep, and I couldn't very well—"

He grunted a laugh. "Half-asleep, she says! Sure,

your ears were bent forward like a bird dog's, and your eyes straining through the curtain.''

''Don't be mad at me, Uncle Brian.''

He smiled shakily. ''No, I couldn't be mad at you, childeen. We've been through too much together, you and I.''

And then she had to ask it, ''Is your heart broken at seeing her again, and knowing she's married to someone else?''

He took a long while to straighten Ben's jacket on the hanger. ''I don't think so, Mavourneen. It's fair shaken at seeing the girl—and not seeing the one I've been picturing all these years. It gives me a queer emptiness.''

Cully set up such a wild scrabbling at the door that they both looked out the window. ''It's Rose and the noisy Indians,'' he said. ''Just say nothing—not yet, anyway—about all that transpired in the kitchen.''

''Don't forget you're having dinner with Grandfather. You'd better get ready.''

''That's right, that's right,'' he said absently. ''Yes, I'd better be making myself ready.''

Stacy was still sleeping in the alcove off Mother's room. Katie Rose lay awake in the double bed, thinking of Colleen and her throwing herself at Uncle Brian. Surely, he had noticed how flabby, how whiney-voiced she had become. Maybe that accounted for his feeling ''fair shaken,'' and the ''queer emptiness.'' But supposing that started his old longing for drink again?

He came home before either Ben or Mother. He stopped at her door, and asked, "Are you awake, Kathleen Mavourneen?" and came in and sat down on her bed.

In a low voice, he picked up the conversation where they had left off this afternoon. "No, my heart isn't broken. That's a strange thing—but now that the shock is over, I feel a lightness I haven't felt for many a day. For many a long year."

In the dark she groped for his hand.

"What a prize fool I've been, bright angel. I'll confess to you, now, that again and again I was drawn to Denver, and I'd leave a job in Bannon to come here. I knew where Colleen lived. Praise God, I hadn't enough guts to go to the door—but I'd drive down the street, thinking mayhap I'd see her in the yard, or on the street, and that she'd come to me and put her hand in mine, and say, 'It was all a mistake. I still love you, and we can go off some place and start over.' "

"That's just what she did say this afternoon, Uncle Brian."

"Ah, but it wasn't the same girl saying it. It was a disloyal, discontented wife. I'll confess something else. So have I driven past Fred's garage. A time or two I saw him at the gas pumps out in front, and the hate I felt was like poison in my veins."

"Don't you hate him now?"

"Not now. It's more sorrow for the man—a stubby, little fellow, who'll be bald before his time—having to go home and listen to a whiney woman."

"Maybe that's why he works late." She added viciously, "I just wish you'd told her that her dress was a size too small for her, and that her face was like a full moon."

"I could never tell a woman that."

"I was afraid maybe you'd be so upset you'd want a drink."

"Aren't you the worrier now! I turned down a drink tonight."

"Not at Grandfather Belford's. He wouldn't offer you one."

"Yes, at Grandfather Belford's. In the midst of our chess game, a friend of his dropped in. This friend wanted a drink, and asked me to have one with him."

"Aw, that was mean."

"That's the first thing a fellow on the wagon has to face. Wherever you go—even at work, or the end of a workday—there's always someone ready to put a glass in your hand. Once I even reached for one, and then shoved it away. And do you know why?"

"No. Why?"

"Because I saw in it your gran and grandda bowed in shame. I heard Rose's heartbroken voice, and saw the disgust in your and Ben's eyes—yes, and the three littles, coming down early, and finding me on the couch, like the drunken sot I was. I swear if I lifted a glass to my lips now, I'd taste tears in it. It was only that Thanksgiving night, that the thirst was bigger than I was. Lucky for me, I had you and that lad to take me in hand. And lucky for me, you were such a skinflint in not giving me money."

He mused on. "I'll have another pay check the fifteenth. It'll be bigger than the others, because of my promotion. You won't forget to pay Flood for his fender work, along with Mac for gas, and the bill at Downey's."

"You've already got more than enough to pay those," she said, thinking of the tight wad of bills in the pink soap box under the floor, not more than six feet from them.

"By heaven, we're capitalists—filthy capitalists, you and I. What do you say, we go Christmas shopping after the fifteenth? We'll give presents together. Be thinking of what each one wants."

"I know what I want for Ben. Another white jacket."

"We'll get him two more," he shouted. "What a time I had ironing that fool thing dry without scorching it today!"

He stood up, and Katie Rose asked, "Can I tell Mom? I mean she'd be so relieved to know you're not still grieving over Colleen."

He turned it over in his mind, before he said slowly,

"Yes, tell Rose—and of course she'll burn up the line to Bannon to repeat it. But that's all right. Just don't go into details, Mavourneen. To tell the truth, I can't help feeling a little ashamed for the woman and her coming to me, and the things she said that were better left unsaid."

Nineteen

✿

THE WHOLE FEEL of the school was different when Katie Rose went back the next day. Everyone stopped, and told her what a knockout she and Ben had been in their song-and-dance number. Everyone said it was good to see her back. Even a *senior,* who was writing up the hootenanny for the school paper, interviewed her.

For the first time Katie Rose felt she belonged at Johnny Q.

Something else wonderful happened. The noisy chatter at their lunch table came to a sudden lull as Mrs. Dujardin, the drama teacher, approached. She singled out Katie Rose to tell her she had been impressed by her singing and dancing, and her "stage presence." She wondered why she hadn't enrolled in the drama course, and Katie Rose, almost choking on a mouthful of banana, said she hadn't thought of it.

"You must sign up for it next semester. At least, you must come out for the musical I'm planning on doing in the spring. There's a part I'd like you to try out for." Her pat on Katie Rose's shoulder was like a blessing.

She watched the teacher's majestic figure weave its way toward the faculty table. She scarcely heard Deetsy's gushing, or Miguel's, "Whatta you know! Stage presence yet," for she was thinking of Jeanie's saying that she would work like an army mule if she got on the school paper. So would she work like one in the drama club.

June broke into her thoughts by telling her that both McGaffey and Bruce Seerie were home with the measles.

Even though Uncle Brian had urged Katie Rose to spare the details to the family about Colleen's visit, she had to tell Jeanie or have spontaneous combustion. She waited until they two were alone in the dressing room, with only their dryers for soft accompaniment, to tell her. She imitated Colleen's, "Don't you know me—Colleen?" and her mincing in on high heels, her coy laugh, and her, "You told me I had a foot of shod air." She went through the motions of Uncle Brian ironing, and made his answers in a deep voice with a thick brogue.

Jeanie, with her shining eyes, made a perfect audience. She broke in with, "Katie Rose, you're a perfect actress. If that Dujardin woman could see you now, she'd give you the *lead*."

Maybe Uncle Brian was right, and all the O'Byrnes were ham actors.

She told of their conversation late last night, and ended with, "We're going shopping when he gets his next pay."

"Can I go with you? I can't think of anything more fun than to go Christmas shopping with Uncle Brian."

After school, Katie Rose walked all the way to the Boulevard to pick out and mail a get-well card to Bruce.

Already the tidal wave of Christmas was rolling in. In the drugstore, Downey and his wife were setting up long tables of enticing gifts. Christmas carols pealed out over a speaker system from the five-and-ten. At home, she found Stacy frowning over her Christmas list, and the inroads it would make on her saving for her Weatherwise coat.

"I did hope to have it for when we go out caroling," she lamented. "How much have you got toward yours, Katie Rose?"

"Not even half."

Bruce was back in school on Tuesday. Katie Rose dawdled in the hall outside of lit, because this hall led to the gym. Her heart announced his swinging, light-footed approach. He was with other boys as usual, but they were not his former football teammates. These three boys were evidently app gym, and eager to get at the rings and bars, for when she said, "Hello, Bruce," and he stopped with his smiling, "Well hi, Kathleen," they stopped too, and looked at him almost reproachfully.

He thanked her for her get-well card, and she thanked him for his. She had so much to tell him. But would June tell a boy about the black tunnel, and her fear that she would never get out? Would June confess, "It changed me. I'm not as mean and selfish as I was"? No, she would not.

But Katie Rose *had* to say, "I haven't seen you since we did that crazy song and jig at the hootenanny. Mrs. Dujardin liked it. And she wants me to take drama next half, and try out for a part—and gee, I'd be in seventh heaven if I only—"

One of the boys said, "Hey, Seerie, we better get going, before the horizontals are taken."

"We're having our app gym tryout Friday," he said hurriedly, "and those crazy measles made me lose a lot of practice on the giant swing."

He started to go, but Katie Rose, certainly not June-inspired, laid her hand on his arm, "Bruce, did you like our song and dance at the hootenanny? And if I do get a part in a show—I mean, I'd like you to come—"

"Sure, sure. And I'll clap like crazy." But he was saying it over his shoulder as he joined the boys.

She went into lit, forgetting to smile at Mr. Jacoby. Would she ever learn not to let the eager side of her show? She had been making headway with Bruce in her June role.

The next week, she and Jeanie had their night with Uncle Brian in the University Hills shopping center. He was in high spirits, which meant that he had to clown as only he could.

They went first to the china department, where a tired gray-haired woman clerk showed them teacups for Mother. Uncle Brian turned to Katie Rose and Jeanie, and asked meekly, "Can I buy these?" He explained to the saleslady that he was on leave from the pen, and these two were his parole officers.

Her amazed look turned to a laugh when Katie Rose giggled. She carried along with the joke and even promised to send him a postcard when he got back to the "big house."

They shopped for bicycle headlights for the three littles. It was in this department, when the girls were idly looking at pencil-sized flashlights, that Uncle Brian called to them in a loud voice, "No shoplifting now. Remember, you promised me with tears in your eyes you wouldn't lift a thing if I brought you."

This time it was a serious young man clerk, who had a startled moment before he decided he needn't call the store detective.

Uncle Brian was a lavish spender. When they bought after-ski boots for Stacy, he cast measuring glances at both Katie Rose's and Jeanie's feet. He gave them a shove and said, "The two of you go down the aisle and look at bedroom slippers for Gran while I poke around here."

Out of his hearing, Katie Rose laughed. "Come Christmas, you and I will both have fur-lined boots."

"Oh, but he shouldn't buy *me* a pair."

"Wild horses couldn't stop him," Katie Rose said.

The girls were full of ice-cream sodas, and all three were laden as pack mules, when they finally climbed into Uncle Brian's car. He made a stop at the lot on the Boulevard where Christmas trees were sold. Miguel was one of the helpers, and it was obvious from the spatters of paint on himself that he had been using a spray gun to turn green trees into silver, blue, and lavender ones.

"We'll have no tree with dyed hair," Uncle Brian said, and selected a natural green one for the Belford hall. "No, Miguel, we won't take it yet. I'll pick it up later." He turned to Jeanie, "And now, my love, my brightness, we'll be taking you home."

Katie Rose and her uncle came in their own side door and deposited their load on the dining table. One glance around the house told them that Liz had arrived from Bannon. There, on the table, was her harp-shaped loom with a pattern of red and white yarn in it. There sat a large bowl of eggs, each still wrapped in paper torn from a catalog; and, at the head of the basement steps, a bushel basket of cabbage.

She came downstairs to greet them, bundled up in a wool robe and puffing for breath as she always did from exertion. She told Katie Rose she was a treat for old eyes, and Brian was handsomer than ever.

"Blarney will get you no place, woman," he told her, and swung her off her feet.

Yes, she had come in for a check-up at the clinic, and to buy a few things for Christmas. "Besides, I've had the boyeen on my mind, and I—"

"You needn't worry about Miguel. His grandparents are home, and he's the best-fed boy at Johnny Q."

"Will you tell him I want to see him, Katie Rose? Indeed, that's one reason I came up."

Christmas came on Wednesday this year.

"It couldn't be perfecter," Stacy exulted. "We'll be out of school the Friday before, and have all those days between to get ready, and the nights to go caroling."

On Thursday, the day before school let out for the holidays, Katie Rose was surprised to see the shiny blue Belford car waiting outside Adams High. Emil was in the driver's seat and Aunt Eustace, in the back, opened her door to call, "Come and get in, Kathleen, and we'll drive you home."

She looked picture perfect as always in her bright red suit, fur stole, and matching hat. She laughed in gay excitement, as Katie Rose sat down beside her. "I never saw anything like the way the holidays are getting jammed-packed with parties and festivities, and I suddenly thought how wonderful it would be to have you share them all. And every girl should get some new and pretty clothes for Christmas. Kathleen dear, it's been too long since you've visited us."

Yes, a long time, but Katie Rose felt anew the old magic spell that her gay and glamorous aunt could always cast over her.

Aunt Eustace continued, "We were so disappointed that you were sick and missed our dinner party—I could tell it was a blow to Bruce. But I'm having another one Saturday to make up to you for—"

"You mean day after tomorrow?"

"Day after tomorrow night. I though it would be lovely if you were hostess with me. And Grandfather and I wondered if you couldn't brighten up our whole holidays by spending them with us. Wouldn't you like to?"

"Oh, I would—I certainly would."

She accepted, not thinking so much about spending the holidays at the Belford mansion, but that at last she would have her inning with Bruce. At last he would see her in the Stardust dress against a regal and fitting background.

"We'll talk it over with your mother," Aunt Eustace said, as Emil turned off on Hubbell Street.

It did seem uncanny, the way Aunt Eustace always

arrived at the worst possible time at their house. Katie
Rose opened the front door, and ushered her into the
hall and a strong, cabbage-cooking smell. When her aunt
came, Katie Rose not only saw through her eyes, but
smelled through her nose. And heard through her ears.
Never had Mother's old portable sewing machine, set
up on the dining table, sounded so clattery.

If only the whole downstairs wasn't so *un*private!
She had no choice but to step into the living-dining
room, and announce, ''Aunt Eustace picked me up at
school and came home with me.''

Mother looked up from her sewing in positive alarm.
And no wonder. It was that purple-striped Gay Nineties
dress she was stitching on; the one with the draped
overskirt and the ruffles that were forever pulling loose.
She snatched it out of the machine, rolled up the whole
rustly mass, and tried to wad it into her sewing
basket.

She stood up and tried to smooth back her hair while
she greeted Aunt Eustace. And then she dropped back
again behind the table and machine. No wonder again.
She wore a shapeless and faded baseball sweater of
Ben's over a pink, frilly, dotted Swiss housecoat. Her
feet were in a pair of the knitted bedsocks Liz dispensed
so freely.

And there sat Aunt Eustace pulling off long suede
gloves that perfectly matched her brown fur stole. So
did her pumps. So did her bag.

And why did that lug of a Stacy have to yell in from

the kitchen door, "Hi, Aunt Eustace. I just made tea. You all want to come out? We sent the littles to the Boul for cakes."

Katie Rose said swiftly, "I'll bring a tray in here." The dinette was all too close to the kettle of odorous cabbage.

In the kitchen, she had an awful moment before she found a lemon to slice for Aunt Eustace. She gathered up ill-assorted cups and saucers, and thought of running upstairs and unpacking the pretty new ones she and Uncle Brian had bought Mother for Christmas. But no, he wouldn't like that.

She carried in the tea things. Aunt Eustace was telling Mother about Grandfather, and how confined he had been through the cold winter. "He misses his contact with young people. So I wondered if you wouldn't let us borrow Kathleen for the holidays. She could help him trim the tree. I hate to think of his feeling lonely at Christmas."

Mother said, "When he phoned a few days ago, I asked him if you both couldn't come here for Christmas dinner. He said he'd love to, if you didn't have other plans."

"I appreciate your asking us, Rose, but, as I say, Father is more frail than we realize. Confusion tires him. That's why I always think it best to have dinner at home. But it would mean so much to him to have one of his grandchildren there. One never knows how many more Christmases he'll be with us."

Mother couldn't argue against that. She only looked at Aunt Eustace and at Katie Rose helplessly, while she took pins out of, and put them back in, the red pincushion on the machine in front of her.

The pincushion was in the shape of a tomato, only many times bigger and harder than any tomato that ever grew. Pins, needles, and safety pins were stuck in it. She hoped Aunt Eustace didn't notice the short garter that had come off a girdle, and was stuck in by the safety pin at the end.

Stacy broke in, "Oh no, Katie Rose! You can't miss our Christmas play at St. Jude's, and all of us going to midnight Mass—and you've always gone caroling."

Katie Rose didn't have time to answer—though she did have time to think: What is tramping about on cold nights compared to an evening with Bruce?—when in clomped the three younger Belfords with a bulgy brown paper sack. Cully was circling about them, his greedy eyes on the bag, and all three excitedly said that Pearl was at the bakery, and just look what she—

Katie Rose's very soul shuddered. Oh no, not with Aunt Eustace here!

. . . Mother had friends every place. She did things for them, and they did things for her. She brought cucumbers from Bannon to Mrs. Wetzel at the store for her kosher dills, and Mrs. Wetzel sold Mother cheese at wholesale. Last spring, when Pearl at the bakery moved into a drab little apartment, Mother found time to paint the walls for her. In turn, Pearl gave the Belfords the "imperfects"; the cookies that came out a queer shape, or doughnuts that were too brown or too pale.

Stacy snatched the sack out of Matthew's hands, peered into it, and screamed in delight, "Cupcakes! Lookee, here's one that looks like a stove-pipe hat." Instead of getting a plate for them, she tore open the sack, and flattened it out on the table. Some of the cupcakes resembled stove-pipe hats that had been sat on and mashed flat.

Katie Rose sat, thinking of how tea was served in the Belford mansion, and winced with shame at their pawing over the cakes, their saying, "Mom, here's one with pink icing." And, worst of all, Stacy brazenly asking Aunt Eustace which kind she'd like.

Aunt Eustace didn't care for any. She mustn't keep Emil waiting, she said. When Katie Rose walked to the door with her, she suggested that Katie Rose come over to the Belford mansion after school tomorrow. "You needn't take your suitcase with you. Leave it in the hall, and Emil can pick it up when he's doing errands. I'm having a party tomorrow afternoon, so hurry over."

Ben came in the back door, just as Aunt Eustace was going down the front steps.

Mother said, "Bring the pot in here, Stacy, and I'll have a fresh cup with Ben." Her sigh all but said, "Now we can relax and enjoy our tea."

You'd think she'd at least say, "Stacy, you should have put the cupcakes on a plate when Aunt Eustace was here."

She said to Ben, though her explanation was meant for her glowering daughter, "I know I'm a sight, but I was ready to drop in my tracks after helping Liz with all her shopping. When I finally got her and Brian off to Bannon—he'll be staying the night—I thought I'd lie down. Then I remembered I had to mend this fool dress—and it was chilly in here with the scalawags fanning in and out."

"You look all right," Ben said. Katie Rose said nothing.

Mother pulled the purple-striped dress out of its hiding place, and fitted it in the machine. She bent closer to look at the needle as she let the foot down. She lifted tragic eyes, and moaned, "Do you know what happened? I broke the machine needle when I yanked the dress out so fast. It's the only one I've got—and the Singer shop's downtown, miles away. God help us, now I'll have to sew this long strip of ruffle back by hand."

"Aw gee, Mom," sounded around the chomping of cupcakes; and, "Maybe I could drive down and get one," Ben offered.

"Oh no, no. It'd take too long."

She pulled the dress back onto her lap, and reached to the pins in the cushion. She looked at Katie Rose, and exploded, "I wish that woman wouldn't come barging in on us, without so much as a by-your-leave, of if-you-please. Her, and her nose tilted high in the air. I wish you hadn't come dragging her in, just when I was—"

Katie Rose exploded back, "You wish it! You don't wish it half as much as I do. I never was so ashamed in my whole life. All of you scrambling over those revolting cupcakes that were probably dropped on the floor and stepped on—and then gathered up, and put in a sack for the Belfords."

"But they taste good," someone said—she was too carried away to know which one.

"Taste! How could anybody taste anything, with the smell of cabbage so thick you could—you could cut it with a shovel."

Ben grunted out, "Spare us your Duchess of Belford act." And Mother snapped, "So! I suppose the smell of cabbage offends your Queen Eustace."

Katie Rose should have been warned by the angry flash of her eyes. But she had to fling out, "Not offends —asphyxiates. I just wish everyone of Liz's cabbages had frozen in their—"

She saw her mother's hand reach out and, simultaneously, felt a hard thump on top of her head. The scratchy weight clung there. For her mother's pitch had turned the tomato pincushion upside down, and the pins and needles caught in the top of her hair.

Ben's deep and hearty haw-haw sounded first, then

Stacy's shrieking giggle, "The latest in tomato hats!"
Katie Rose ducked her head, and the tomato hat
dropped with a thud at her feet. But the garter, its
safety pin caught in her hair, still dangled before her
eyes.

She stood as frozen as she had just wished Liz's cabbages were. What was more mortifying than to be hit
on the head with a clinging pincushion, and then to have
everyone double over in glee? Well, everyone except
little Brian, who only smiled shakily, and her mother,
who sat there as though she were as stunned as her
daughter at the whole happening.

Stacy stepped up to her. "Hold still," she said, and
untangled the black hair from the catch on the safety
pin. "You had it coming to you," she added, and then
she looked at Ben and they both doubled over in
laughter again.

Very, very funny! For a few seconds, she stood
there, her heart pounding. What was the *hurtingest*
thing she could say to Mother? She said it with a sneer,
"You should talk about the Floods being common as
pig tracks!"

On that parting shot, which no one answered—they
were still laughing—she walked out of the room and up
the stairs. She went into the room she shared with
Stacy, banged the door shut, and bolted it. Even then
their laughter rang in her ears.

Twenty

❁

THE NEXT MORNING, when Katie Rose thought the family would be at breakfast, she slid the bolt on her door, and stepped out. She was dressed for school. She carried her overnight bag and over her arm was the white mohair wrap. Except for a sortie to the bathroom late last night, it was the first time she had emerged from the room since her humiliated retreat the day before.

Last evening, Ben had come up and rapped on the door. She wanted to hear him say, "I didn't mean to hurt your feelings by laughing." Instead, he announced casually, "Supper's ready, Katie Rose."

"I don't want any supper," she answered coldly.

Later, Stacy had tried the door. Maybe she would say, "Aw, Katie Rose, you know how we always laugh when Mom whams one of us." If she had said it, maybe Katie Rose could have laughed just a little herself; for part of her had to admit that she must have looked funny with that oversize tomato stuck slantwise on her head. But Stacy only yelled through the door, "Open up, for Pete's sake, so I can go to bed."

She had gathered together Stacy's ravelly nightgown, her comb and brush, and opened the door just wide enough to push them through. Let her sleep again in the alcove off Mother's room.

She was glad Uncle Brian was spending the night at Bannon. If he had thumped on the door, and said, "Let me in, Mavourneen," he would have been harder to put off.

She had reached the stair landing with her bag and wrap, when Ben started up with a cup of coffee. "Wait till I take this to Mom, and I'll give you a hand," he said. "She was so beat, I told her to stay in bed. The railroad men had a Christmas party at Giddy's last night, and she was playing 'I've Been Working on the Railroad' till two in the morning."

He needn't think he could play on her sympathies. She answered, as one stranger to another, "Thank you, I don't need any help."

He gave her his old dark look as he passed her.

The overnight bag, which Emil would pick up later,

she set in the hall, and folded the wrap on top it. She was hunting for her trench coat in the closet, when Stacy stuck her head out of the kitchen. "Breakfast's on, Katie Rose. I fried you an egg."

Had they all held a conclave and decided to pretend that she had never been hit on the head with a hard tomato pincushion, and that they hadn't all held their sides in high glee? Without looking at Stacy, she said, "I'm not eating breakfast here."

The littles were suddenly in the hall. One muttered that her coat was in the living room, and they all scrambled to bring it and her purse to her. She accepted both with a cold "Thank you," and put on her coat, feeling for gloves that weren't there. She'd go without, rather than take time to look for them.

Ben was standing on the lower stair and, as she started toward the door, he ordered, "Katie Rose, you march right back up those steps, and say good-by to Mom."

She stood for a vacillating moment with her hand on the knob. If old bossy Ben had even said her mother would feel bad if she left without a word, why then— then— She couldn't answer for the ache in her throat. She only opened the door and went out, half-fearful that he might grab her arm and pull her back.

No one tried to stop her. But before she reached the corner, little Brian came running after her with her gloves. He said pleadingly, "Don't be mad at Mom. I mean—well, once when she was mopping, and me and Jill and Matt tracked up her floor, she whacked us all with the mop—but we just laughed—we just laughed and laughed. And then she laughed, because we all had wet behinds.''

That was different. Everyone had laughed together. This time everyone had laughed *at* her, rejoicing to see her made a fool of. She couldn't answer him either for the lump in her throat.

She stopped at Wetzel's store and, from the little change in her purse, bought two bananas, and ate them on her way to school.

All morning she went through classes feeling numb and hollow and sickish. Such a disorganized day, this final one before the holidays. Pupils who were part of the choral group were ducking out of classes to practice. ''Peace on Earth, Goodwill to Men'' seeped out of assembly and echoed in halls. But teachers had no goodwill to the measle absentees, when it came to making up and handing in the work they had missed.

All morning she tasted those bananas until a lunchroom tuna sandwich pushed them into place. She ate it alone, while she proved on paper that all angles in an equilateral triangle are equal. As though it mattered! Jeanie had stayed on in French to translate four pages of *L'Abbé Constantin* for Madame. Miguel had to catch up his history notebook. He said before he went loping off, ''I'll be looking for you after school, Petunia. My day of reckoning is at hand, and I need your moral support.''

She didn't see Bruce. Perhaps Mr. Jacoby was cracking the whip over *him* for some past assignment.

At school's end, she waited long in journalism for Jeanie, who waited to turn a story in to the teacher, who was off somewhere in the building. They stepped out into the cold, sunny afternoon, and Katie Rose said, ''I can walk past your house with you on my way to Aunt Eustace's.''

Oh, to step inside the serene order of the Belford mansion, and feel *wanted* and made over!

''You going there? For how long?''

''For the Christmas holidays. And tomorrow I'm to be hostess with her on a dinner party for—''

''For the Seeries, I suppose?''

''Yes.''

And oh, to have a beautiful, unbroken-into evening with Bruce!

''Did you see Miguel, and help him through his dire reckoning,'' Jeanie asked.

''Miguel? Heavens, I forgot all about it.''

''That's one thing you should have remembered,'' Jeanie said in such a cross-grained way that Katie Rose hesitated to tell her of the humiliating fracas at home.

They walked on in silence until they reached Jeanie's house. Her mother was standing in the doorway of the house directly to the south of them, and Jeanie said,

"Come on in with me, and meet our new neighbor. Remember my telling you about the newlyweds moving next door? Well, not exactly newlyweds, because she's going to have a baby in April. Did you ever know the Malones that live on Barberry on the other side of the Boul?

"I know who they are. We had to read Martie Malone's columns for current events at St. Jude's."

"This is Beany Malone—Beany Buell now. Mom knew her and her husband through her Mount Carmel nursery work. She told them about this house being for sale, and so they're buying it. Come on in with me. I'm just crazy about Beany."

So was Katie Rose the minute the door was opened and she met Beany Buell's wide, hospitable smile. "Come on in, both of you. We're a little short of chairs to sit on, and rugs to walk on, and glasses to drink out of, but just think!—we're in our *own home* for Christmas."

This house was much smaller than the Kincaid's next door. Even so, it looked quite bare to Katie Rose, with nothing in the living room but a red damask love seat, a few scatter rugs, and a rough-looking plank table. The bowls, bookends, and knickknacks were wedding presents, the hostess explained.

Katie Rose had never thought freckles becoming, until she saw them sprinkled over Beany Buell's nose. A green smock brought out the green of her eyes. But it was her happiness that was so contagious, that almost shouted, "Be happy with me."

I'd like just to sit and soak it up, Katie Rose thought.

Jeanie's mother said, "I've been helping her hang her draperies. Her girls' club at the community center helped her make them."

"They're turquoise sheets, with miles of brown fringe stitched on them." Beany chuckled. "My brother Johnny says Carl and I are now 'Three sheets in the wind.' And you're Katie Rose Belford? Then you're one of the Belfords that goes around caroling at Christmas. Oh, be sure and come here. Because we want to invite you all in to break bread with us—only it'll be cookies—so Carl and I'll feel like real householders."

"Katie Rose won't be out caroling," Jeanie said. "She's spending the holidays with her aunt Eustace."

"Maybe you know my aunt Eustace, Mrs. Buell?"

"Just call me Beany. I still think of *Mrs.* Buell as Carl's mother. I know who Eustace Belford is. I was always so impressed by the society editor in the *Call* printing every year, 'Happy Birthday to Eustace Belford, Denver's loveliest.' "

"She's entertaining this afternoon, so I guess I'd better be going."

She and Jeanie started out together. Jeanie took a minute to run to their mailbox at the curb to see what mail was in it. In the doorway, Beany said to Katie Rose, "You have eyes like my oldest sister's. Some day boys will be writing you poems, the way they did her, about your violet eyes. But did anyone ever tell you that they tell too much?'' She added surprisingly, ''Oh, Katie Rose, don't be unhappy over Christmas.''

Katie had a sudden longing to stay on, and talk out her woes to this new friend—she would understand. But Jeanie gave the mail to her mother and said rather curtly, ''Come on if you're coming, and I'll walk to the corner with you.''

Jeanie walked beside her, scuffling with the toe of her boot at the snow that rimmed the sidewalk. She looked ahead to the turreted stone house, sitting loftily on its high ground, and burst out, ''I can't understand you, Katie Rose. Wanting to spend Christmas there, when you've got a family of your own.''

''It so happens that I'm a complete outsider in my own family.'' Maybe now was the time to tell Jeanie the reason why.

But Jeanie said with crimped lips, ''I think it's mean, mean of her to lure you away from your folks at Christmas.''

''You're crazy as a bedbug. She did not lure me.''

''Like fun, she didn't. All her talk of wanting you to be hostess with her. And waving Bruce Seerie in front of you like a carrot to a donkey.''

''What's so mean, mean about her wanting her own niece to spend Christmas with her? Or her not wanting Grandfather to feel lonely?''

"She's the one who's afraid of being lonely."

"I won't listen to any more of your running her down," Katie Rose said in fury. She stepped off the curb to cross the street.

Jeanie caught her arm. "You'll listen to this much more. She's got what Dad calls a queen complex. Okay, she was the most beautiful girl on the campus, and Homecoming Queen, Ice Carnival Queen, Maypole Queen. She was presented at court with three feathers in her hair—see picture. So she's gone on expecting everyone to look up to her. She craves adulation."

"Whatever that means," Katie Rose sneered.

"I'll tell you, goose girl. It's what you give her, and that's why she lavishes gifts on you—"

"Just because you don't like her," Katie Rose screamed, "you needn't think you can change me." She shook Jeanie's arm off roughly, and strode off without a good-by or backward glance.

Why, her knees were wobbly under her. She kept on walking fast and mumbling, "You needn't think you can change me." But by the time she was walking the last block, she was mumbling in shocked disbelief, "It's Christmas. And Jeanie and I had a fight. I never thought we would."

Twenty-One

❁

EMIL'S WIFE, Vera, answered Katie Rose's ring at the Belford mansion. From the vestibule, Katie could hear the babble of voices, and see guests spilling over from the living room into the foyer.

Vera was not the graven image her husband was, nor the dignified old family retainer Mrs. Van was. "Hello there, Miss Kathleen," she greeted her. "You want to go in the way you are? There's some in sweaters—though some, of course, are dressed to the nines—so you look good enough. Unless you want to go upstairs and freshen up first."

Katie Rose edged around the people in the foyer, and up the stairs to her room, not only to freshen up but to take a minute to get hold of herself. Her fingers were shaking as she put on lipstick.

Downstairs, Aunt Eustace greeted her fondly, and went through introductions to a great array of women, both old and young, and a few scattered men.

Her aunt stood out like the star on the stage in a *señorita* costume, its full, creamy-white skirt and fiesta blouse heavily embroidered in beads. The white mantilla, held in place by a high, jeweled comb, made a lacy frame for her dark hair. If only Jeanie could see how much more beautiful and sparkling she was than all the other women in the room put together. . . . But Jeanie had admitted she was beautiful. . . .

Grandfather gave her his firm handclasp, and presented her to the men he was talking to in a corner. She sipped her eggnog, and reached hungrily for hors d'oeuvres on the trays Vera passed. He bent over her, and said low, "I'm about to duck into my study before she shows the pictures."

Emil had set up the projector and screen. A woman called Irene handled the slides, while her aunt told her guests about her Christmas in Mexico last year. There, in color on the screen, was Aunt Eustace buying a Christmas tree, another of her placing flowers on a roadside shrine, another of her at what she called a *piñata* party.

The forty or fifty guests finally departed. Emil put away the picture-showing paraphernalia. The velvet draperies that marked off the dining from the living room were drawn while the table was set for a late dinner. Irene, Aunt Eustace's friend, stayed on.

Aunt Eustace, flushed and happy, talked with girlish gaiety about the party all through dinner. What a flatterer Irene was! When Aunt Eustace told about a guest exclaiming that she hadn't changed a bit in ten years, Irene said promptly, "Not in twenty! Everyone says they don't see how you stay so young."

They were talking about their young days when Katie Rose went up to her rose and silver room. The draperies were drawn, and the bedlight was on. The carafe of water sat on the bedside table. Her new gown and challis robe were laid out on the bed.

Just think, she told herself as she always did, no arguing about whose turn it is to clean up the dishes. No Stacy cluttering up this beautiful room and bath. No worry in the morning about whether Ben spilled ketchup on his white jacket or not. She waited to be filled with *euphoria*, that double-crostic word meaning a sense of buoyancy and well-being. But she felt empty.

Always before when she came to Aunt Eustace's world, she gave never a backward glance to the one she left. She did now. Why? Was it because now she had a definite niche in her own world? She was Uncle Brian's bright angel. The littles wanted no lemonade except what she made. Ben grumbled when Stacy ironed his jacket, because she didn't put a crease in the sleeve.

Mrs. Dujardin had urged her to join the drama group.

She walked to the closet and looked at the Stardust dress Vera or Mrs. Van had hung on a padded, scented hanger. She said aloud, "Tomorrow night, Bruce will see me in it." He might ask her to go out after the dinner. She fingered the fluffy jacket which, thanks to Rita's cleaner, showed no trace of greasy smudge.

But other thoughts nagged at her. . . . Miguel had said he needed her. Maybe he had looked all over the school for her, while she waited in journalism for Jeanie. . . . Jeanie? What would life at Adams be without her? . . . Had Mother waited upstairs this morning for her to come and say—well, at least good-by?

She breakfasted with Aunt Eustace in her upstairs living room the next morning. A table was laid in front of the fire in the onyx fireplace. Aunt Eustace, in a powdery blue housecoat, with lace frothing at the neck and wrists, poured coffee. Katie Rose wore the challis peignoir she would never dare wear for breakfasting at home. Not with bacon spattering as she fried it, not with the littles forever tipping over milk at the table.

Mrs. Van brought hot popovers and said that Vera was helping Emil put ornaments on the Christmas tree that had been delivered earlier.

"But I thought Grandfather and I would trim it," Katie Rose said.

Aunt Eustace smiled at her. "I wanted it up for our

party tonight, and I was afraid it would crowd you for time. Because you and I are going shopping this morning.''

Katie Rose saw the tree in the foyer as they went out—a tall, silvered one, reaching almost to the high ceiling. Vera, on a stepladder, was hanging fragile, lustrous blue ornaments on it.

"I'm so weary of a mishmash of decorations. That's the blue of the Mediterranean—I ordered them specially at the Riviera shop.'' Aunt Eustace laughed with girlish delight. "And I had Madeline send away for a silver lamé dress, so I'll match our Christmas tree.''

If only a person could look at something and just see it, without tag-ends of memory pushing up. Katie Rose thought of the very embattled angel that would go on the highest tip of their tree at home. And of the *crèche* under it, with the one sheep with its broken leg. It had to be stuck on with chewing gum every year.

Again Emil drove them to Madeline's. In the fitting room that was bigger than the bedroom she shared with Stacy at home, Mrs. Neff brought Aunt Eustace's silver lamé for her to try on. She and Katie Rose both told her how beautiful she looked in it.

"And now,'' Aunt Eustace said, "we want a new coat for Kathleen.''

Mrs. Neff brought in polo coats, plaid coats, imported tweed coats, all with handsome silk linings. But Katie Rose kept shaking her head. "All the girls at school are wearing what are called Weatherwise ones.''

Mrs. Neff said they carried only "name" coats.

Katie Rose could have told Aunt Eustace, "Sears has them," and coerced her into their store in this same shopping center. What *was* the matter with her? Was it because Jeanie had flung out, "She buys adulation from you"? Was it because she and Stacy had both been saving for Weatherwise coats, and she, Katie Rose, would feel—well—crumby to go home in one that had simply been handed her.

"This coat I've got—it's all right," she insisted.

They lunched at a little French restaurant. Emil then dropped off Aunt Eustace at Jean-Paul's beauty shop to keep her appointment, and drove Katie Rose back to the Belford mansion.

Vera was in her room, vacuuming the thick rose carpeting. She flicked off the hum of the cleaner to say, "I won't be much longer. I'm only giving it a lick and promise, so I can help Aunt Van get ready for the doings tonight."

"How many are coming to the dinner?"

"She's changed it to a buffet supper. Fifteen—maybe sixteen—because she figured she might as well pay back a lot of obligations."

Katie Rose had thought it was to be an intimate small dinner.

"Is Grandfather resting?" she asked.

"No, he's got company right now in his study. Maybe you'd like to go in Miss Eustace's room till I finish here."

She went through her aunt's immaculate bedroom and on into her sitting room. She sat down and got up, feeling extra and useless in this big house.

Book shelves were built over Aunt Eustace's desk. The lowest shelf was wider to accommodate all her green leather scrapbooks. Katie Rose knew so well the write-ups and pictures that were in them, from poring over them on other visits.

She took one down and idly turned the pages. *Miss Eustace Belford greets Count from Italy. Miss Eustace Belford attends opening Symphony.* Hmm-mm! Here was, *World-famous writer, Michael Parnell, presents hostess, Miss Eustace Belford, with autographed book.* So that tall, gangling man was the writer Liz had boarded in Ireland, and whose book she treasured; the writer Madame Mee-lair recommended so highly to her students.

All those scrapbooks. The later ones, she noticed, were not as thick with clippings as the earlier. Suddenly she wanted to get away from the half-thoughts that kept struggling to the front of her mind. She thrust the book back in its place, and hurried out and down the stairs to Grandfather's study.

He was alone. He replaced the telephone and smiled at her. "Sit down, my dear. I'm trying to run down a certain McCormack record for your Uncle Brian for Christmas."

She asked suddenly, "Grandfather, is your heart— is it very bad?"

He looked into her troubled eyes, and shook his head. "No, not now. The doctor tells me I'll be cluttering up the landscape for quite a while. Which makes me very happy, for I have years of work ahead on my Chaucer and Hoccleve manscript."

But Aunt Eustace always intimated that each Christmas might be his last.

She had to ask another question, "Do you get awfully lonely?"

"Loneliness, Kathleen, is not a matter of being alone. It's a lack in the mind—or heart. After your father died—yes, I felt a great lack. Often, I'd have Emil drive me down to the Ragged Robin for a cup of coffee, so I could fill the emptiness by seeing and talking to Ben. No, I'm far from a lonely man. My life is very full."

But Aunt Eustace had told Mother her visit would save him from being lonely.

Vera came to the door to tell them Miss Eustace had returned, and Mrs. Van would be serving tea in the living room. She added, "Her friend Irene is here too. She's one of the supper guests, but she came early. She'll help show the Mexico slides again."

Grandfather explained to Katie Rose, "Years ago, when Eustace was Ice Carnival Queen or Football Queen, I can't remember which, Irene was her lady in waiting."

They entered the living room to hear Irene telling Aunt Eustace that Jean-Paul's new styling of her hair was utterly adorable. Aunt Eustace, flushed and pleased, poured tea with the gingerly movements of one conscious of a fresh manicure on her long nails. She held them out for Katie Rose's inspection, and laughed. "I know it's silly—that silverish cast—but it's just for over Christmas."

Mrs. Van was passing cups when the musical chimes sounded, and she went to answer the door. Katie Rose's fingers suddenly stiffened on the cup's frail handle at sound of a familiar voice. She looked at the wide doorway to see Miguel's loose-limbed trot taking him past Mrs. Van, and into the room. His eyes lighted on her, and he said in his abrupt, zany way, "Petunia, I need you."

She saw that he had scrubbed at the paint spatters on his chin, and combed his unruly, straw-colored hair. But the knit cap he swung in his hand had mussed it, and both his plaid shirttails were tucked in crookedly.

Joy surged through her. It was like seeing someone from the planet she had left. And right then she knew what she hadn't known before; that her restlessness and depression were just plain homesickness. She got up, and hurried to him, "Oh, Miguel, I forgot all about waiting for you yesterday."

She managed introductions to her grandfather and Irene, and said to Aunt Eustace, "I guess you remember Miguel?"

"I remember him very well," Aunt Eustace said, but with little warmth.

Miguel spoke to the roomful, "The reason I could get off early today was because we sold every Christmas tree on our lot. There're still a few to be picked up though. But I've got to see Mr. Knight—he's our principal. It won't take very long. So could I take Petunia with me?"

She could have cried out, "Yes, take me back to my old world." Aunt Eustace's luxurious—even pampered —one wasn't enough. Once it had been. But that was before her own was warm and packed full of promises.

Aunt Eustace said, "I'm sorry, but Kathleen is busy. We're having sixteen guests this evening." And Irene added gushingly, "Yes, and time goes faster than one realizes. I always have a horror of not being dressed when the first guest arrives."

Sixteen guests for a buffet supper, and one of them Bruce Seerie. Katie Rose stood still, feeling the familiar tug at her heart. But she'd had enough of straining to be the kind of a girl to please or impress Bruce. She wanted to be herself, and go tramping from house to house, singing carols. She wanted to stop in at the scantily-furnished house next to the Kincaids', and bask in Beany Buell's happiness.

She reached for Miguel's hand, and said, "Sure I'll go with you. And, Aunt Eustace, I'm sorry about the supper party, but you'll have so many here you'll hardly miss me." She had to swallow hard before she added, "I'm sorry—but I want to go home for Christmas."

Grandfather said, "I think you should, my dear. I thought all along your place was with your family. They'll miss you."

She looked at Aunt Eustace. She couldn't say, "I'll go on loving you, but not with the old awe and adoration"—Jeanie's word was *adulation.* "I won't be under a spell." She was even given a glimpse of the years ahead when her love for a woman, who was desperately trying to hold on to her glamorous youth, would be real and tender.

But because she couldn't say any of that, she dropped Miguel's hand, and stooped over the tea table and kissed her. "You're wonderful, Aunt Eustace. You always have been. I wouldn't leave only—only I've so many things to do—and places to go."

Perhaps her aunt sensed the subtle change in the relationship, for she said slowly, "You've got other places to go?" She rallied then and said with a gay laugh, "Oh, don't I know! When I was your age, there weren't enough hours in the day or night."

Irene added loyally, "There still aren't. Gracious, Kathleen, your aunt can only accept about one out of every three invitations she gets."

"I know," Kathleen agreed, feeling suddenly older. "I know how popular and sought-after Aunt Eustace has always been."

Twenty-Two

✿

THE TOP of Miguel's little car was down, and the
leather of the bucket seat felt icy cold as Katie Rose
dropped into it. They drove off with the wind ruffling
her hair, and the suitcase in the back nudging her
between her shoulder blades.

"Gee, Petunia, maybe I shouldn't have come horning
in like that and gumming everything up for you."

She laughed, feeling quite at home in the rackety
car. "You really *un*gummed things for me. Are you
going to Mr. Knight's and tell him about changing
your transcript? Do you know where he lives?"

"I sure do. I drove up there yesterday, and then I
lost my nerve and didn't go in. I think I'll drive down

· *291* ·

to the Christmas tree lot, because when he bought his tree he said he might be wanting a few extra boughs. I'll gather some up, and maybe they'll be kind of a peace offering."

He stopped at the dismantled tree lot on the Boulevard, and gathered up an armful of green branches. They scratched her on the back of her neck as they drove on.

Just as they reached the corner by Wetzel's store, Miguel braked so sharply that she rocked in the bucket seat. "There he is now!" he said.

Yes, there was Mr. Knight, ruddy of face, and tweed-overcoated, coming out of Wetzel's. He was joggling a sack of groceries, with an end of crusty rye bread poking out the top. Miguel didn't move. He sat paralyzed, while Mr. Knight walked toward his own car.

"Miguel, you'd better yell to him."

He even opened his mouth, but no yell came. Instead he muttered, "Looks like he's in a hurry. Maybe I'd better wait. Maybe this isn't a good time."

Katie Rose took one look at Miguel's scared face. She called out, "Mr. Knight! Mr. Knight! Miguel wants to see you." Even that wasn't enough. She had to dig her elbow into him and shove. "Get out, you zany zombie. You've been putting it off long enough. You might as well get it over with. Here, take the Christmas boughs with you."

They reached Mr. Knight's car as he deposited his

groceries in the back seat. He thanked Miguel for the greenery. Miguel only stood, brushing pine needles off his plaid sleeves. Katie Rose prompted again, "Miguel has something to tell you, Mr. Knight."

On that, he blurted out, "I wanted to tell you I changed my transcript that I brought up from the school in Mexico. I changed my name on it."

Changed his name? Katie Rose had always supposed he had changed a grade.

Mr. Knight waited.

"The name was Parnell, and I made a B out of the capital P, and I crossed the double ll's and made them double tt's. It just took a couple of pen strokes to change to Barnett."

Parnell? Parnell? And Miguel was Spanish for for Michael—

Mr. Knight didn't look surprised. He said quietly, "I know, Miguel. I knew five days ago. We were pretty slow getting a verification of your transcript from Mexico. But when the school secretary did write us, he said there had been no Miguel Barnett enrolled last year. He thought perhaps we were referring to Miguel Parnell, son of Miguel Parnell, the writer, who had left to attend school in Denver. So I got out your transcript for a closer look, and saw where the name had been changed. I still can't figure out why. I should think you'd be proud to be Michael Parnell's son. What's there to be ashamed of?"

"It wasn't that I was ashamed, sir. But just once I wanted to be *me*. I mean I didn't want to get by on being the son of a famous writer." He looked at Katie Rose's amazed face, and back at Mr. Knight. "You don't understand how it's always been. When I'd go to school in all these different places, the teachers—and even some of the kids—would play up to me because I was Michael Parnell's son. Only sometimes it'd be the opposite. Like in France. I guess what Pop wrote about the revolution didn't sit well with a few. Gee, I had one teacher that needled me day in and day out."

They both listened with puzzled looks on their faces, as Miguel hurried on, "I guess I wouldn't have thought of it, if Grandma and Gramps hadn't been gone when I got here. I was broke, and I needed a job—just any kind of a job. I wanted to see if I could get one on my own. Other jobs—like last Christmas when I worked in a bookstore. But gee, they just hired me because of Pop. I always had a lot of friends, but I was never sure it was me they liked. Because when a kid at school would ask me to his house, he'd say, 'My folks read your old man's books, and they want to meet you.'" He looked uneasily at Mr. Knight. "Maybe none of this makes sense to you."

It did to Katie Rose. Because she remembered all his talk about trying to prove something.

Mr. Knight said gravely, "Yes—yes, it does in a way, Miguel. But tell me this, because I'm curious.

Are you telling me because your father is coming back or, for some reason, you'd be found out?"

"No. Pop won't be leaving Alaska till summer. And Grandma and Gramps stick pretty close to home. Even when Liz—she's a relative of Petunia's—told me I couldn't go on sailing under false colors, I knew she wouldn't go blabbing it around. No, I'll tell you what kept bugging me—it was your giving me the guitar. I got new strings for it, but I knew everytime I played it I'd think of how you'd been so swell—and how I lied on the transcript. I'd have told you sooner, only I was scared. That's why I brought Petunia—"

"Did you know about this, Kathleen?"

"No, sir," Miguel said quickly. "All she did was lend me a purple pen. She even told me I'd have a day of reckoning if I changed my transcript."

Mr. Knight laughed his hearty, booming laugh. "I don't think any of us at Adams' will either lionize you or needle you just because you have a famous father. But I'm glad you told me. I decided to let it ride awhile, hoping you would."

He wished them both a Merry Christmas, and climbed into his car.

"I love that guy," Miguel breathed.

"I love him too," Katie Rose agreed.

Even after he had driven off, they still stood. So Miguel was Michael Parnell. He was the boy een Liz had mothered in Ireland.

"The idea of your telling me all that tommyrot about your father being an itinerant worker," she accused him.

"He's the most itinerant worker I ever knew."

"All that about his gathering plums and sorting them!"

"He does. A lot of sorting and discarding before he puts them in books." He helped her into the front seat again. "Thanks for that hefty shove out of the car, Petunia. I didn't have what it took on my own. Now I can string up the old guitar—" He sang out in his cracked falsetto:

All is ca-halm, all is bri-hight—

Then he asked, "Next stop Hubbell Street?"

All was not quite *ca-halm* and *bri-hight* with her yet. "No, I'd like to stop at Jeanie's first. And maybe you'll have to shove me out this time." Because it wasn't the easiest thing in the world to go to someone and say, "I'm sorry we quarreled. Please, let's be friends again."

As they drew up and stopped in front of the Kincaid house, Jeanie was standing in the door, signing for a delivery package. And Katie Rose had only to walk partway up the flagstone walk and say. "I'm going home with Miguel," for Jeanie to throw her arms around her, package and all.

"I'm so glad, Katie Rose—gosh, I'm glad. Ben's

getting off work early, and he's coming here for an early dinner so we can go caroling—we had such a time finding coal oil for the old lantern—and Beany, next door, is borrowing glasses to serve punch—"

"And Miguel is taking the guitar Mr. Knight gave him, because it doesn't weigh on his conscience, because we've seen Mr. Knight, and he confessed about changing his transcript. And it wasn't a grade, but a name —and you'd never guess what his real name is."

She couldn't give her time to guess, but said, "It's Michael Parnell. He's the son of the writer Madame is always talking about."

"I'll be a monkey's uncle!" Jeanie said unbelievingly.

They both looked at Miguel who was at the car adjusting the overnight case, and folding the seldom-worn fluffy wrap. They looked at each other, and laughed on the same thought: Miguel would go on being the same Miguel, always rumpled, always hungry, always winning everyone with his scapegrace but warm grin.

Jeanie shifted her mood from gleeful to sober as only she could. "Are you feeling lower than a snake's big toe because you're missing the Seerie dinner party at Aunt Eustace's tonight?"

"Buffet supper," she corrected absently, trying to sort over her feelings for Bruce that had brought both ecstasy and pain. "It doesn't seem to be in the stars, as Miguel says, for Bruce to see me in my Stardust dress. You remember telling me once that I ought to move him into a sort of storeroom for future reference?''

''And you said you couldn't—because of that rose-colored aura surrounding him. Could you now?''

She nodded slowly, ''He'll always be somebody special but now—'' She felt a new inner stiffening. *I am I, Katie Rose Belford, with a chance for a part in the school musical. I am Uncle Brian's bright angel, and once Ben called me the Rock of Gibraltar. I don't have to waylay any boy in the halls—*

Jeanie's mother rapped on the window, and pantomimed for Jeanie to come in and get a coat, or else ask Katie Rose in.

''I'll be seeing you later tonight when we go caroling,'' Katie Rose said.

Jeanie's parting words were, ''Throw a dust cover over you-know-who to protect his dazzling smile.''

Again Katie Rose settled herself beside Miguel, and he drove on. He stopped at a stop sign, and she voiced her thoughts, ''Miguel, all the time you've been proving you were *you,* I've been trying to prove I was somebody that wasn't me.'' She had tried on roles as one would dresses—the gush-glib one, the literary-light one, the complacent-June, complete with Mona Lisa smile. She wasn't sure what the real Katie Rose was—not yet—but she knew it wasn't any of those.

"You stay you, or I'll bash your teeth in," Miguel said.

He turned off Hubbell Street and stopped at their side gate. Cully was her first greeter, and his welcome was so overwhelming she had to fight him off. "I'm not sure the family will be glad to see me," she said uneasily, as Miguel walked to the door with her.

"Wanta bet?" He opened the door, shoved in her overnight case, and said, "I'll be back shortly."

Inside the dining room, she leaned for a minute against the door. Every pore of the house oozed the feel of Christmas. The littles were wrapping presents at the dining table, amid a great clutter of colored paper and ribbons and stickers. Mother, in her scarlet Gay Nineties dress, stood on a chair in the living room, hanging a sprig of mistletoe from the center light. Uncle Brian sat at the piano in the hall playing "Adeste Fidelis," and scolding Stacy, "Not fi-dell-is, you dolt—fee-*day*-lis."

They all turned surprised eyes on Katie Rose. She said thinly, "I've come home," and then, to her surprise, started to cry. And she had been so sure the puckerin' string to her heart was the tight kind!

Uncle Brian cried out, "Our ewe lamb is back," and reached her first, and pulled her to him. Mother was next with a rustle of silken skirts.

Mother didn't say in so many words, "I never meant to throw the tomato pincushion at you." But her, "Oh, lovey, I'll make you fresh tea—there's nothing worse than a lukewarm brew,'' said it for her.

And neither could Katie Rose say, ''I'm sorry I said you were common as pig tracks, and that I left in such a huff.'' But her, ''I got homesick—at Aunt Eustace's,'' said it for her.

The littles shouted, ''Don't look, Katie Rose—don't look! We're wrapping up your present.''

They all escorted her to the dinette. Mother made fresh tea, and Uncle Brian cut cold meat. Everyone talked at once. Stacy said, ''Hey, can't we open the fruit cake for Katie Rose that Pearl sent us from the bakery?'' (Maybe it *had* baked lopsided, but right then Katie Rose didn't care.) And Mother was explaining that she had dressed early because Guido was having a Christmas tree party for all the staff before the dinner rush started.

Unpredictable Mother! She said, ''I'm going to be nicer to Aunt Eustace. After all, she's family. Brian and I were saying that it's time he and I stopped being childish about her. We're going to visit back and forth more—'' She broke off with her rueful but infectious laugh. ''Listen to who's talking! I'm always vowing I'll be easy and friendly, and then she comes in and makes me feel like a scullery maid—whatever a scullery maid is—and I get my back up. So, Katie Rose, you help me be nicer to her.''

At that, she had to hurry into the living room to settle a battle between the twins over who should use the last sheet of wrapping paper.

Then suddenly the family went scampering in all directions. Uncle Brian drove Mother to Giddy's, and the littles wanted to be dropped off on the Boulevard for more wrapping paper and ribbon. Stacy ran across to the Novaks' for the mittens she had left there.

Katie Rose sat alone, drinking her tea in nice content. The sugar bowl, with its broken handle, sat on a corner of the table. Probably the poor half-a-bath fund was sadly crippled by all the Christmas demands. So were her savings for a Weatherwise coat. But right then it didn't matter.

She lifted her eyes to the clock. If she were at Aunt Eustace's, she would be zipping up the blue brocade about now. Again she tested herself for a sharp pang. Just a small stirring of regret. *And you, with feathers,* she admonished, *you just stay perched, until I tell you to soar.*

She was looking up the words to "Adeste Fidelis," when a thumping at the side door interrupted. She opened it to Miguel and their bushy Christmas tree. He panted out, "I thought I'd better get it before they closed up the lot and took down the lights. Grab that tip-end, while I wangle it through the door."

Between them they carried it into the hall and leaned it against the piano.

"Here's where I came in, Petunia," he said with the same appealing grin that had melted her heart the very first time she saw him. "I'll help you put up the tree, if you'll give me something to eat."

About the Author

LENORA MATTINGLY WEBER was born in Dawn, Missouri. When she was twelve, her adventurous family set out to homestead in Colorado. She attended school in Denver, and has lived and worked there ever since.

Her well-loved stories reflect her own experiences. As a mother of six and a grandmother, she is well equipped to write of family life. Her love of the outdoors, her interest in community affairs, and her appreciation of warm family relationships help make her characters as winning as they are. Mrs. Weber's first love is writing, but she also likes to ride horseback, swim, and cook for her large family.